Vol. 2 Lucy Aged 10.25 and the Secret Room! 2

Darren John Charlton
Illustrated By Lily Jessica Charlton

Written in 2021 by Darren John Charlton
1st published in 2022.
Illustrations by Lily Jessica Charlton

Published by
Out Of This World Publishers
PO Box 5996
Dronfield
S18 9DZ
United Kingdom

Paperback ISBN 978-1-8380553-3-2

.

Health and safety consultants – Stuart, Kevin and Bob. Their report is as follows:

We would like to issue a joint statement expressing our concern over the content of this book.

Before reading this, make sure you have enough room to roll around on the floor laughing. On a serious note – it's best to read this book in pairs so you can prod each when you start to fall asleep.

Have tissues on hand for crying or in case you are allergic to amazeball books.

If you are the kind of person who gets so engrossed in a story that you don't want to stop and go for a wee, it's probably best you read it on the toilet or outside, certainly not on a bus.

Turn your phone off; those annoying beeps can be so off-putting. The only exception is if you are texting your friends about how fabulous this is or if you are ordering more copies. Oh, and if you are getting chased by a man with an axe.

Don't read while on your bike (I've seen someone do this!) unless it's a tandem and you're at the back.

Reading this book COULD increase your intelligence, therefore, we would advise you to take care, as we believe it is best to be silly for as long as possible. Right, race you to the fruit bowl. BANANAS.

www.lucyandthesecretroom.co.uk

I wanted to thank the children who were the first people to review Lucy and the Secret Room and with their comments and feedback gave me the encouragement and motivation to write this sequel.

Thank you to:

Eleanor, Max, Daisy, Dylan, Isabel, Ben, Lily, Rose, Amelia, Jasmin, Rosa, Liv, Emily, Emily and to the remaining children whose names I don't know but their comments were invaluable.

Contents

Hopefully you will find some of this useful.
Words in the text which are underlined have their
brief meaning, for this story, included in the glossary at
the back of this book. This is designed to help adults
as well as some of the children.
Some children have found it easier to read the section in the
glossary that corresponds to the chapter they are
about to read before starting to read the chapter.
It is not important to fully understand some of the
science or maths within this book to enjoy the story.

The illustrations within this book have been drawn by my daughter.
This is so they will resonate with primary school age children. All of the pictures
depicted in here are designed to look like Lucy's drawings from her notebook,
journal and schoolbooks.

Introduction

(*A brief summary, or recap, from* Lucy and the Secret Room Vol.1.)

After having a bad day at school, 9-year-old Lucy scours her new bedroom for a distraction.

She spots a book on her bookshelf, *Cosmology – Reach for the Stars*, which she is well aware she doesn't own. Whilst trying to remove this book from her bookshelf, she realises it opens a secret bookcase door which unearths more than she could have possibly imagined.

Lucy decides to investigate further – her late father was also very inquisitive, and she owes a lot of her characteristics to him – against her better judgement of telling Mum.

Realising the task at hand too great for her alone, she invites her best friend, Jamie, to help her explore these new rooms under her house. Each room needs a code to enter, which Jamie and Lucy have had to decipher together.

They discovered rather annoying, and potentially dangerous, rock monsters and some gigantic Venus flytraps, but their favourite find was a rather odd creature not dissimilar to a little bear; like a real-life teddy bear that may have been left outside for far too long. They named him Wocky, as he did remind them a little of an Ewok, but Wocky has three humps on his back and a very strange, long, forked tongue for catching flies.

In the last book, Lucy has explored all of the basement level, with the exception of one door in the first room, and there was that staircase leading up to another level too.

Join Lucy and Jamie once more as they continue their journey and reveal the secrets to those final mysterious rooms.

Most importantly, will she tell her mum?

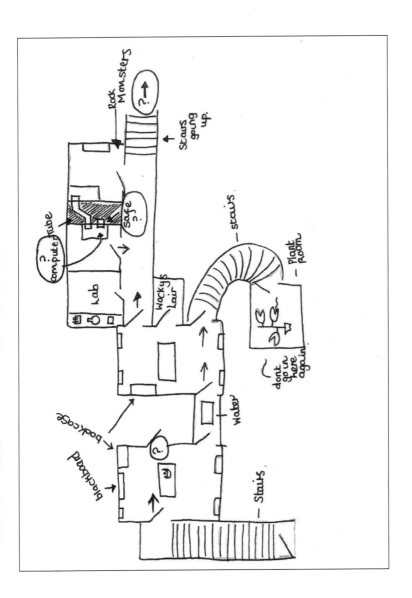

11

Chapter 1
Sleepover, what sleepover?

I glance at my oxygen monitor. I still have twenty minutes left, so I carry on digging.

"Dr Lucy, look at this! Look how far I can jump. I'm going to mark out a long jump for us, and we can have the first Olympics on the moon," Jamie exclaims excitedly over the inter-helmet comms. He picks up a moon rock and gently throws it back towards me. My first thought is that he hasn't thrown it hard enough but, because of the low gravity here, it travels surprisingly far. Wocky bounds after it like a like a giddy puppy (even though he's more like a bear than a dog).

Wocky's specially made spacesuit fits him well; it really <u>emphasises</u> his three humps on his back. Oh no. Before he gets to the rock, Wocky looks up at me and hurtles in my direction. I don't have time to gesture for him to stop and, in an instant, he leaps in the air and into my arms. I close my eyes as his enormously long, lizard-like tongue rolls out. I'm expecting to get slimed again but, as I open my eyes,

I can see some gloopy goo oozing down inside *his* helmet. He looks very <u>bewildered</u> until he licks it back up again and burps.

"Wocky, Wocky, over here." Jamie gestures him over not wanting to miss out on the fun.

"Jamie, we are supposed to be working." I can't be mad with him, though. No one can stay mad at J for long, he's so childish but adorable.

"What are you digging for again?"

I'm not going to explain 'astrobiology' *again* to him, especially in these spacesuits with – I glance back at the monitor – fifteen minutes' oxygen left. "It's time to be heading back to the lunar base now, J."

"It's a good job, as I *need* a wee," he replies.

"Don't do it in your suit like last time!" I warn. Just then an overwhelming urge comes over me. I need one too.

I wake up with a start and look around. It was a dream. It was so real and so is my urge to wee. I hate it when that happens. I dash to the toilet – fortunately Mum isn't in there and at least now I don't have to remove a spacesuit to go!

After washing my hands, I return to my comfy bed and close my eyes again. Back to that dream once more, I'm on the moon with Jamie. I try for several minutes to carry on with my dream but, it's no good, I can't seem to focus on it any more.

I look down at my damaged arm and frown. This wrist brace is a nightmare. Weeks have passed by, and

I haven't been able to visit the secret rooms. Feeling a bit down, I grab my journal from under the bed in the hope that I can find something to cheer me up. I open it up on the last page I have written in. I study the Year 5 love map.

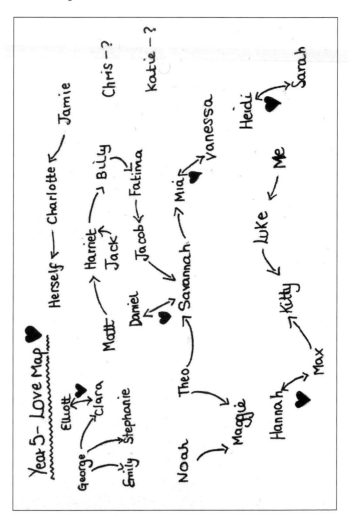

Last week, I had tried to figure out who I could help get together, but it is *so* complicated. There is no way Stephanie (or Emily for that matter) likes George. So, I can't do anything about that. I need to talk with Maggie, as both Noah and Theo are nice and I'm sure I could pair one of them up with her. I'm keeping away from Harriet, though, because the last time I tried to set her up with someone it didn't work out and she bit my head off (not <u>literally</u> – obviously).

If only I could be as sweet as Kitty, then maybe Luke would like me more than her. I'm a little bit glad Jamie hasn't got a girlfriend yet as I would miss him too much, but it wouldn't get in the way of our friendship because that's far too important.

It's been months now since he came over here and we found the secret rooms, Wocky, the rock monsters and that safe. I look back through the pages of the journal to try and remember where the weeks have gone.

We had planned a few sleepovers before the summer holidays, but it never worked out as Mum was starting work earlier and earlier in the mornings. This meant earlier nights for her and less chance for me to sneak out, explore more, and play with Wocky. Wocky – I'd hardly seen him at all. Sometimes my visits to him were four weeks apart, but he always seems to be OK. He must be getting some food from somewhere, but where? So many unanswered questions.

We made plans to have an extended sleepover in the six-week holiday. Jamie was away for the first two weeks, and then his family were visiting for five days. Mum and I were hoping to book a short holiday to somewhere warm, so we had to keep those weeks free. Our holiday never happened though, as the car was playing up and cost a significant amount of money to fix.

Then, disaster struck. Jamie was supposed to be staying over in the last week of the school holidays but, as Mum had to work, she had signed me up for gymnastics kid camp for two days. I remember I was so looking forward to it as well. I had done gymnastics a lot when I was younger and got my bronze badge with British Gymnastics so I was expecting these two days would be lots of fun, especially since Heidi, from school, also goes.

On that first day, as I was swinging between the parallel bars, I lost my grip, slipped off and landed on my left wrist. I don't think I've ever cried as much (well except only once, when Dad died). I looked at the pictures of the cast I'd stuck in my journal. I can't remember what type of break the doctor at the hospital said it was, but I told everyone it was the worst one possible. I remember getting a lot of sympathy from everyone, including the teachers, my friends and family (especially my grandad) and even some from strangers in the supermarket, but not as much as I had imagined. When Clara broke her arm last year, she seemed to get loads of attention and I joked to Jamie I couldn't wait to break something. How foolish was I? The attention doesn't last for long, but the broken arm, and the pain that goes with it, does. At least now the pot is off and because I've been given a wrist support, I can take it off and wash properly, which is a relief!

I flop backwards on to the bed and rest my journal on the bed to the side of me. I close my eyes and start to think back to how hard I found it when I was still getting used to only having one arm. The good thing is I'm right-handed so I could still write, but it was the little stupid things like showering and trying to put my socks on that I found so frustrating. Just getting ready for school was a nightmare! Fortunately, Mum had bought me some slip-on shoes so that helped.

A smile comes across my face. PE, I did miss taking part in PE lessons, but it was very funny watching from the benches. I never noticed certain things before when I was on the court but sitting on the 'sidelines' you see so much more. I remembered Dylan always seems to be nowhere near the ball. The more I watched him the more I realised he actually moves away from it, and I never saw him run once. Then there's Katie. I think she spent more time sat down next to me than playing because I know she doesn't like PE. Although she's one of my close friends, it was always, "Miss, I've hurt my ankle", "Miss, I feel sick", "Miss, I feel dizzy". She always seems fine as soon as the teacher isn't looking, though.

I did enjoy helping the teacher out though. I learned a lot from *not* playing. I got to help set things up while everyone else was getting changed, and I got to use the stopwatch and even <u>referee</u> some games.

Mum disturbs my thoughts as she comes into my bedroom. "Morning, Lucy, did you sleep well?" she asks in a cheery voice.

"Hi, Mum. I did, but I'm really tired. What day is 'Superhero Day' at school, Mum?"

"Oh, I'm not sure. I'll have to check the school newsletter, because you've also got the prom coming up and Human Solar System Day, so I need to check on the dates for all of those. Why are you asking about Superhero Day? Are you worried you're going to get pranked like Jamie did last year?" Mum stifles a giggle.

"Oh yeah, I remember. Chris sent him a message reminding him to get dressed up that morning, and Jamie being Jamie just thought he had forgotten. He didn't realise that Chris was being mischievous and telling him on the wrong day! He wore his underpants over his trousers!" I say, shaking my head in disbelief.

"Yes, it's a good job he was coming here first before school so he could get changed again. It would have been really embarrassing otherwise."

"It's a good job he had put clean pants on to start with!" I add.

"Well, I just took that for granted, Lucy," Mum laughs. "Now, are you coming down for breakfast yet?"

"Soon, just give me time to come round."

"I'll be downstairs," says Mum, as she closes the door behind her. Now she's mentioned food, I realise I'm suddenly hungry, so I decide to get up and go down for breakfast now.

I see Lucas (my little monkey teddy) on the floor. "What are you doing down there?" I ask him whilst placing him back in my bed. "You can't lie on the floor at your age. You keep warm in my cosy bed." He's nearly as old as me and, in teddy years, that's quite old!

"Oh, still in your pyjamas I see. You still look tired," Mum comments.

"I am. I was having an amazing dream about being on the moon with Jamie. Jamie could leap really far, and Wock…" I stop myself instantly. I feel sick to the pit of my stomach. I tell Mum everything, but the one thing I've kept from her is the secret rooms and my furry friend. Do I come clean now, or do I just explore a little more so I have some answers to this mystery? *Think Lucy, think*, I urge myself. What do I say?

"Wock?" Mum asks, rather confused.

"I didn't say Wock, I said *what* an amazing dream it was." I think I've got away with it.

"What a curious dream. On another note, though, while you're sat down and can't run away, has anyone invited you to the school disco, sorry, 'the prom' yet? It will come round quicker than you think."

"No one's asked me yet, but…" I think for a minute. "I was thinking about asking Luke."

"Luke? When am I going to meet him? You know what Dad would have said. He would need to <u>interrogate</u> him for days before he would be allowed to even hold hands with you."

"What does interrogate mean?"

"To question him."

I take a sip of orange juice whilst I think of Dad. "What was that perfume Dad said he would get for me?"

"He said he would swap out your 'Impulse' for 'Repulse' to keep the boys away," she says, laughing.

"That's mean. Thanks for the toast, Mum," I try and say whilst ramming a slice in my mouth.

"You're welcome."

I look at the pile of papers all around us. "What's all these papers on the table, Mum? Are you working on something?"

"Yes, it's for work. They've asked me to complete this 'positive mental attitude' course."

"We've done this at school. I can help you." Mum looks surprised. "You need a 'growth mindset'. The teacher said you can do anything if you put your mind to it. Except… well, Coby thought he could fly."

Mum's mouth is wide open as I continue.

"We told him it doesn't work like that, but he kept jumping off tables."

"Oh no," Mum says, <u>tentatively</u>. "What happened to Coby?"

"He's in hospital now with a broken nose!" I quickly finish my toast. "I'm going back upstairs now."

"Would you like some fruit, Lucy?"

"Not right now, I'll grab some when I come back down."

Grandad always says "An apple a day keeps the doctor away" and he's <u>ancient</u>. I wonder what he does if he *does* need to see the doctor, does he just hope he hasn't eaten any fruit already! I head back upstairs and jump on to my bed. I open my journal again and gather my thoughts.

So, this was the start of Year 5: a broken wrist; bye to my favourite teacher so far, Miss Needham; hello new teacher, Mrs Malikinski. Everyone is scared of her (even some of the other teachers, I think), but I still haven't made up my mind. She has been nice to me so far. But I've always been good, unlike Daniel who's constantly in trouble, and she really *does shout* at him. I was hoping he wouldn't be in my class again this year, but I can't complain as I get to be with Jamie once more.

My tenth birthday has come and gone; I quite like being one of the oldest in my school year. Not like Jamie who is one of the youngest which means there's nearly a whole year between us! It was nice at the cinema watching *Paddington 2* with Jamie, Maggie, Rose and Emily. I could just about hold the popcorn with my pot on, although Emily was kind enough to lean over and hand me my drink when I wanted it.

I was hoping for an iPhone13, but that didn't happen. I wasn't surprised though, as Harriet doesn't even have one yet.

Turning the page of my journal, I look at the list of presents I received.

I got David Walliams' *Blob* book from Jamie. I still need to read that. His books are so funny.

A make-up set from Emily.

A craft kit from Rose.

Sketch pad and art set from Maggie.

Mum and Grandad got me a spa session with a mani-pedi, but we've not been able to go yet because of my wrist.

I am now 10! And still no sign of another sleepover. Then it hit me – Michaela.

Michaela used to babysit me. I just need to convince Mum to have a night out and for Michaela to come round and 'look after' me. Michaela would spend the whole night on her phone to boys, no doubt (although not always the same one), whilst watching Netflix. Who says girls can't multitask? This would give me all night to explore my secret rooms and play with Wocky, as she wouldn't come up to check on me.

I study the secret codes that I've written on the map. I've worked all the codes out that I can at this stage. I need to find the key to the safe behind the rainbow picture and investigate where the stairs lead to. But first, I will need Jamie's help to get across the water obstacle. Wait a minute… I have a ladder in the garage. I now have a plan!

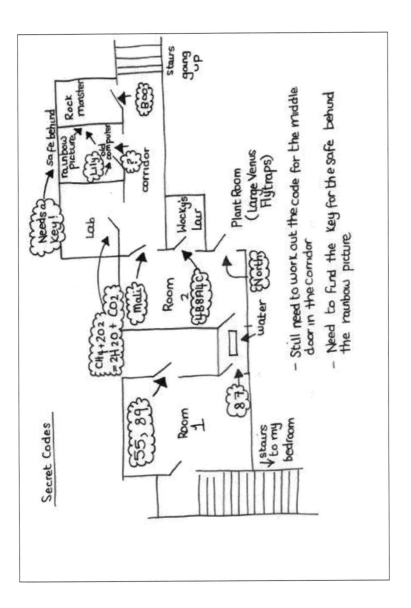

Secret Codes

Room 1

55, 89

87

stairs to my bedroom

$CH_4 + 2O_2 = 2H_2O + CO_2$

Mall

Room 2

4B8Al4C

water

North

55, 89

Lab

Needs a Key!

Wacky's Lair

Plant Room
(Large Venus Flytraps)

safe behind

rainbow picture

Lily

old computer

? corridor

Rock monster

Boo

stairs going up

- Still need to work out the code for the middle door in the corridor

- Need to find the key for the safe behind the rainbow picture

23

Chapter 2
Michaela to the rescue

I open the notes on my phone and set myself reminders of what I need to do, as there is so much to think about, I don't want to forget anything. What shall I call it, progress update? No, I'll call it status update.

When I've finished with my notes, I send Jamie a text message.

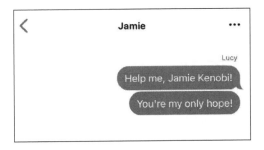

It's the distress code we use for each other, as we are both big *Star Wars* fans. He should reply quickly, even though this isn't strictly an emergency. I can't wait any longer, so I <u>FaceTime</u> him. It's ringing. Come on, come on. Where is he?

"Hello, what are you up to?" chirps Jamie, cheerily.

"I've had a great idea."

"Oh no, what this time?" he asks, hesitantly.

"Listen, here me out."

"OK," he mutters.

"I am going to convince my mum that she needs a night out, and I can get Michaela to come over, and then…"

"Wait, she's the really good-looking one, isn't she?" he says rather excitedly.

"NO! Well, she is pretty, just a bit <u>unconventionally</u>. Is this the girl you said you wanted to ask out two years ago who you never stopped talking about?"

"Maybe," Jamie replies <u>sheepishly</u>.

"She's nearly twice our age, Jamie! And she has a boyfriend."

"I'm defo coming round, though. I'll get my mum to ring yours. They could go out together, and I'll get to come round for a sleepover. I can't wait. It'll be awesome."

"Er, you're not coming over just to drool over her," I clarify.

"No, of course not. We can carry on exploring together, besides, I've missed Wocky. You never know, she might let me take a picture of me and her now. I am two years older."

"Jamie! Stop kidding yourself. She might even bring her boyfriend!"

"Oh," sighs Jamie.

I could hear a song in the background at Jamie's. "What you listening to?"

"Oh, it's One Direction, 'Story of My Life'. What about you?"

I wasn't listening to anything; it was perfectly silent. "Nothing now, but yesterday I couldn't stop playing 'Shut Up and Dance' by Walk the Moon."

"Cool, sounds awesome," says Jamie <u>enthusiastically</u>.

"Have you ever heard of them?" I ask, curiously.

"No, but I like the name. I'll look them up. Will your arm be better by the sleepover? I bet you still can't get across those monkey bars."

"You're right, I can't right now. I might be able to in few more weeks. At least my pot's off now and, with the wrist brace, I can do a bit more so I'm <u>formulating</u>

26

a plan. I have a ladder in the garage, so we could carry it upstairs and use it bridge the water. The only problem is I don't know if it's long enough."

"You will have to measure the ladder and measure the length of the water before we arrange the sleepover."

"I'll do that and get back to you. I do hope the ladder's long enough!"

"If not, Luce, we could warm it up like we did in that science homework last year."

"Warm it up? What?"

"Don't you remember, heat makes things expand and the cold makes them smaller? If we heat up the ladder it's bound to fit... isn't it?"

"I like your logic, Jamie, but in <u>reality</u>, it would only expand by a few <u>millimetres</u> and, even if that's all we need, what happens when it cools back down again? We would lose the ladder and maybe you as well!"

"Why me?"

"Because you would go first to test it, obviously."

"Ha ha," he replies, <u>sarcastically</u>.

"Speaking of homework, have you done yours yet?" I ask.

"What? We have homework? I've not done anything. Mrs Malikinski's going kill me."

"We only went over it in class the other day."

"I remember now. It's too big of a problem. There is no way I can do it."

"It might look like a big problem, but it's just several small problems. Break it down into small sections and tackle them one by one."

"No, I still can't do it. I'm going to get expelled," he exclaims.

"You've not even looked at it yet. Don't be a drama queen. Look, don't worry. I'll take a photo of mine and send it to you. Just don't copy it word for word."

"Thanks, Lucy, you're a lifesaver. I'll go and work on my mum now and start to plant the seed for a night out, she won't take any convincing."

"OK, talk soon."

"Bye. Over and out."

"Bye, Jamie." I press the red button to disconnect the call. Right, I need a plan. Take pictures of homework and send to Jamie. I'm doing this at the same time as going over the plan of action in my head. If I don't do things as I think of them, I am likely to get distracted and forget something.

Next, measure the ladder in the garage. I start to head downstairs. After this I've got to measure the water in the secret room, so I need to find a suitable time to do this.

"Lucy, who were you talking to?" Mum shouts from her room.

"Hi, Mum. Oh, it was just Jamie. He's got some questions about his homework."

"OK, I've got to pop round to Carol's next door and help her with her computer – it's not printing again."

I was going to make a joke about computers not printing things only printers do, but I think better of it as Mum seems a little stressed.

"I'm just going into the garage to look for something." I couldn't think of anything off the top of my head so hopefully she won't ask what it is I'm going to look for.

"Alright. When you come back in, I will go next door. I won't be long, because I need to start dinner."

Swiftly, I head outside to the garage. Right, I need to find the ladder. The garage is quite cluttered. There are still a lot of Dad's things in here: tools, bits of wood, boxes of 'stuff' and an exercise bike. I start to move a few things. Here's what I need. Right, tape measure. I know where that is, as I used it last week for our 'measuring things in your home' homework. It's a shame I hadn't measured the ladder though. It's very difficult using a tape measure with only one hand, but after practising last week, I'd learnt that there is a sliding lock on it so I can put the tape between my legs and pull out the measuring part slowly without it recoiling back and whipping me; which hurts!

The ladder is 9 feet – exactly.

I put the tape in my pocket, and I race back upstairs to write it down in my journal.

"Are you done now, Lucy? Can I go next door?"

"Yes, Mum. How long will you be?"

"About a half an hour." With that, I hear the front door slam, as Mum heads next door.

I look out of Mum's window. I wait until I can see George's mum, Carol, has let her in.

Right, measure water, I recall my list from memory.

I grab my spare rucksack from under my bed. I always keep it fully stocked with the things I may need for any last-minute trips to my secret lair. Quickly, I slip on my old gym shoes. I now keep the laces loose after fighting with them last time. I've done this so many times before it's like second nature, I could probably do it with my eyes closed.

I close my eyes and walk over to the bookcase. *BANG!* I open my eyes then close them again, as if no one saw me having a sneaky peek at where I was, and I start <u>fumbling</u> around for the <u>cosmology</u> book. Where is it? As I pull on different books some fall on to me before hitting the floor. I take another peek. Then I put my hand straight on it. I pull the book and hear the click. The bookcase pushes inwards. I shuffle round and push it closed. I am just about to attempt the stairs with closed eyes when common sense gets the better of me.

I open my eyes. THAT'S A LOT OF STAIRS. I grab the rail and efficiently make my way down to the door at the bottom.

Not to waste any time, I whizz through the first room, heading straight for the right-hand door. I type in the memorised door code '87'. I push the door open and stare at the water. How AM I going to measure this? I start by extending the tape measure out as I did when I measured the ladder, but the tape measure bends and drops into the water when it's only reached about halfway across. I retract the tape measure, splashing a little water my way. I <u>apprehensively</u> peer into the water to see if I have disturbed anything. Small ripples appear on the surface as the water settles. No monsters seem to be awakened as yet. I don't want to risk that again. As I look up, I wonder if I can measure the distance between the bars and multiply it by the number of bars there are, but I disregard this idea immediately, as I know from the number of times I've clambered across the monkey bars that some of the bars aren't equally spaced. Then it occurs to me. I've got some rope in my backpack and it's certainly long enough to reach the other side (and then some). As I remove the length of rope, I smile. I had already marked the rope in 300mm sections using small pieces of ribbon. This brings back memories of playing tug of war in the park with my friends. I can't believe the markers are still there.

I count nine sections. So that's nine multiplied by 300mm and, as 300mm is equal to 1 foot, that's 9 feet in total.

> **300mm = 30 cm = 1 foot = 12 inch**

I lay the rope out on the floor but, because it's so long, I have to continue laying it through the door I've just come through and into the first room I enter when I come down here. As I stare down at the 9-foot rope, simulating the length of the ladder, I try and visualise this over the water, but it's no good. I can't quite tell if it's going to be long enough or not. There would be no point trying to get the ladder down here and then finding it's just too short. I decide the only thing for it is to throw a long section of rope to the other side and then I can count the sections between the edges of the water. One end of the rope has a little metal hook on it and this added weight will help me throw it across the water. I'm finding this whole process very tiring, as I'm still not used to doing too much with one hand.

Take aim. Three, two, one – throw. There is an almighty splash as the metal hook followed by the coil of rope hit the water. I haven't thrown it far enough. I cover my face and step back to avoid getting too wet but, just as I do, I see the coil of rope whizzing past me and into the water. I lunge forward, stamping my left foot down on the floor as if I'm trying to squash an angry wasp, even though this looks more like a snake trying to flee than a wasp.

MISSED! There isn't much rope left now. I will lose it forever if I can't get the end. I sharpen my senses and <u>anticipate</u> how long it will take for my foot to hit the floor and where the rope is likely to be at that point (just like when you are at the fair and you are trying to throw a ball at a moving target. You need to anticipate where the target has moved to by the time the ball hits).

STAMP. Got it. I quickly crouch down and collect all the rope, moving back away from the water as I do. I'm still unsure what might be in there. For a second, I imagine the rope is a snake and I nearly let go of it again. I do a quick double take to reassure myself.

The rope is a lot heavier now it's wet, and I'm not sure if this is going to help me or not, but I'm conscious I'm running out of time. All I have to do is throw it higher and harder to reach the other side. This time I will keep my left foot on the other end. I push down firmly whilst tugging on the rope. There, that's going nowhere.

I calm myself down by taking three large, deep breaths in and out whilst I focus on my target. I need to go longer and higher than last time, so I'm aiming for the top corner of the room at the other side. The rope is long enough and the more of it I can throw over, the less likely it is that it will slide back into the water.

I muster up one big, gigantic throw that is worthy of the Paralympics. (I do only have the use of one arm!) The wet rope shoots up into the air. It's going to do it. I'm just about to let out an enormous cheer when the metal hook goes through the last rung of the monkey bars and coils back round. It's alright, I'll try again. That was so close I could taste success. As I start to retrieve the rope, the metal hook, which is attached to the far end of the rope, has latched on to the monkey bar. I tug on it forcefully several times, but it's well and truly <u>anchored</u>. Collapsing on to the floor, I felt like I could cry as I'm so tired now. If I had both arms I might even be tempted to swing across like Tarzan.

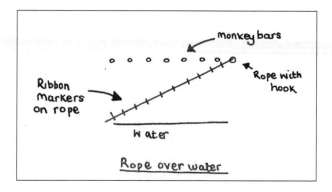

Rope over water

I look at the ribbon on the rope. I can at least estimate the length now. I carefully count the sections. Ten. It's 10 feet or ten multiplied by 300mm. I quickly calculate in my head. Because I'm multiplying by ten, I just need to add an extra zero really, so the length equals 3000mm or 3 metres. But that doesn't help, as the ladder is 9-feet long, so I'm still not sure. I glance at the time on my phone and realise I need to get back. I place my rucksack on the rope to hold it in place while I go back into the main room to look for something that will hold it in place until Jamie and I can come back down. I empty out the plastic fruit from the bowl and then place the bowl on to the rope. This isn't going to work. I need something heavier. I grab a few large books off the bookshelf and place them into the bowl to weigh it down.

"That should do it," I say out loud. After grabbing my bag, I race back up the stairs and carefully open the bookcase door. No sign of Mum. Good. I enter my bedroom and close the door behind me before slouching down on the chair in front of my desk.

All that effort and still no closer. I phone Jamie.

"Hello there." Jamie seems quite chipper.

"I can't do it," I exclaim. "I've tried." I regale the rope and water saga to Jamie.

"Did you say the ladder is 9-feet long and the rope is 10-feet long at a diagonal? It sounds like it will be close. We will just have to take the ladder down and hope for the best."

As Jamie is talking, I start to sketch it out in my notebook.

"Wait a minute. This is just like a right-angled triangle. The rope is the longest side, the <u>hypotenuse</u>. So, the water will be less than that."

"You lost me on triangle," chuckles Jamie over the phone.

"I'll call you back. I should be able to work this out using <u>Pythagoras</u>."

"You are going to work what out? Eating pie?"

"I'll explain later. Bye, Jamie."

"OK, save me some pie."

I disconnect the call and continue with my drawing.

Pythagoras

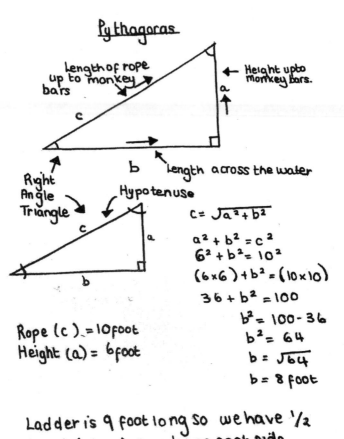

Length of rope up to monkey bars → **c**

Height up to monkey bars ← **a**

↑ **b** ← Length across the water

Right Angle Triangle →

Hypotenuse

$$c = \sqrt{a^2 + b^2}$$

$$a^2 + b^2 = c^2$$
$$6^2 + b^2 = 10^2$$
$$(6 \times 6) + b^2 = (10 \times 10)$$
$$36 + b^2 = 100$$
$$b^2 = 100 - 36$$
$$b^2 = 64$$
$$b = \sqrt{64}$$
$$b = 8 \text{ foot}$$

Rope (c) = 10 foot
Height (a) = 6 foot

Ladder is 9 foot long so we have ½ foot (6 inch) over hang each side.

Excellent - this plan will work! ☺

I know the height of the bars is about 6 foot, as they are roughly the same height as the ones at school. And the hypotenuse is 10 feet. So, using Pythagoras, I can work out the length of the water.

$A^2 + B^2 = C^2$

A equals the height, so that's 6 <u>squared</u>, or 6 multiplied by 6, which is 36.

B squared is the water, so I'll need to try and work that out.

C squared is the diagonal length of rope, which is 10 squared, or 10 multiplied by 10, which is 100.

By taking away 36 from one side of the equation I also need to take it away from the other side. So, 100 minus 36 equals 64.

That leaves B squared equals 64.

To get B on its own I take the squared off the left and move it to the right and do the opposite of squared to the 64. The opposite of squared is <u>square root</u>. So, the square root of 64 is 8, as 8 times 8 equals 64.

So that leaves B equals 8.

So, the length of the water is 8 feet. The ladder is 9 feet, so the ladder should overhang either side by about half a foot, which is the same as a small ruler; 6 inches or 150mm.

I ring Jamie back. "I've done it!" I shout <u>triumphantly</u> down the phone at him before he can even speak.

"Done what?"

"I've worked it out using Pythagoras."

"I thought 'pi' was for circles?"

"Pi is, as in pi r squared. But Pythagoras is for working out lengths of right-angled triangles and, guess what? The ladder is long enough. We just need to arrange a time for you to come round and help me get it down there before the sleepover; maybe after school one night." I ramble on so quickly that Jamie can't get a word in edgeways.

"Yes, excellent, sounds good. Got to go now, I'm just having my tea."

We say our goodbyes, and I hang up the phone. I can't wait for him to come round now. Even with only one arm, there's nothing holding us back.

Chapter 3
The confrontation

"QUICK LUCY, QUICK," shouts Maggie, as she and Emily come running over to me. "Jack and his bully boys are picking on Jamie again. I wish they would all just grow up. Those boys, again! Whatever's wrong with them?"

We race over to the corner of the tennis courts. I can see Jamie up against the railings. He is standing tall with his shoulders back and, although he doesn't look scared, I know he hides it well. I also know he won't fight back, especially as he is outnumbered. Jack, on the other hand, is slouching over – like so many people do when they are naturally tall. I know Jack will fight if he outnumbers his opponent.

"BACK OFF, JACK," I demand, as I get closer.

"Well, well, your girlfriend's here, Jamie. Lucy to the rescue."

"She's not my girlfriend."

"Why do you have to pick on people all the time, Jack? There's just no need for it. What's going on this time?" I say, crossly.

Matt pipes up, "He's stood in our place, aren't you, weirdo."

"Really! You're pathetic. This is just as much Jamie's space as yours, and mine for that matter." I glance around. "All this space around us and you still have to find someone on their own to pick on. It was Rosa last week, wasn't it? Picking on a girl. You should be ashamed of yourselves."

"We can't all be perfect like you, Lucy. Go on, scuttle off and go and play with your dolls or something," Jack mocks.

"OR WHAT?" I shout with more aggression and conviction than I knew I had in me.

Jack seems a little taken back. He's not used to challengers. Matt and Billy step back slightly.

"I'm not scared of you, Lucy."

"What are you going to do, Jack? Beat us all up? I don't think so. You will all be expelled." I look over at Matt. "And what would *your* mum say, Matt?" He lowers his head in embarrassment. I know his mum well and he knows this.

Jack steps forward as if he's going to push me over, so I get ready to step back and catch him off balance. Before I need to, Jamie lunges forward and almost gets between us.

"That's enough," Jamie says very <u>assertively</u>.

"Why are you sticking up for him anyway? He's not worth it. He can't even play football!" Jack asks me.

"It's not all about football," Jamie replies.

"It sure is," Jack mouths.

"Well, it's a challenge then. Girls against boys at football. Tomorrow lunch. IF YOU DARE," I say with a raised voice.

"You've got no chance," Billy interjects for the first time.

Jack is silent. It's like I can hear the cogs in his head going round.

"WHO'S SCARED NOW!" I look straight at him. I notice his eye twitches when he's nervous. The last time I saw this was when he lost his trousers after PE and he had to wear a lab coat. It looked like he had a dress on!

"We need time to practise. We'll play the match next week," he stutters.

"NO, if you are that good, you don't need to practise. Tomorrow. Or shall I just tell everyone that you're too scared to play?" I look over at Maggie who's got her phone out ready.

"I'm on it," she says.

"Alright, tomorrow then. I'll get Mr Hall to referee," Jack concedes.

"Oh no you won't! He'll favour you lot."

Matt pipes up. "Mr Hall, yes, referee he will," he says, waving his arm from left to right.

I interrupt him. "Your Jedi mind tricks don't work on us, Matt, so I'll ask Mrs Meadow because she's fair."

"But she's *your* PE teacher," he protests.

"She's fair, unlike Mr Hall who doesn't think girls should play football!" I turn to Maggie. "Maggie, send it. They're too scared to play."

"FINE. We'll play tomorrow. Mrs Meadow can ref. You don't stand a chance."

"If that's the case, then you need to tell your voice that. It sounds a bit shaky."

"I don't know why you're hanging around with losers like him," he points at Jamie.

"Jamie's more of a boy than you are. You'll understand one day." I turn around and fist bump Jamie. "See ya then. You best go and get practising. You don't want to lose to girls now do you? That *would* be embarrassing."

Matt smiles and gives me a small nod in admiration.

Maggie is already posting online about the game tomorrow. Emily and Jamie just look on in amazement. I don't know who is smiling the most. Jamie's cheeks though have gone slightly more pink than usual.

"I don't need you sticking up for me all the time, Lucy. I can hold my own," Jamie says, quietly.

"I know you can, but you would do the same for me. It's what friends do."

The bell sounds.

"Back to lessons then," Emily says and skips off with Maggie.

I notice that Jamie has spotted Charlotte walking towards us in the distance.

"Close your mouth, Jamie," I whisper.

"Hi Charlotte, do you know which big school you'll be applying to next year?"

"Big school? No one says that Jamie, it's secondary school," Charlotte scoffs, as she walks away.

"Did you hear that, Lucy; she knows my name."

"That's not what I think you should take away from that conversation!" I say, shaking my head.

The next few lessons pass without incident. Before I know it, I'm at home with Mum having my tea.

"So, Lucy, what have you been doing today at school?" Mum asks while we're sat at the table.

"Jamie is being picked on again by Jack and his friends. We challenged them to a girls v boys football match."

"It's awful he gets picked on all the time. I feel for him, because it's not nice. It's good he has some friends to talk to, as I know he finds it difficult to talk to his mum or dad. Please let me know if it carries on. He really needs to try and find a way to open up to his parents more, I know they would understand and try and help him if they knew."

"I'll let him know, but he's fine. It seems to bother him less and less. Oh, in science club today we got the whole class involved," I say, changing the subject.

"Oh yes, did you do the 'matters of state experiment' in the playing field?"

"Yes, how did you know?" I ask, as I put another mouthful of potatoes in my mouth.

"It's in the school email. They said it went well and you all enjoyed it."

"Most of us enjoyed it," I correct. "Jamelia and Ben nearly got crushed when we all hugged together at first, pretending we were a solid. Some of the boys were pushing too hard. Me and J weren't even in the middle, and we were panicking a little. It felt like that time I got stuck in my sleeping bag and the more I wriggled the worse it felt."

"I remember. Can you remember what that's called?"

"A NIGHTMARE!"

"No, it's called <u>claustrophobia</u>. An irrational fear of confined spaces," Mum confirms.

"I thought 'claus-a-phobia' was fear of Santa?" I say trying to contain my laughter.

"You are missing the 'tro' off. It comes from <u>Latin</u>; phobia meaning fear and claustro meaning bolt. As in a bolted door so you are trapped."

"Thanks, Mum. I'm sure I'll have forgotten that before I've even finished my broccoli!"

"Well, you can't remember everything, Lucy, and most people only remember what they want to or need to. But you will find a lot of words have Latin origins and there are lots of phobias that different people have."

"Talking of eating, why is 10 afraid of 7?"

"I don't know, Lucy, why is 10 afraid of 7?"

"Because 7, 8, 9! Get it, 7 ate 9."

"Ah, very good," giggles Mum. "You do like your numbers."

Why is 10 afraid of 7?

because 7, 8, 9

"So, going back to my story, Mum, we all survived being squashed into a solid, but only just. Next it was time to spread out and move around a little to simulate being a liquid." I paused while I finished off my carrots. "Finally, we all spread out across the whole field moving around freely. Can you guess what state we were in then?" I was trying to catch Mum out, as this is what she does to me to see if I'm listening.

"You were a gas."

"Yes, that's correct. You can have my parsnip for getting that right, Mum."

"No, I don't think so, missy. Nice try, but you need to eat it."

"Dang-it. Can we get a dog, Mum?" I ask, rather hopefully.

"No, Lucy. We've had this conversation several times now." Mum looks frustrated.

"But Max gives his dog all the bits of his tea he doesn't like, and his dog, Dougal, loves it."

"Dougal? His dog is called Dougal? That's a funny name for a dog." Mum switches the conversation back to school. "Talking of states of matter and school, the school email said you will be learning about temperatures and pressures next week."

"Yes, they told us already. We have homework to put in the fridge."

"What do you mean?" Mum asks, a little confused.

"We have to use a plastic water bottle or balloon and fill it half full of water. We then have to place in somewhere cold like in the fridge or freezer. The air and the water compresses the colder it gets."

"The liquid water will start to turn into a solid and the air will also compress." Mum understands now why it will have to go in the fridge.

"Yes, and the bottle will crush inwards. We watched a video on it in lesson. We then have to place it somewhere warm, and the bottle will expand."

"That sounds cool. We can do it over the weekend. It reminds me of the time when we went abroad on the plane about three years ago," Mum says, thoughtfully.

"Why?" I ask. I'm not really sure what that has to do with my homework.

"You bought a bag of crisps at the airport and didn't eat them, do you remember? When you took

46

them out of your rucksack on the plane the bag was ready to explode."

"I do remember. I thought it would pop open. We magically had more crisps," I smile.

"Well, not quite. There weren't any more crisps in there just the air pressure on the plane was lower than the pressure in the bag, so the bag expanded. The opposite happened when you had a drink of water on the plane and resealed your plastic bottle. The bottle looked fine until we landed and then it was squashed."

"Why?" I'm still confused.

"The air pressure on the ground is slightly higher than the air pressure introduced to the bottle when you opened it on the plane. That caused that air inside the bottle to compress and suck the bottle in when we landed."

"Can we go on a plane this weekend and I'll video it for school?"

"Yes, OK, we'll just fly to Spain for a few hours," Mum laughs.

"REALLY!" I say, excitedly.

"No. Not really."

"Mum, you got me really excited then." Sometimes I struggle to understand when she's being sarcastic.

"You all done now?" Mum asks, as I push my plate away.

"Yes. All finished. Oh, Mum, what do you want for your birthday this year?"

"I'm glad you asked. I know exactly what I want, but I'm not sure you can buy it. I think you will have to make it for me."

"What's that? I love making things."

"You know I struggle with all the different emojis? Well, I would like an emoji dictionary."

"Mum, you are so old," I shake my head. "No worries though, I've got this covered. I'll soon have that sorted."

"Thanks, Lucy. Now, do you want to help me wash up or are you going to read?"

"Definitely read, if you are OK tiding up?"

Mum nods, and with that, I race upstairs to grab my book.

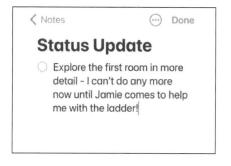

Emoji Dictionary

Happy

Laughing

crying

love

Whining

puppy eyes

Chapter 4
A picture is worth a thousand words

While Mum is tidying up the garden on this unusually nice day, I'm going to take this opportunity to explore the first secret room again. I need Jamie's help with the ladder, so I'm limited to the first room only, but I've always raced through it without stopping to take a better look around, so it will be good to spend some time in there exploring.

As I make my way down the <u>numerous</u> stairs, I feel the air getting colder the lower I go. I enter the first room again. Every time I come in here, I instantly glance at the fruit on the table and I feel hungry. It's probably a good job the fruit is plastic, because after the amount of time they have been down here, even the maggots eating them would be <u>fossilised</u>.

I look up at the blackboard at all the <u>gibberish gobbledegook</u> on there. I take a deep breath. I can't even begin to think about most of that right now. I forgot how complicated a <u>conundrum</u> it was, and now I remember why I didn't write much of it down in my notebook when I came down before. This is obviously going to be a maths problem that I'll tackle another day (or maybe never!). On a positive note, I have already worked out that the five rows of numbers written on the board equate to five names by using the simple code of A equals 1, B equals 2, but I naively thought the rest of it would be just as easy. How wrong I was.

<u>Alphabet Code</u>

A = 1
B = 2
C = 3
D = 4
E = 5
F = 6
G = 7
H = 8
I = 9
J = 10
K = 11
L = 12
M = 13

N = 14
O = 15
P = 16
Q = 17
R = 18
S = 19
T = 20
U = 21
V = 22
W = 23
X = 24
Y = 25
Z = 26

I start looking round the room. The walls in this room seem newer and smoother than the ones in the other rooms, which are rough stone walls similar to the kinds of walls in an old castle, but I could be mistaken as it's been a while.

I've only been down here five minutes, but I'm getting cold now. As it was warm outside, I didn't think to put on a jumper to come down here. Goosebumps start to appear on my arms. So much for having a good look around, now all I can think about is heading back upstairs.

I decide to have a quick look at the bookcase before I head back. There doesn't appear to be any fiction books, they are all information books: engineering, maths, physics, biology, chemistry, oceanography, robotics, astronomy, *Understanding Latin Uses Within Science*... and many, many more. Oh, that's strange, there is one novel. It's *The Lion, the Witch and the Wardrobe* by CS Lewis. All of the books in here appear old and dusty. But what stands out the most is that they don't appear to be in any order; not alphabetically, or by size, or even by colours! I feel compelled to rearrange them but not now, I am too cold. One book catches my eye as I'm starting to leave, *Secret Coding for Beginners*. I pick it up and flick through the pages. I place it in my backpack so I can read it later. I tell myself I'm not stealing it, just borrowing, as I have every intention of returning it later.

I'm just about to leave when I notice the three pictures on the wall. I looked up at the first one.

I try to read it whilst doing star jumps to keep warm.

The answer to life and the universe is Goldilocks.
Not too hot, not too cold.
Not too big, not too small.
Not too easy, not too hard.
Everything in moderation.
Everything just right.

I decide to take photos of all three pictures and study them upstairs, with a jumper on and maybe a hot chocolate. A smile appears on my face and a warm sensation flows through me. I quickly take out my phone and photograph each picture, taking care to allow it time to focus. I've got so many blurred images that I'd be an adult by the time I've gone through them all and deleted them!

I head back up the stairs. It's always harder going back up. Well, I think that's my exercise done for today.

After closing the bookcase door, I race over to the chest of drawers and remove the thickest and fluffiest jumper I can find from my middle drawer. As I rub my arms to keep warm, I decide that this jumper will do nicely.

Mum bursts into my room. I jump out of my skin; that was a close call.

"Lucy, why have you got a jumper on? It's lovely and warm outside. Go and get some fresh air."

"On one condition…" I negotiate.

"What's that?"

"Can you make me a hot chocolate, please?" Mum looks <u>flabbergasted</u>.

"Hot chocolate? On a day like this?"

"Please, Mum, pretty please." I'm so cold I can feel it in my bones!

"OK, I'm ready for a drink as well. I'll treat myself for tidying the garden up, and I'll have one as well."

"Good for you, Mum. I'm going to get my notebook and draw in the garden."

I grab my phone, my pencil case and notebook and head downstairs with Mum. She puts the kettle on whilst I head outside.

I get myself comfy on the bench and rest on the table whilst going through the photos I've just taken.

I've already decided I'm going to copy them into my notebook, as everything goes in there.

I phone Jamie.

"Hello there." It didn't even ring. "I'm <u>tele-pathetic</u>," Jamie announces.

"I think you mean <u>telepathic</u>. There is nothing pathetic about you," I correct him.

"I know; I was just being funny. I was just going to ring you, as it happens."

"Great minds think alike. What are you up to?"

"Nothing much, just been on <u>Roblox</u> with Dylan, but he's off out to go for lunch with his relatives."

"Poor Dylan."

"I know. He started coughing and put his head next to the radiator and told his mum he had a temperature, but she wasn't buying it."

"It was worth a try." I make a mental note to remember this trick for the future.

"What are you up to?"

"I've taken some photos of the pictures in the first secret room. I'm going to copy them out into my notebook and try and work out what they are."

"Sounds exiting… NOT! What pictures are they? I can't remember any apart from the sunrise."

"They're not pictures as such, more statements, so I can see why we really didn't notice them before."

I spot Mum coming towards me with my mug of hot chocolate, topped with whipped cream and rainbow marshmallows.

"Thanks, Mum. I'm just on the phone with J."

"OK. HI JAMIE," Mum shouts a little too loudly.

"Mum's just brought me a hot chocolate."

"That's more like it. I wish I was there now. Can you talk?"

"Yes, Mum's gone back inside now. I'll put you on hands free then I can talk you through the pictures." I quickly activate the speaker button and place the phone on the table by the side of me.

"Right, the first one is of <u>Goldilocks theory</u>."

"You've got a fairy tale on the wall? That doesn't make any sense. Just like that plastic fruit doesn't make sense, actually."

"I think it relates to the nursery rhyme but there is more to it than that." I read it line for line back to Jamie.

> ## Goldilocks Theory
>
> The answer to life and the universe is Goldilocks.
>
> Not too hot, not too cold
> Not too big, not too small
> Not too easy, not too hard
>
> Everything in moderation
> Everything just right

"The answer to the universe – REALLY?" he says sarcastically.

"I remember my dad talking to me about this. I think it relates to the earth being in the Goldilocks zone in space. Not too close to the sun and not too far away either. So, the conditions are just right."

"I get that, but really, the answer to the universe?" Jamie doesn't sound convinced.

"Well, it could be. This is similar to how evolution works. Animals that are too extreme in one way or the other may not survive in the long term as conditions change."

"I don't get what you mean, Luce."

"Well, take a wild bird for example. If it has a plentiful supply of food and doesn't need to work hard for it, it becomes obese and lazy. If the food supply runs out, they might be too slow to find any alternative food sources. This could wipe them out all in one go."

"But if they are small, they would be OK?"

"No, on the other hand, if the food supply is scarce the birds would be small and weak then they would be prone to being eaten themselves."

"So, what's the answer?"

"Goldilocks, of course. Not too big and not too small. I know it's a very simplified answer and it doesn't explain evolution fully, but you get my drift."

"Got it now. It's a bit like when I ask for chocolate at the supermarket. If I don't ask, I don't get any, and if I ask for too much, I don't get any. But if I'm not greedy, I'm more likely to get some?"

"Well, I don't think the Goldilocks theory was written for chocolate, but I do see your logic," I giggle. Jamie is very good at relating things to food.

"What other pictures have you got? Hopefully, nothing as complicated as that!"

"SI units."

"What is that?"

"I'll forward the photo to you. It looks like measurements, but I'll let *you* research it and come back to me."

"Homework? You're giving me homework!" Jamie sighs.

"Well, I'm sure you owe me. All the homework I've helped you with."

"Fair point. I'll get back to you on that."

SI units
Length – Metre (m)
Time – Second (s)
Amount of substance – Mole (mol)
Electric current – Ampere (A)
Temperature – Kelvin (K)
Luminous intensity – Candela (cd)
Mass – Kilogram (kg)

"There you go. I've sent it."

After a few moments, Jamie confirms he's received the picture. "The first two are easy. <u>Metres</u> and seconds, and isn't the last one, mass, the same as weight?"

"Yes. Mass is the same everywhere, but weight is your mass with the effects of gravity."

"It says here, there are seven base units and all other units can be worked out from these units. All conversions using this metric system are done by moving the decimal point to scale it up or down. It also says that all seven base units can be accurately reproduced and is the world's most widely used system of measurement," Jamie adds.

"You've just looked that up?"

"Of course, I did. There, my homework's all done," he announces, proudly.

"Wow, you're on fire, J."

"What else do you have?"

"Just sent it. <u>Ohm's law</u>."

Ohm's law
Volts / Amps = Resistance
Volts / Resistance = Amps
Resistance x Amps = Volts

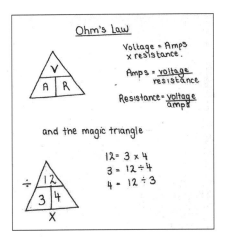

"What's all that about? Do I really want to know?"

"It's actually really simple," I explain. "The triangle helps you work out the equation for the answer you require. So, imagine you put 12 at the top of the triangle and below it you put a 3 and a 4. Three times 4 equals 12. Twelve divided by 3 equals 4. Twelve divided by 4 equals 3. I use this triangle formula a lot in science and maths lessons."

"Now you put it like that it does seem simple."

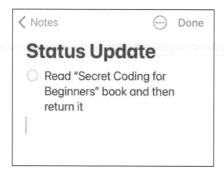

Chapter 5
The prom

"Mum, I was going to ask Luke to the school prom, but he's already going with Kitty, so I've asked Jacob instead. He said yes."

"Like the man from Del Monte," Mum laughs and I'm confused. "Never mind. I'm pleased for you, Lucy, but you haven't really mentioned him before. Is he the new boy that transferred from another school last month?"

"Yes, that's right. I've been showing him round and helping him make friends. He seems nice even though he didn't say yes at first," I explain.

"You managed to convince him."

"I think he was embarrassed to say yes in front of his friends. He kept saying he doesn't like dancing and probably wouldn't be going."

"Do you want me to pick him up on the way so you can arrive together?"

"No. I've already suggested that, and he said he would meet me there. Can you order that purple dress I like, please? Pretty please, Mum." I give her my best puppy eyes look that I know she can't resist.

"Yes, OK. I'll order it today so it will come in plenty of time."

"Thanks, Mum. I'm going to <u>DM</u> Emily and Maggie, so we don't end up all going in the same dress."

"When I was your age DM stood for Danger Mouse!" Mum snorts as she laughs!

"What? Danger Mouse? What IS that?"

"It was, and maybe still is, a children's cartoon. I'll look it up for you."

"No, don't worry, Mum, I'll check it out later. DM is direct message, <u>FYI</u>."

"I know. I was just saying…"

"I know, Mum. You are old," I laugh. I wouldn't dare say that to anyone else.

"Cheeky. Is Jamie not going? I know he generally doesn't go to these kinds of things."

"No. It's not his thing."

I pick my phone up off the table and message the Lucy/Maggie/Emily (LME) girls' group chat.

LME

Lucy

My Mum's getting me that purple dress. What r u both wearing?

Maggie

I've still got that red all-in-one that I wore for my birthday

Emily

I haven't decided yet. Is Jacob still going with you?

Lucy

I think so. He said he would meet me there. But he did say he might have football 1st.

Maggie

I hope he showers!

Emily

Doubtful! I still think he's messing you about. He's told the boys he's not going!

LME

Lucy

I'll stay optimistic - until he tells me otherwise!

Maggie

He's a boy, not a gentleman. I think it's wishful thinking on your part

Lucy

That reminds me of a song my dad used to play all the time - 'King of Wishful Thinking' I think it was called. I'll dig out one of his mix CDs later

Maggie

Are you still going with James, Em?

Emily

Yes. Anyone asked you yet?

Maggie

No and I'm glad! I don't need the drama. I'm going with you guys regardless

It's finally the big day, and I'm still frantically trying to get my hair to look like the girls in the videos I've watched many times over the last few days. I don't want to be late, though.

"Are you nearly ready yet, Lucy? You are going to be late," Mum shouts up the stairs.

"Nearly. I'm just adjusting one of my hairgrips."

"Stop messing with your hair. I've not spent an hour curling it, for you to just mess it up."

"Mum, I want it to be perfect. Jacob said he's wearing a suit and tie and everything, and he's had his hair cut especially for tonight." I'm a little <u>exasperated</u> that Mum doesn't seem to understand the importance of this. "How do I look?"

"Perfect, like always."

"No, you always say that. I need to look better than how I normally look."

"You look amazing."

"Do you think Dad would agree?"

"He would, but I think he wouldn't approve of that dress and all that make-up. He would probably lock the door to stop you from leaving."

"He would want me to be happy. I know he would."

"He would, but he would say you are growing up far too fast. Right, shoes on, we don't want to keep Jacob waiting too long." Mum starts to put her coat on.

"Can you just fasten the strap on my shoes, please? I can't do it myself."

"Of course, Your Highness." Mum does a sarcastic curtsey, as she helps me with my shoes.

The drive seems to take forever. I can't wait to see him. I'd asked for a picture of his suit, and he said he didn't want to spoil the effect. I'm so excited.

Mum drops me at the gate where Mrs Hudson is there to greet us and sign us all in. I say goodbye to Mum and, as I hurry towards the entrance, Mum shouts after me to confirm what time she will come and pick me up. That seems like far too short a time, so I race in as quick as I can and look for the smartest dressed boy.

Em and Maggie join me.

"We've not seen Jacob," they confirm.

"He says he's coming. He can't wait to show off

his new suit."

"He hasn't got a suit," interrupts James. "He hates them. He's just pulling your leg."

"Come on, Lucy, come with us and get a drink. He'll find us when he arrives," suggests Maggie.

"I'll just wait here a bit longer so I can see him arrive. You carry on. We'll find you as soon as he gets here."

I take my phone out of my little matching purple shoulder bag. No messages. Come on Jacob. I message him.

That's disappointing. I should have insisted we pick him up. I head over to find everyone else. People are still arriving and hardly anyone is dancing yet.

"Told you he's not coming," laughs James.

"James don't be so insensitive," scolds Emily.

"I can prove it. You just don't want to believe it, that's all."

"Prove it then," demands Maggie.

James takes out his phone and shows us the 'Oresome boys' group chat.

None of us made any reference to their terrible spelling of awesome.

He hesitates. "I shouldn't really show you this, actually. It is sacred, boys only."

All three of us are staring at him. He instantly realises has no choice now and holds the phone up so we can all see.

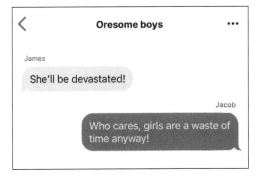

"How inconsiderate." Maggie is furious. "Who does he think he is?"

"He's a boy, what do you expect?" Emily replies.

"Cheers," remarks James.

"You're no better. How dare you let this happen. Begone with you, I say," Emily says angrily.

"Come on. I was the one who told you he wasn't coming," James protests.

"Disappear. You are no friend of mine."

James skulks off looking for his silly mates.

I slip away while this conversation is happening (although, as Emily is angry, the conversation is quite loud, so I can still hear everything that's being said). I look back, Maggie and Emily are looking round for me, but I'm nearly out of sight now.

I quickly sneak into the toilets and lock the door. I'm sure my mascara is ruined, but I'm reluctant to wipe my eyes.

I do the only thing I know I can – text Mum. I'm sobbing so much my breathing is <u>erratic</u>, and I know I wouldn't be able to get any words out if I tried to call her.

A message pings through from Jamie.

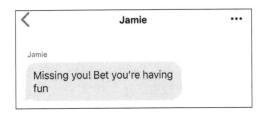

I dial his number, as I've regained control of my breathing now.

"Thought you'd be too busy to chat to me," he remarks as soon as he answers the phone.

"He's stood me up." I manage to get the words out.

"No way! What's wrong with him?" I can always rely on Jamie to understand how I'm feeling.

"I think it was a bet. Did you know anything about it?" I really hope he doesn't, but I want to be doubly sure.

"Certainly not. I would have warned you. But, then again, they don't speak to me anyway."

"I normally give people a second chance, but he's blown it," I say, definitively.

"Too right. What a fool. Do you want me to come? I will do, you know."

"No, it's OK. That's really kind of you. But I know how much you hate these things. Besides, Em and Maggie are here."

"OK. I'll take my coat back off. As long as you are OK."

"I will be. You always make me smile. You can carry on playing *Roblox* now," I offer.

"How did you know?" Strangely, he sounds a little surprised.

"You are always playing it!"

"True."

"Talk soon. Thanks J."

As we say our goodbyes, I unlock the door, and I'm greeted by my other two besties.

"There you are. I thought you had done a runner."
Maggie looks relieved to have found me.

"Here, hold still," Emily says, as she wipes my eyes
with some tissue. "Good."

Charlotte walks in. "Come on, quick. I've
requested 'Dancing Queen' and the DJ's playing it now."

We all run out on to the dance floor.

♪ *You can dance,*
You can jive,
Having the time of your life,
Ooh, see that girl,
Watch that scene,
Digging the dancing queen. ♪

We all sing in unison. Maggie tries her best, but
she is the first to admit – she can't sing.

What   had   gone   from
#WORSTNIGHTEVER was now becoming
a great night, and I'm starting to have a great time. I
glance over and see George on his own in the corner.

I can't help myself. Nobody puts George in a
corner, not even himself. I dance over, but he's looking
at his phone.

"What are you looking at?" I startle him a little, as
he is so engrossed in his phone he hasn't spotted me.

"Did you know that your body produces 1.5 litres
of mucus, bogies to you and me, most of which you
swallow?" I'm nearly sick in my mouth!

"Er, not me. Why are you looking at that?"

"The mucus is to wash particles out of your lungs and keep you safe from infections."

"Stop saying that-word," I insist. If he carries on, I may seriously be sick.

"Do you want to see some images?" he offers.

"No! George, put your phone away." I remove a face wipe from my bag and pass it to him. "Wipe your hands."

He does, without hesitation and, rather well, I think. I pull him up from his chair.

"Let's dance." His face lights up.

"Look, Harriet's got one of those doggy bags!" he points and laughs.

I glance around wondering what horrors he is referring to.

"George, don't ever say that again. She will kill you. A doggy bag is something completely different. Harriet has a Radley bag! I know it has a dog on it, but it's NOT a doggy bag." I was trying really hard not to laugh.

"Oops," he laughs along. I'm not sure if he realises his mistake or not.

There is an expression 'dance like no one's watching' and clearly, George knows this well. He's bouncing on the spot, like he has a pogo stick up his bum. When he's in the air, he reaches up as high as he can. On the way back down, he quickly lowers his hands as if he was trying to jump over something.

> PUT YOUR HANDS IN THE AIR AND DANCE LIKE NOBODY'S THERE

"You've got some moves there, George." I don't think he's heard me. He's definitely in the moment.

Suddenly, Elliot tries to cut in.

"May I have this dance? I'll save you," he says winking with his back to George.

"Sorry, Elliot, I'm dancing with George." His confidence drains from his face, and he vanishes as quickly as he appeared. I'm not really dancing *with* George. He's now unstoppable. He has his own grooves. I haven't realised that most of us have stopped dancing now and we are all <u>mesmerised</u> by him, as he had dropped to the floor, on to his back, and was doing some kind of spinning and breakdancing – but not the kind anyone, EVER, had seen before.

We are all clapping him on. #BESTNIGHTEVER!

Chapter 6
Operation ladder

It's an inset day today, so we are off school. Mum has also taken the day off, but I know she has a very important video call to be on at 11 a.m. for at least an hour. This is the perfect time to get the ladder.

It's 10.30 a.m. now, so I text Jamie.

I go downstairs. "Jamie will be here in a few minutes, Mum. We're going to do some homework upstairs while you are on your call."

"OK. Don't have your music on loud, no singing or pillow fights!"

"Don't worry, Mum, we'll be quiet," I reassure her.

Mum sits down at the kitchen table and starts setting her laptop up.

"No, you are not having your call in here, are you?" I panic.

"Why?"

"Er… I think, er… It will be quieter in the lounge. Plus, we might need to come back down for a drink. We don't want to be in your way," I improvise, trying to think of a plausible reason for her not to stay in the kitchen.

"Good point. I didn't think of that. Help me move my things into the lounge will you, sweetie."

As soon as I've carried my mum's books and things through and have helped her set up, the doorbell rings.

I can see Jamie outside jumping around. He's either extremely excited or he needs a wee! His mum has only just got out of their blue Ford Focus.

I run and open the front door.

"Hi, Jamie, do you need the toilet?" I ask.

"No! Why?" He comes in for a hug.

"Hi, Alison," I smile, as she reaches the front door.

"Hi, Lucy. Jamie's really excited to do homework with you. I'm glad you have a positive influence on him. I've been asking him for days to do it."

Mum walks up behind us in the hallway. "Hi, Alison. Are you doing anything fun with your day off work today?"

"I wish. Just catching up with housework and food shopping. Pete's left me to do the dishwasher. I bet he checks it when he gets home, because he thinks he's the only one who can load it properly."

"Really?"

"You best believe it. He reckons he's got <u>NVQs</u> in loading it! Have you ever heard anything more ridiculous than that?"

"You know what? I could do with NVQs in emojis."

"Tell me about it. I just pick any silly face, no idea what any of them mean."

Me and J are just looking at each other obviously thinking the same thing: *Parents – how embarrassing!*

"Bye, Mum, time to go. Jenni's got to start work now," Jamie adds forcefully whilst ushering his mum out of the door.

"Jamie's right. I'm on a call in a minute," Mum confirms.

With that, we all say our goodbyes. As I'm closing the front door, I notice the back of Jamie's dad's car.

"You've still got that Tesla sticker on your car, I see," I say with a smile.

"Yeah, I don't know who my dad thinks he's kidding by removing the Ford Focus badge and replacing it with a Tesla one. It doesn't even look anything like one."

"Maybe he's just buying a Tesla one piece at a time," I offer.

Mum seems distracted for a moment but then says, "Fancy doing schoolwork on your day off school, Jamie!"

Jamie looks horrified for a second, but then he remembers that this is just our cover story.

"Yes, Jenni, at least Lucy and I are together and can help each other."

"Did Lucy tell you that I need it to be quiet this morning as I'm on an important call? I'm doing an online training course," Mum clarifies.

"I did, Mum. Come on, Jamie, let's go to my room."

Jamie nods to Mum, as I grab his arm and pull him away from the conversation. We need to go before Mum figures out something is amiss.

"Right, we'll go over the plan one more time," I suggest when we're in my room and out of Mum's earshot.

"Do we have to, Luce? We've been over it a thousand times now!"

"Have you brought your waterproof trousers and a towel?" I ask.

"What? What are you talking about?" Jamie looks horrified, for the second time in as many minutes.

"Someone's got to go into the water and secure the ladder at the other side." I try to keep a straight face.

"That wasn't in the plan. I'm not going to get wet. You know I don't like water."

"I'm only joking," I reassure him.

Jamie doesn't look amused. "Well don't. I got worried then that I had forgotten the plan."

"Lucy, Lucy," Mum shouts up from the foot of the stairs. "I'm going into my call now."

"OK, Mum. Close the lounge door."

"Good idea," I hear her shout before I hear the lounge door close. I put my finger to my lips and look at Jamie.

"What are we waiting for?" whispers Jamie.

I'm not ignoring him, but I'm just listening intently. I can hear Mum on the call.

Jamie is looking over at my journal. "What's this?" he asks, as he starts to flick through the pages.

"I've been redrawing a section of the summer night sky. You can still see Cassiopeia even though it's not summer yet. You don't need a telescope – just look for a big 'W' in the night sky." I show him in my book.

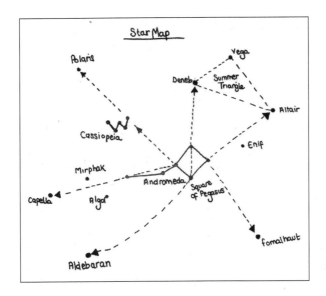

"Oh, you'll never guess what I saw the other night?" he excitedly asks.

"The moon?" I hazard a guess.

"No, well yes, but I was talking about the ISS."

"The International Space Station," I confirm. "I missed it, but I've seen it many times before."

"My parents let me download the app, so I now get alerts when it's visible. It's the first time I've seen it."

"It's fast isn't it? It moves just like a plane through the sky and looks like a star. Come on, close that up, we are wasting time. Mum's started the call, so we need to get going." I usher him towards the door.

"Operation Ladder," Jamie says with the deepest voice he can muster.

"Why does everything have to be about the military with you?"

"It's because of my brother. He's obsessed with the military, so we like to play our war games with each other."

Jamie starts his timer on his phone, so we can keep track of the time.

"Good idea, Batman," I say, as he looks up at me.

"So, I'm Batman now. Does that make you Robin?"

"No, I think I'll be Batgirl or Supergirl."

"Whatever. But I'm Batman. Say I'm Batman again – I'm going to record you, so I can remind you in the future that *I'm* Batman, just in case you forget!"

"I don't think so. Right, let's do it. No time to waste." Jamie nods but without the same level of enthusiasm that I have.

We creep downstairs. I point to the creaky eleventh step as I pass it. Jamie gives me another nod as if to say 'I know, you've told me a thousand times', and he motions me to carry on with a couple of flicks of his wrist.

We pass the closed lounge door, go through the hall and into the kitchen.

We creep out of the kitchen door and head to the garage. It's another cold morning again, not a glimpse of the sun anywhere. I let Jamie open the side door to the garage, as it's always a bit stiff and everything seems a lot harder with my wrist brace on.

He spots the ladder straight away and picks it up like he's a superhero.

"It's lighter than it looks," he chuckles.

"Yes, its aluminium. It's a light metal."

Just then, he knocks over a couple of boxes as he tries to <u>manoeuvre</u> it through the door.

"Hang on. Let me help you." I grab the front with my good hand. "You move to the back and close the door."

"OK. Sorry about the boxes."

"I'll tidy them up tomorrow," I sigh.

"Slow down," Jamie says breathlessly from behind me. "I'm almost jogging."

I slow down. We're not quite in sync with each other.

"It's just like the first time we did the three-legged race, and you went storming off and pulled me over and even then, you didn't stop, you just kept on dragging me, do you remember?"

"I was determined to beat Sophie and Eleanor." I recall it vividly. My competitiveness got the better of me that day.

"Well don't pull me over again."

We reach the kitchen door. I slowly open it and peer in. I look back at Jamie and nod to him to confirm the coast is clear. We both carry the ladders into the house. Jamie pulls the door to behind us, and we make our way up the stairs. There's an unmistakable sound of the creak from the eleventh step. I glare at Jamie. He just shrugs and flashes me his charming smile, which seems to be his special power.

When we make it into my bedroom, I'm a little taken aback. The ladders seem a lot bigger in here, and we're struggling to do anything with them.

"Are these telescopic ladders? They seem to have extended." Jamie seems rather <u>bemused</u>.

"No. It's all relative. They looked small in the garage and outside because they are bigger spaces. My bedroom is a lot smaller, so the ladders look bigger. It's how illusionists do their magic. It fools your eyes. I must admit, when I planned this out in my head, I didn't realise how big the ladders would be in this little room."

"Careful, Lucy, it almost sounds like you are admitting making a mistake."

"Some of the best ideas come from making mistakes." I sound just like Mum.

"If that were true, I would have had loads of brilliant ideas by now," Jamie laughs.

"There's still time, Jamie. Right, I'm going to rest my end on the corner of the bed. You stay still otherwise you'll knock Charlie's tank over." Charlie is my red and blue Siamese fighting fish.

I place the ladders down, pull on the cosmology book and push the secret bookcase door open.

"Right, let's carry these ladders down the stairs and place them in the first room. I opened the door at the bottom of the stairs earlier so it would be easier for us while we're carrying the ladders."

I pick up the ladders and we very slowly descend the stairs. This is incredibly <u>precarious</u>. I instruct, "Left… right… left… right," just as we had done when we were perfecting the three-legged race for the second year. Our timing has to be <u>impeccable</u> right now. And it is.

"Great job, Jamie. I'm at the bottom."

"Keep going then," comes his reply.

"Er… I don't seem to be able to. The ladders are stuck!"

Chapter 7
Teamwork

"What do you mean the ladder's stuck? It's a shame they don't have a bendy bit in the middle," Jamie muses.

"That would be a little pointless, as you wouldn't be able to climb it! I've got an idea. Just pull it back a little. I just need to angle it down in the corner more. There, done it. Lift your end up higher, Jamie, and slowly walk down the steps. Watch your fingers going through the door," I warn.

"Nearly there. <u>Wowsers</u>! We did it. I'm <u>gobsmacked</u>."

"Right, leave them here, I just need a rest," I say, slightly breathlessly.

"Me too, that was difficult with two arms. Can't imagine how hard it was for you."

"We'll lay it on the floor."

"Whatever happened to that 'boys vs girls' football match, Lucy?" Jamie asks.

"Jack keeps rearranging it. I doubt we'll ever get round to playing it."

"I don't remember these pictures on the wall." Jamie's distracted now from the football conversation and is looking at the room around us.

"Yes, they've always been here. You don't think I've started decorating down here, do you?" I say whilst moving my arms around to try and get the feeling back in them.

I open up the door, using code 87 that I have memorised. The rope is still there weighed down by the books and the fruit bowl from the last time I came down here.

"Right, Jamie. Let's carry the ladder through here and place it over the water."

"Okey-dokey."

We both pick up an end of the ladder and carry it over to the area of water.

Jamie stops at the water's edge. "You keep walking, Luce, and I'll feed the ladder past me and over the water."

This seems to be working until the farthest end of the ladder is very close to the edge of the other side of the water and then, catastrophe, it gets too heavy for us both to hold and the majority of the ladder falls straight into the watery abyss. We quickly pull it back and drag it out.

"I'm sorry, Lucy, I didn't mean to drop it. I know this isn't part of the plan."

"It's not your fault. It was never going to work, and I should have anticipated this. You were acting as the <u>fulcrum</u>. So, when you are holding the middle of the ladder its balanced perfectly, but the more I passed to you the harder it is for you to hold on to it."

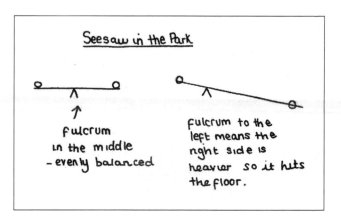

Seesaw in the Park

fulcrum
in the middle
- evenly balanced

fulcrum to the
left means the
right side is
heavier so it hits
the floor.

This unexpected issue has thrown me. I can hear Jamie mumbling about something, but I'm trying to think on my feet.

"I can't concentrate, Jamie." I start doing my deep-breathing routine. Breath in for four seconds, hold it for four seconds and then out for four seconds.

"You OK?" Jamie sounds concerned.

I compose myself. "Yeah, fine now. Sorry, what were you saying?"

"I've got an idea. How about tying the rope to your end of the ladder, and I'll try and throw the ladder so my end goes to the other side. We can use the rope to pull it back if I miss."

"Great idea." I'm genuinely impressed with Jamie's suggestion.

"Really?" sounds a very surprised, Jamie.

"I think it's too large and heavy for us to throw it over, but using the rope is an excellent idea." I remove the rope from under the fruit bowl and loop it under the first rung on the ladder nearest the water's edge. "Right, Jamie, you hold on to this end of the rope, and I'll push the ladder across.

"Pull the rope a bit more," I suggest, "that will keep it out of the water."

"This is starting to work. The ladder's like a drawbridge, like in a castle, Luce."

I smile back at him. "Slowly release some more rope and lower it back down." I have to get down on to my knees now and keep pushing.

"Don't fall in, 'cos I'm not rescuing you. And you won't be able to swim with that dodgy arm of yours." He has a point about the <u>latter</u>, but I didn't believe him about the <u>former</u>.

There's a clunk as the metal hits the stone surface on the other side.

"We did it," comes a triumphant cry from behind me. I stand up and turn around to be greeted with a high five and then a fist bump.

"Teamwork! Thanks for your help, Jamie. I couldn't have done it without you. Just pass the end of the rope over this last rung." I point up to the monkey bars.

Jamie loops the end of the rope over <u>effortlessly</u>.

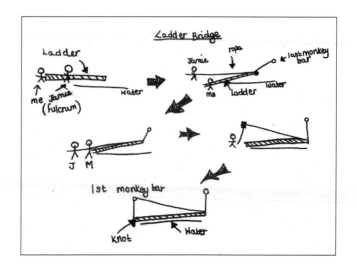

"I feel like a cowboy now. I have so many adventures with you. If I was at home, I would just be on *Minecraft* or some other game all the time."

"We do have a lot of fun together. It wouldn't be the same if you weren't here." I tie a little <u>bowline knot</u> to hold the rope in place to the ladder. Jamie watches with interest, so I explain what I'm doing.

"First, I make a little loop over the straight piece (1), loop round again and feed that under and through the first loop (2)."

"Got it," he nods.

"Then, feed the end under the straight piece (3) and back through the original little loop (4)." I slide the large loop over the end of the ladder and tighten the knot.

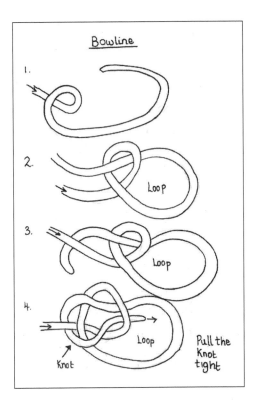

Bowline

1.

2.

Loop

3.

Loop

4.

Loop

Knot

Pull the Knot tight

"Look, we can now hold on to this rope to help us cross."

"You're on fire with great ideas." Jamie pauses. "Wait, who's going across first?"

Just then there is a ringing from Jamie's phone.

"Oh no, it's the timer. We'd better get back upstairs," Jamie says whilst silencing his phone.

"Can you just help me put these books on the table and I'll carry the fruit bowl."

We quickly carry them through and place them on to the table before we race back upstairs.

"The coast is clear," he says when he reaches the top and beckons me up with a quick wave.

I pull the bookcase door closed when we're both back in my room. I feel a sigh of relief come over me, as I recall what we have just achieved. Thinking back, there were two occasions I thought the whole plan was in jeopardy. I was so focused on whether the ladders would be long enough to go over the water and when me and Jamie would be able to sneak them out of the garage, I'd forgotten how big they actually were and if they would get around all the obstacles in our way. And then, I had also overlooked how we would get the ladders across the water.

I collapse on the bed, feeling glad that we had pulled it off, whilst Jamie is staring at the periodic table on my wall.

"You just need some group 1, period 4, Lucy, and then you'll be 'Lucky'."

"What do you mean? What is in group 1, period 4? I can't see it from here."

"Potassium."

"I don't get it." I'm still puzzled and not quite sure what Jamie is talking about.

"You want me to explain some science to you? That's a first. Potassium is K."

"Yes, I know that."

"If you add K into your name, you get Lucky."

A section of the Periodic Table

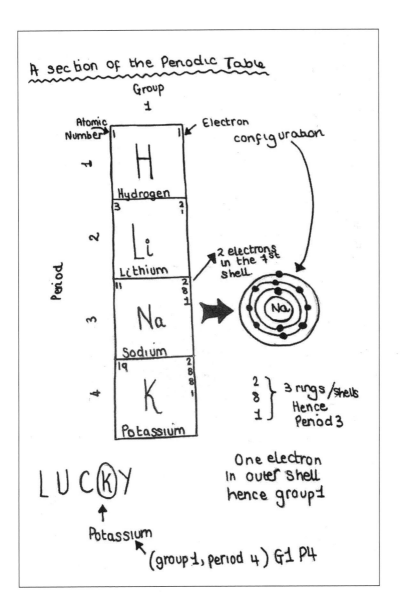

Group 1

Atomic Number →

Electron configuration

1	1
H	
Hydrogen	

Period

1

2 electrons in the 1st shell

3	2 1
Li	
Lithium	

2

11	2 8 1
Na	
Sodium	

3

Na

19	2 8 8 1
K	
Potassium	

4

2
8 } 3 rings/shells
1 }   Hence Period 3

One electron in outer shell hence group 1

L U C (K) Y

↑
Potassium

(group 1, period 4) G1 P4

"Well, I never thought of that. I'm already quite lucky as I'm part Irish, on my dad's side. Grandad regularly reminds me – we have the luck of the Irish."

Jamie doesn't seem to care or understand. He turns around and starts watching Charlie swimming around.

"Charlie's tank is looking a bit dirty, Lucy."

"I know, I haven't cleaned the water in a few days. I normally syphon a bit of the water out, about 20%, and refill it with fresh water. After all, fish do swim in their own toilet!"

"Ugh. That's gross now you think about it. So… when we swim in the sea…" Jamie thinks aloud.

"No, just think how big the sea is. All the fish poo is all very <u>diluted</u> down. Anyway, I bought a test kit with my spending money last week. I can test Charlie's water to see if it's safe. It tests pH, ammonia, nitrate and nitrite. On the pH test it turns red for acid, green for neutral and blue for alkali. And nitrates are good for the garden, so I use the water that I've syphoned out to water Mum's plants. And…"

"Lucy… no… stop talking, you lost me at red and blue," Jamie says confused.

"OK. It's just you looked interested."

"Well, I was for about a millisecond. I want to be like Charlie – I don't think he has a care in the world."

"You are probably right," I agree.

"Did we have any homework for tomorrow?"

"You are such scatterbrain, J. We had to draw that

graph from the table of numbers."

"Which one?" He genuinely doesn't remember the homework we were given.

"The miles to kilometres conversion graph. Can't you remember? I was really excited, as there are a lot of science measurements that use both imperial and metric figures so I thought this would be great."

"I thought everything is metric now though?"

"If you ask your dad how far your car has travelled since it was new, I bet he will tell you in miles not kilometres."

"Can you show me your graph?"

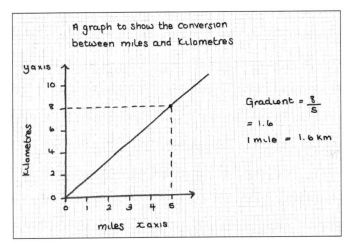

"Look, 5 miles is equal to 8 kilometres."

"Got it. Hey, my brother told me a joke yesterday."

"I'm surprised you can remember it!" I laugh.

"Knock, knock."

"Who's there?"

"Robin."

"Robin who?"

"Robin you – 'of your homework.'" And with that he takes out his phone and photographs my graph.

"You're so cheeky, Jamie!"

"I know. He told me another one as well. Ready?" I nod. "Why aren't skeletons very good at lying?"

"Don't know. Why aren't skeletons very good at lying?"

"Because you can see straight through them."

"I like that one," I giggle.

"I'm done now, guys," Mum shouts up to us from downstairs. "Does anyone want any lunch?" At the mention of food, our ears prick up and we both dart for the door.

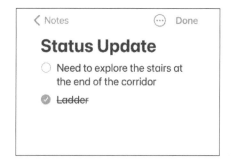

‹ Notes   ⋯   Done

Status Update

○ Need to explore the stairs at the end of the corridor

◉ ~~Ladder~~

Chapter 8
The balancing act

It's evening and Mum has settled down to watch a <u>romcom</u> for the night. The coast is clear, and I've got a couple of hours to go and explore. I've been waiting for this opportunity since Jamie left, now that I've got my bridge in place.

I'm so excited. I slip on my old gym shoes (they still fit but only just). I'm actually a size bigger now, but these are so worn, they still fit. I'll have to look at getting another pair, as I remember Mum saying if my shoes are too small my toes won't grow straight – and I don't want wonky feet! But these will do for tonight. I grab my rucksack. It's been all stocked and ready to go for ages. It's time to go on my <u>clandestine</u> journey. I listen intently at my bedroom door. I can hear the film. Somebody's in love with someone else – that's all I can make out. I race over to the secret bookcase door and pull on the cosmology book. The door pushes in. No time to waste. After pushing it closed, I skip down the stairs with giddiness and, before I know it, I'm looking at the ladder bridge. I stop in my tracks, though. My subconscious is wondering if this is actually a good idea. If I slip and fall, nobody knows I'm down here, so nobody is coming to my rescue. Maybe I should wait until Jamie's around again. I'm full of <u>trepidation</u>; after all, I've only got one working arm at the moment!

DON'T BE
AFRAID TO
FAIL –
BE AFRAID TO
NOT TRY

I look at the ladder. I was good at the beam when I use to go to gymnastics. But on the other hand, that was a long time ago.

I can do this, I reassure myself. I've got the rope for extra support. Besides, it could be weeks until Jamie can come for a sleepover again and I can't wait that long before going exploring.

I hook my left arm, with my brace on, over the rope, so I've still got my good arm for balance (and to grab the ladder if I slip).

I work my way along carefully and confidently. The hardest part is the start. I'm halfway now and my mind is starting to wander. I think of Wocky. I really can't wait to see… Argh, my foot has slipped, and I can see the water getting closer. Panic suddenly kicks in, but the fall almost seems to happen in slow motion.

I try to grab the edge of the ladder with my right hand, but it won't reach. I'm dangling by my left arm, which thankfully is looped over the rope and has stopped my fall. That will teach me to pay better attention. *Focus on the moment, Lucy*, I tell myself. I regain my footing and stand back up. My heart is racing, and I suddenly feel really hot.

"Concentrate, Lucy," I say out loud this time. The rope I'm holding on to gets lower the closer I get to the other side, so I can't make any more mistakes now. I regain my <u>composure</u> and continue, slowly and carefully, to the other side.

"Done it!" I yell, whilst doing a little victory jump. That's the hard part done. Now, it's time to go and see Wocky. I open the door and place my bag on the table. I can't believe how hard it is the find the digestive biscuits, that I put in here, with just one hand. They could make this into an <u>Olympic sport</u> (if it's not already!).

Found them. I take two out of the packet and place them on the table. I look at the door on the right and shiver a little, as I remember the horrors of the giant Venus flytraps which are in that room. I march over to the middle door and enter the code **4B8A4C**. This was my favourite door, so I made a point to remember the combination code for this lock. Time to see Wocky.

An <u>elated</u> Wocky comes bounding out. It's so amazing to see him again. He almost pushes me over, because he's jumping up like a small child wanting to be picked up.

He's enormously fascinated with my wrist brace, smelling it intently and licking it. Wow, I'd forgotten how long his tongue was. He licks the whole brace.

"What have you been eating, Wocky? Your breath stinks; it really does reek."

He tilts his head slightly, lets out a small growl, as if he doesn't understand me, and then carries on investigating my brace.

I reach for a biscuit and hold it up in the air. His nose twitches. Aha, something more interesting and tastier than my arm. I throw the digestive in the air and, woosh, his tongue shoots out and grabs it.

"You like <u>devouring</u> biscuits, don't you?" I giggle.

If we were part of a travelling circus, the things we could do together. We could be famous.

"Right, Wocky, we must carry on exploring. I'm glad we're together because, if I'm honest, I'm a bit lonely without Jamie." I was going to give him the other biscuit but, as I look over at the table, I notice it's already gone.

"Wocky!"

He's licking his lips, and he kind of shrugs as if to say, 'wasn't me!'

"I know you took it, cheeky. You should have asked. I might have wanted it." I don't think he understands. "It's a shame Liv isn't here. She could teach you sign language and then we could communicate."

He suddenly shoots off chasing a fly that whizzes past. I notice the pictures on the wall in this room too. I remove my phone and take a photo of each of them to study later.

I open up my bag again and find my notebook. "Right, the password for the next door – 'Where is Timbuktu?' The answer is Mali, which I remember now." I'm obviously talking to myself. Even if Wocky could understand me, he's more interested in chasing the fly at the moment.

I type in the code, grab my bag, and enter the corridor. The light is already on. That's strange, because the lights only come on when the sensor detects movement when someone enters the room.

I glance round. Wocky is still behind me. So, what, or who, triggered the light? I wish Jamie was here right now.

I can't see anything in the corridor, so I enter cautiously. Could someone be hiding round the corner up the stairs? I can feel my heart beating faster and my breathing is becoming a little erratic. Goosebumps appear on my arms, and I start to shiver. One step at a time, I start to move forward trying to stay in control of the situation.

Suddenly, there's a barking from behind me but, before I could turn around, Wocky has raced past me and shot up the stairs. Something has sparked his curiosity. I start moving more confidently to follow him. As I get to the end of the corridor, I look up at the sensor and notice a spider walking across it. So that's what it was. Relief washes over me. I should have known. This has happened in my house before. I put that to the back of my mind and swiftly climb the spiral stairs to find a strong metal security door blocking our path. Wocky is scratching away at it but, so far, isn't even making a mark.

"That's strange, there's no door handle," I remark, oblivious that he obviously can't understand me.

There's a panel on the wall and a keypad with a noticeboard above it. I push on the panel which looks like a giant button for someone with big hands, but nothing happens. I look up at the noticeboard. I decide to take a picture of it first then decide to write it out in my notebook anyway. I'll start a new page. As I'm writing, I try to look for a clue to the door code.

Good things come to those who wait.
Opinions change over time.
Love makes the world go round.
Do something that makes you happy every day.
I believe in you, you should too.
Life is short, cherish every moment.
Oh, don't forget to exercise three times a week
Children are the future.
Keep your friends close and your enemies closer.
Star Wars **– the best story ever.**

Well, that doesn't make any sense. Then it hits me. I remember one of the codes in the *Secret Coding for Beginners* book that I was reading the other night. The first letter of every sentence – it spells Goldilocks. Just like the picture from downstairs.

```
G | ood things come to those who wait
O | pinions change over time
L | ove makes the world go round
D | o something that makes you happy every day
I | believe in you, you should too
L | ife is short, cherish every moment
O | h, don't forget to exercise three times a week
C | hildren are the future
K | eep your friends close and your enemies closer
S | tar Wars - the best story ever
```

I type in the code with <u>gusto</u>. I hear the clunk of the lock, but the door still doesn't open.

In frustration, I push the panel with the palm of my hand, and it <u>illuminates</u> immediately. There's another clunk. The door unlocks and opens inwards slightly. A bright, white light shines through. It almost blinds me for a minute. As I look away, I see Wocky scuttling back down the stairs.

After my eyes adjust, I peer in.

Chapter 9
A spaceship? Aliens?

As I look in, I can see an immaculately clean corridor. There's a futuristic feel to this place. Could this be a time portal or a spaceship? I have to find out. I thought I could hear animal noises for a second, but as I listen more intently – nothing. It must have been my imagination (or could it have been my stomach?).

I push the door open and step into the corridor. There is a 'clean' smell, like disinfectant. It's like a hospital kind of smell, and the floor and walls are white and smooth. It's a complete contrast to the rooms downstairs which remind me of an old castle.

I've only moved about a metre from the door when I hear it clunk shut and lock behind me. I'm committed now, and I feel like a stranger in a strange land. As I look back, I can see where I have walked. Tiny grit particles from the stone floor downstairs have come off my trainers and left traces. If it had been anywhere else you wouldn't notice it, but in here it stands out like a sore thumb.

I'm just about to bend over and try and wipe it up, when I hear a beeping from further down the corridor. Quickly, I dive through the nearest door I can see, which is just ahead of me on the left-hand side. This could be <u>out of the frying pan into the fire</u>, as I have no idea what I'm hiding from but, equally, no idea what is on the other side of this door.

The lights come on instantly as soon as the door is opened and, fortunately, it's a storeroom. Probably the neatest, tidiest storeroom in the world, though. I wish my bedroom cupboards were this tidy!

There appears to be lots of containers, cages and empty fish tanks (?), bottles and cans of chemicals among other stuff but, before I can take in any more, my attention focuses on the beeping coming from outside. I open the door just enough to peek through, but I can't see anything. But something is squeaking. It reminds me of when I used to have a squeaky wheel on my skateboard that just needed some oil. I look around. I have just seen a can of oil in here, somewhere. Oh no! I peer again. I thought I saw movement out of the corner of my eye, but it's gone again. I remove my phone from my pocket, open the camera app and hold it up to the crack. There! No, it's gone again. I move the phone up and down and from side to side so it's working like a <u>periscope</u>. Then I spot it. It's a robotic vacuum cleaner. It's just a bit smaller than my skateboard but circular. I bet it doesn't even come above my socks. I've seen one of these before, though. I remember Harriet showing me a video of hers a couple of years ago. But this looks far superior, and it doesn't look out of place at all in this futuristic environment. As I watch, I can see it <u>meticulously</u> manoeuvre from side to side whilst it cleans the whole corridor floor. It beeps periodically, but it consistently squeaks as it turns. I work out it is its left wheel that needs oiling. It's scanning the floor in front of itself with a red laser beam. I decide to retract my phone and push the door slightly so it's only open a fraction, because the robot vacuum is getting closer.

I can just make out its shape as it passes the door. I can hear it sucking up the grit that I'd <u>inadvertently</u> left on the floor. It makes a couple of beeping noises, probably to indicate it has finished, and there's no more 'sucking' sound. I listen as it squeaks, whilst it turns again, and heads back past the door. It then makes a cute reversing sound, similar to that of large vehicles. *Beep... beep... beep... beep.*

I open the door and peer out again. I have to see what's happening. The robo-vac seems to be reversing on to, what I assume to be, a charging platform further down the corridor on the opposite side to me. The noise stops, the red scanner has switched off and it just starts flashing.

I feel safe now that it has shut down. I'm just about to step out of the room, when I look down at my shoes. I quickly decide to take them off and carry them. I don't want to leave any evidence that I've been <u>trespassing</u>.

The floor is surprisingly warm. I notice some cupboards recessed in the wall next to this door. I decide to carry on exploring rather than stop to look in them.

There is a door on my right-hand side. I try the handle, but it's locked, and the keypad is digital. This is also far more advanced than anything downstairs. I press the enter button. The screen lights up. I read the display.

DNA…
A to T…
G to…?

Oh, I know this. I start to bounce with excitement, because I've seen this on a TV programme. I can't remember what they stand for, but 'A' always pairs with 'T' and 'G' always pairs with 'C' in DNA. It's strange how you remember things. I remember Grandad saying he had an AT-GC, as he knows I love *Star Wars* and it sounds like AT-AT (All Terrain Armoured Transport). He explained his AT-GC was his 'All-Terrain Golf Cart' which was effectively like a quad bike which was why he was eventually banned from the golf course. He churned up most of the grass and made quite a mess, apparently.

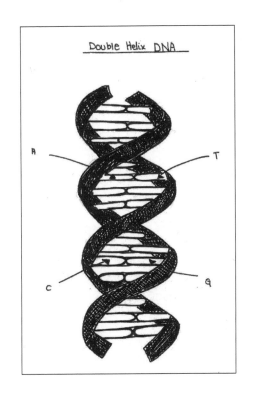

I press 'C' on the keypad and the door opens automatically. I cautiously enter. My senses are suddenly overwhelmed. There are several lights already switched on in here, but it's a different kind of light. It seems warmer in here, somehow, whereas in the corridor it seemed cooler, more <u>clinical</u>.

There is also a different smell. I can smell animals. It doesn't smell as bad as a pet shop but, as I listen, I can hear an extractor fan running that must be filtering the air. I also hear the animals. The door closes behind me. I don't know where to look first. To my left, on a shelf at my eye level, is a row of several fish tanks and <u>vivaria</u>, each one having different species of animals in them. I don't know what half of them are, though. On the opposite wall, at the same height, are more tanks. One or two of them have frogs in them and some have lizards, I think, but I can't see anything in the others.

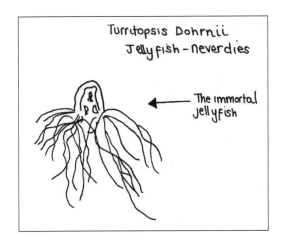

Turritopsis Dohrnii
Jellyfish - neverdies

← The immortal Jellyfish

Gecko-
Ability to walk on ceilings.

I bend down and take a look on a lower shelf. There is a tray of mushrooms and some cages housing some little creatures. They look so cute. I notice a list on the wall, and it seems to be a list of animals in the room; brown tree frog, mussels, mushrooms, blind cave fish, jellyfish, octopus, starfish, geckos… The door opens. I feel myself freeze with fear for a moment, but then I quickly drop to the floor and roll under the bottom shelf. Thank goodness for <u>adrenaline</u>.

I can hear myself breathing heavily. I need to calm myself if I'm going to be able to stay hidden.

I can't believe my eyes. A silver robot enters the room. It has arms but moves on tracks, like a tank. Where am I?

Could these be aliens from another planet collecting animals from earth?

What would they do if they found me? These thoughts aren't helping me calm down. But one thing is for sure – I SHOULDN'T BE HERE!

Chapter 10
Robo-Noah's ark?

I watch as the tracks move closer, and it comes to an abrupt halt right in front of me. I think my heart has stopped. I've never been so still. Not even when I was cast as a signpost in the infant's nativity play!

I listen to a mechanical whirring noise. I expect it to bend down to get me, but it seems to be extending. It picks up one of the glass animal tanks and wheels back out of the open door. The door then closes by itself, as if by magic.

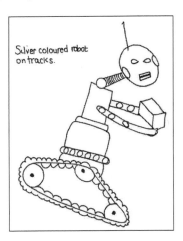

Silver coloured robot on tracks.

I suddenly need a wee. I'll have to hold it. I need to get back home and think about what all this means. This isn't what I had expected tonight, and I just can't understand what's happening. Slowly, I move towards the door, looking for the handle. There isn't one. Instead, it opens automatically. As I wait for the door to slowly open, I have a final glance around the room and that's when I notice some folders on a shelf. I want to have a look, but I really feel like I should get out of here, plus I want to see which direction the robot is heading. There is one thing going in my favour, with my shoes off I can move silently along these floors. I watch the tracked robot smoothly and effortlessly move along the corridor. If I was carrying a tank of water, half of it would be on the floor by now. I can't even carry a cup of tea across the kitchen without spilling some! I suppose the tracks help, as it's not rocking from side to side like we do when we walk. I wonder where it is going. As I step into the corridor, the door closes by itself and I slowly move in the direction of the robot, away from the door I've initially come through. It stops in front of the next door on the right. I shuffle back and try and hide in the door frame. I'm sticking out a bit, but I don't think it's seen me. The robot slowly turns ninety degrees to the right and faces the door. The door seems to open by itself, and it wheels in the fish tank. I move along the corridor in the same direction, but my brain feels torn. One half is saying 'must go back, it's too dangerous', the other half is saying 'need to find out what's going on here'. I'll just have a little peek then I'll head back, I tell myself. I reach the door and <u>fortuitously</u> it has a window in the top half of it. This room is a laboratory, but it's nothing like what I have seen downstairs and is far superior to the one we have at school. This is a lab of the future, and it's spotlessly clean. The robot is placing the fish tank carefully down on the workbench.

The urge to wee has subsided. Although I really should be getting out of here, I am far too curious and need to know what is in those files. I have an opportunity now to get some answers.

I decide I can risk another minute. I retrace my steps back to the other door and type 'C' into to door lock. Why are automatic doors always slow when you're in a rush? Once in, I head straight for the folders. There seems to be a folder for each of the animals in here. I open up the first one entitled '*Blind Cave Fish*' – it seems to imply they <u>regenerate</u> their own heart tissue. The next one is about the geckos. They have a special ability to walk on ceilings, apparently. Some <u>unpronounceable</u> type of jellyfish is next; they don't die at the end of their adult life, they just regenerate. Octopus and chameleons have an ability to <u>camouflage</u>.

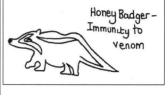

Honey badgers have strong <u>immunity</u> to <u>venom</u> from snakes and scorpions. Mussels' adhesive proteins could be used for surgical glues? Folder after folder, it lists all the animals and their special abilities. But why? What is happening here? There must be even more rooms than this, as I find a folder on dogs and their sense of smell, cats' hearing abilities and hawks' eyesight. I haven't seen any of these animals though, so where are they? No way – even one on sperm whales – where are they keeping that? Apparently, their <u>circulatory system</u> is <u>unique</u>. They only need to breathe every ninety minutes. Wow, that would be cool if I had that special ability. My mind begins to wander, but something distracts me. Is my <u>sixth sense</u> kicking in maybe? I feel that I've overstayed my welcome here, and I haven't got time to look at all these folders right now anyway.

I hear another noise from further along the corridor. It sounds like another door has opened. Right, that's me done. The door never closed, as I was still too close to it, which makes it easier for me to exit quickly. I tiptoe back the way I came, as fast I can, when I suddenly realise that the urge to go to the toilet has returned with a <u>vengeance</u>! As I reach the big, strong metal door that brought me into this corridor originally, the robo-vac's front scanner switches on as if it's waking up. As I look for the door handle, I remember the large push button on the side. I touch it with my finger, but nothing happens. Out of the corner of my eye, I notice the robo-vac has started to move. I place my palm on the button and press as hard as I can. The screen lights up and the door begins to open. I'm through it in no time and, just as I pull it closed, I glance back. The robo-vac is heading my way, but its red scanner hasn't reached me. I think I've got away with it, but I'm shaking. I'm not doing this again without Jamie, I decide.

I race back through the rooms, grabbing a couple more digestives from my bag as I go and throw them down for Wocky. I compose myself, as the only hurdle left is to cross the ladder. Grabbing the rope, I slowly make my way across. I don't look back. I race up the stairs like an Olympic sprinter, swinging open the bookcase door and then slamming it closed behind me when I'm safely back in my bedroom. I've never wanted to get in bed as much as I do right now. I just have to divert to the toilet first for a much-needed wee.

As I lie in bed, I wonder how difficult it would be for alien robots to open my bookcase door. Then I remember the silver bot doesn't have legs, just arms, so he couldn't get across the ladder bridge or negotiate stairs. I grab my phone; Jamie has messaged several times. It's too late to ring him, but I need to reply. When I message him, he replies almost immediately.

I don't reply. I was going to run through everything that had just happened and try to <u>rationalise</u> it in my head, but I can feel myself getting really sleepy. I grab Lucas, my monkey teddy and cuddle him tightly as my eyes begin to close.

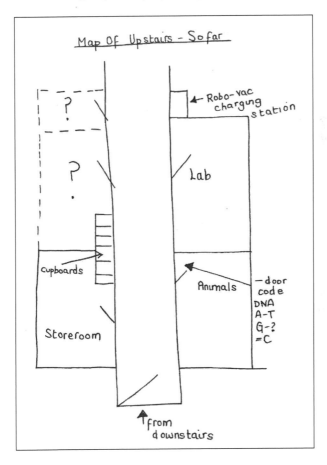

Chapter 11
Scratching at the door

My sleep is disturbed, as I keep hearing a strange noise. What is that? I look around then pull the curtains back a bit more to see if there is something at the window. No, nothing, but it is sunny this morning. I hope it's not a mouse. Emily had mice at her house, and they had to move out for days until they were all caught. I remember back at our last house, we did have the odd mouse get in. Dad said they were just field mice because we lived near a farm, but that never bothered me as we had Shelly, our very agile hunter cat. The number of funerals we had in our back garden was <u>notorious</u>. All of them, we think, had something to do with Shelly. There were birds, mice, a squirrel, spiders, flies, woodlice and even a fox, but that may have suffered at the hands of something else seeing as it was a lot bigger than Shelly!

I jump out of my skin as the scratching starts again, but it's a lot louder this time. I can feel my heart thumping in my chest and my breathing is getting more erratic. I grab my torch and, as I look around the room, I grab my... Harry Potter wand – that's the best thing I can find to protect myself!

Right, let me look under the bed. I don't want to look, but I have to. Nothing. Aha, there's Daisy's headphones, I'll have to get them back to her. There it is again; the noise is coming from the... bookcase. OH NO!

As I head over to where my bookcase stands, my stomach is in knots. After pulling on the cosmology book, I push the bookcase door open. Immediately, Wocky darts in and dashes around my room, just like I do when I'm being dragged round the shops but then I suddenly see the toy section.

He takes me by surprise. I'm so glad it's him and not something else! But out of the corner of my eye, I notice my bedroom door is not fully closed. Whilst Wocky is sniffing at something under my bed (maybe last week's socks?), I sidestep over and push the door closed. Wocky pulls all my bedcovers off and starts moving blindly around my room. It looks so funny. I wish Jamie could see this. But he can! I grab my phone and start videoing. Without warning, Wocky bumps into my bedside table and knocks over my glass of water. It seems to happen in slow motion. The glass starts to fall to the floor then the remaining water splashes out, just missing the book I had started reading. But the plug for my electric light and my phone charger are also on the floor. I dread to think what might happen next. I remember what Dad always used to say – water and electrics don't mix. I can't recall why now; whether it might cause a fire, damage the device or stop all the electrics in the house from working… That's it – you can get <u>electrocuted</u> as water is a <u>conductor of electricity</u>. I'm part way through my slow-motion lunge to catch the glass when I stop myself from getting too close. Wocky, covered by my bedcovers, dives over the plugs pulling my bedside light down with him. Everything returns to normal speed, in a flash. The water soaks my bedding and there is a bang as my lamp hits the floor. The bedding isn't moving. My heart sinks; Wocky isn't moving. I freeze. My immediate thought is 'can I do <u>CPR</u> on him'? I have done basic first aid <u>resuscitation</u> at school, but it was for humans, not for Wockies! I love him, but I don't know I can give him the kiss of life! I start to move over to him when I hear my dad's voice in my head. "Electric and water don't mix, always turn the power off." My eyes start to well up. I don't know why, it just happens. Pausing for a brief second, my clarity returns. Quickly moving around the plugs and the bedding, I unplug everything from the wall before moving over and slowly lifting the bedding, dreading what I might find.

Wocky jumps up to greet me like he was playing dead and saying peek-a-boo. I cry with joy, as he starts to hug me and lick me with his unusually long tongue (which always takes me by surprise).

My joy suddenly turns to panic once again, as I hear the unmistakable sound of our creaky eleventh stair. MUM'S COMING!

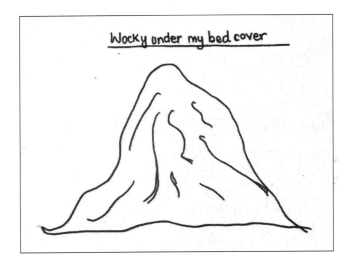

Wocky under my bed cover

Looking around the room, I try to take in the situation and formulate a plan. Wocky pops up from under the sheets looking like an adorable lost puppy – he obviously doesn't comprehend the gravity of the situation I'm faced with right now. *Got it*, I think to myself whilst quickly grabbing my phone. I FaceTime Jamie. He immediately answers and, before we speak, I point the phone at Wocky then turn it round and mouth, "HELP ME!"

Jamie's smile suddenly disappears, and he says, "I've got your back" and he hangs up. My bedroom door starts to open, so I quickly dive under the covers with Wocky.

"Lucy! What is all that commotion? And what ARE you doing? Your bedroom is like a pigsty!"

"Sorry, Mum, just making a den and playing hide-and-seek with Jamie on FaceTime."

"How does that even work? And Lucy, you've knocked your water over and your lamp off, you could have broken it! I thought I heard a bang." Mum does not sound happy.

Wocky starts to make a growling noise then proceeds to lick my toes. It tickles me, and I start to giggle.

"It's not funny, Lucy. Tidy your room up. Come on, I'll help you change these covers; you've had them on for a while now."

I hear Mum start to walk towards us, and she grabs the corner of the bedding.

I'm done for now. How am I going to start to explain this? I feel immensely sad, as I have managed to keep this a secret for so long.

The phone rings downstairs in the lounge. Mum turns and heads back down. "I'll be back in a minute. Tidy your room, please," she pleads.

My phone starts to ring too. It's Jamie.

"I've bought you a few minutes. I've got my mum to ring yours to discuss some fundraising my mum's doing."

"Thanks, Jamie, I owe you."

"Don't I know it. Quickly, get Wocky back and then let me know what happened," he replies.

I hang up and close the bedroom door. I look round to see that Wocky has seen his reflection in my full-length mirror. He barrels over and bumps into himself before falling backwards. He's probably never seen himself or another Wocky before. He quickly jumps to his feet and starts to lick his reflection. I bet that doesn't taste like he expected!

"Come on, Wocky," I gesture, trying to usher him away and over to the bookcase. As I glance back, I see a globule of slime running down my mirror. Ugh. "Wocky! How gross!" I say in disgust, as I open the secret door once again.

"Come on, Wocky, time to go back home." I lure him with another biscuit from my bag, and I manage to get him back to his lair. When I'm back upstairs, I take out my phone and dial Jamie's number.

"Thanks, Jamie, you're a lifesaver."

"What happened?"

"I realise now that I'd left all the doors open which aided his escape. He gave me the fright of my life. I wondered what it was."

"You were very lucky," Jamie confirms.

"It could have been worse. Besides, you say I'm lucky at everything. Like when I beat you at sports day, you said I was lucky then, but I'd been training for weeks. And what about last week, when I completed that puzzle? You thought it was lucky, but actually there's a lot of skill involved in puzzles!"

"Yes, I remember. You keep telling me the harder you practise the luckier you get."

"It's true, though. Thanks again, bestie."

"You're welcome," he says in his best Dwayne Johnson voice.

"You still can't do it. You'll never make it to the *Moana 2* auditions."

"I'll keep practising. Maybe I'll get lucky like The Rock."

"Er, don't besmirch The Rock."

"Be-smirch? What in the world? I'm sure you just make these words up," he laughs.

"Maybe I just got lucky reading the dictionary."

"Who does that? Apart from you, of course."

"Besmirch means to damage someone's reputation."

"I've forgot the word already, though!" he giggles.

"Jamie! I'd better get my room cleaned up before Mum comes back up."

"Won't the clothes fairy pick them up for you when you leave the room?" he asks, very innocently.

"What!" I'm <u>dumbfounded</u>.

"Well, that's what happens in my house."

"That's your mum, Jamie. My mum doesn't do that. She'll go <u>apoplectic</u> if I leave a pile of dirty clothes on my bedroom floor."

"Talk later?"

We say our goodbyes and end the call. I look round my room. Everything looks <u>topsy-turvy</u>. If only if I could click my fingers like Mary Poppins.

Maybe…

"<u>Abracadabra</u>. Abracadabra." Well, it was worth a try.

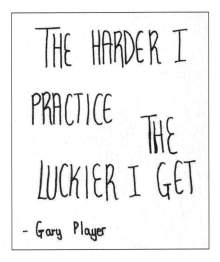

THE HARDER I PRACTICE THE LUCKIER I GET

- Gary Player

Chapter 12
The letter

After safely returning my uninvited, but most welcome, guest, I look around at the devastation in my room. I pick up the glass and mop up the spilled water with an old T-shirt I find under the bed. After picking everything up and checking my lamp and plugs (which surprisingly are still intact and dry), I plug them back in and test them. A smile returns to my face as the lamp works and nothing has exploded. Ah no, the mirror! This is going to need more than a couple of face wipes to clean the slime off. I continue to clean the mirror down and, as I do, my mind wanders to a scene in *Ghostbusters* when someone has just been slimed. The wipe will need to go straight into the bin. Yuk. Right, all done. My bed's a mess, but Mum did say she wanted to wash it today.

Probably a good job, because Wocky might have fleas! I wonder if you can get a flea treatment for Wockies?

I grab my phone and search for our local vet down the road. Found it. I dial the number. It seems to ring like – forever.

"Hello," the voice on the other end sounds rather exasperated.

"Hello, my name's er... Beth. What different flea treatments do you have?"

"What's it for? Dog? Cat? And do you want flea or flea and worm?"

"Worm?" I wonder out loud.

"Come on, I haven't got all day," the lady says, rather rudely.

I wonder why the lady at the vets is so short with me. She doesn't know me, and she obviously doesn't know what I have just been through with a Wocky in my room. If anything, it should be me who was feeling distressed and irritable. But nevertheless, I keep my composure.

"Ah yes. I'll have flea and worm. Do you do one that's for all animals?"

"No! Dog or cat that's what I said. Which is it?"

"It's kind of in between. It's a cross-breed."

"You'll have to bring it in then."

"Bring it in! No, I can't do that. Do you do anything for bears?"

"Don't waste my time!" she scolds, and she immediately hangs up.

That went well – not! I don't suppose they get many bears around here, and I don't really know what kind of day she was having either. Maybe I caught her at a bad time. Never mind. I know – I'll contact a zoo.

After doing another search on my phone, I find a contact us page for 'Zoos R US' and follow the instructions.

To help us answer your query better, please help us by answering the following questions:

Are you enquiring about an animal? Yes.

Is this animal a vertebrate or an invertebrate? I quickly open another webpage on my phone and Google this. Ah, vertebrates have backbones. Does Wocky? Yeah, I'm sure he does. I tick vertebrate.

Is the animal warm-blooded or cold-blooded? He seems warm so I tick that.

Is it a mammal or a bird? Well, I know mammals have boobs. Not sure about Wocky though, but he's not a bird, so I decide to opt for mammal.

Does the animal live in water, on land or is it amphibious? Come on! How many questions? This is ridiculous! I tick land.

How many legs does the animal have? It would be quicker to catch the bus to the zoo and queue up for a zookeeper tour than send an email, I conclude, but I persevere. I type in four legs.

Can the animal climb? This is absurd. How many different departments are there asking questions?

I don't know the answer to this, but I suppose Wocky could climb a little. Koalas do and he is a little like that. I answer yes.

Is the animal a carnivore or herbivore? Well, I know carnivores are meat eaters and herbivores are plant eaters but what's Wocky? Digestive biscuits aren't an option I can select. I know he eats flies because I've seen him and there are no plants around, but Koalas are plant eaters – what should I put? <u>Ironically</u>, I have his DNA, or slime to be more accurate, in the bin so theoretically I have all the information I need to create an identical copy of him, but I still can't answer these simple questions.

Sorry a fatal error has occurred. Please try again. The website has crashed.

"That's just great!" I decide to have one more go before I give it up as a bad job. After quickly reloading the contact us page, I notice a *SKIP* button at the bottom. I skip through all those questions; they weren't <u>mandatory</u> after all.

Type your message here:

Dear Head Zookeeper,

My name is Lucy, and I'm doing a project for school about weird animals.

I was wondering what you do when you discover something new that you haven't seen before, like for example a type of bear with a lizard tongue. How do you look after it? What would you feed it, apart from digestive biscuits, of course? If a strange animal were to, say, get in your bedroom, would it be best to wash your bedding? And can you buy flea and worm medicine from the zoo gift shop?

My school project is all <u>hypothetical</u>. No such Wocky exists. But if it did, what should I do?

Yours faithfully,
Lucy Castleton.
9 Hillcrest Rise,
Cavernly,
Derbyshire,
UK,
Europe,
Earth,
Our solar system,
Milky Way galaxy,
The known universe.

I hit send. I should have read through it first, but I'm so eager to send it before it crashes again, I don't bother.

I am now at a bit of a loss after all that excitement. I am about to ring Jamie but, as I grab my phone, I remember... the photos of the pictures from the second room.

I look through the three images:

The <u>butterfly effect</u>.

<u>Newton's three laws</u>.

An eye test?

The butterflies look pretty. I decide to spend the next half an hour copying these images to my notebook. Except the eye test – I'll just print that off, I think.

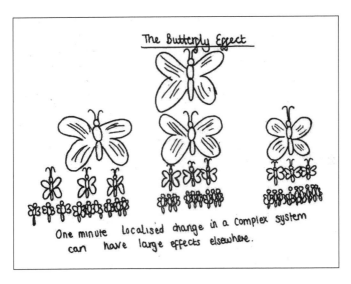

The Butterfly Effect

One minute localised change in a complex system can have large effects elsewhere.

Newton's laws

Newton's 1st law:

An object will not change its motion unless a force acts on it. This is the law of inertia.

Newton's 2nd law:

The force of an object is equal to its mass times its acceleration (F = m x a)

Newton's 3rd law:

When two objects interact, they apply forces to each other of equal magnitude and opposite direction.

Eye test

You don't need to see every letter to have great eyesight.

E
N A
O U
T C E -
L B U O C
N Y O I E A
L M E Y H O A
U T R H F N A C
T N H O E N R A

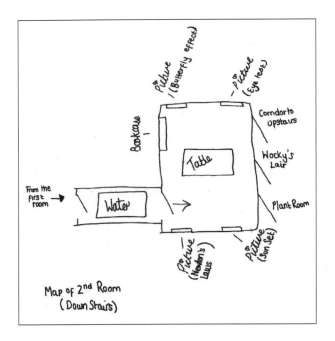

Map of 2nd Room
(Down Stairs)

My phone starts buzzing. Someone's messaging. I check WhatsApp. It's the 'Penguin Club Chat'.

I grab my Penguin biscuit out of my school bag. It's a bit squished though, so this could get messy.

I try and straighten out my biscuit wrapper, as

that's all that's left now, to reveal the joke on the back. Oh, I like it. I might win this time.

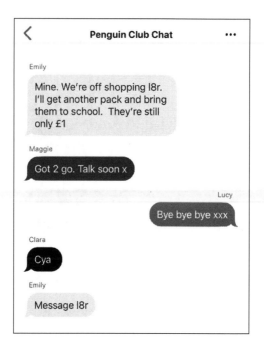

Penguin Club Chat

Emily

Mine. We're off shopping l8r. I'll get another pack and bring them to school. They're still only £1

Maggie

Got 2 go. Talk soon x

Lucy

Bye bye bye xxx

Clara

Cya

Emily

Message l8r

I do love a Penguin.

Chapter 13
The lift

It's the weekend, so I phone Jamie.

"Hi, J."

"Hello, Lucy Lu. I was just about to ring you; I heard a joke off my brother that's right up your street."

"Go on then."

"OK… When a chemistry teacher buys a new house and is looking round for furniture, what type of table do they buy?"

"I don't know."

"A periodic table of course. Boom boom!"

"Love it! OK, I've got one for you now on the same theme," I offer.

"Go for it."

"What's a chemistry teacher's favourite pet?"

"I don't know what is a chemistry teacher's favourite pet?"

"A mole!"

"I don't get it. Why a mole?" Jamie sounds confused.

"Because moles are an amount of substance in chemistry," I explain.

"Are you making this up? It's a bit like going to the supermarket and someone saying how many apples do you want? Oh, I think I'll just have five dogs' worth of apples today. Crazy lady."

"A mole of one substance contains the same number of particles as the mole of any other substance. Just like a dozen contains 12 of something. Like, for example, a dozen red apples and a dozen green apples, you will still have the 12 apples of each type even though they will weigh different amounts. Imagine the apples are <u>atoms</u> and are so small you can't see them to count them, but you could work out how many you have by knowing what a mole of each is."

"So, atoms are far too small to count?" questions Jamie.

"Yes, so this is a way of counting atoms. I haven't fully grasped it myself at the moment, as we don't cover it in science for four more years."

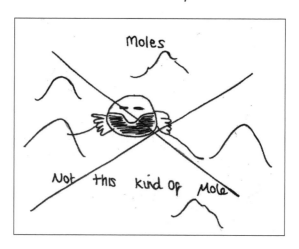

"Well, thank goodness for that! Where do you learn this stuff, Lucy?"

"I did see it on TV. I was flicking through the channels one day and this seemed interesting."

"We've got a different idea of interesting, Lucy. When I'm watching TV, that wouldn't be a channel I would have found!"

"Why, what sort of things do you think about?"

"Well, for a start at school, I'm trying to work out the quickest way home so I can beat my brother to the TV then I can put on CBeebies."

"Do you still watch that? I didn't realise it was still on."

"You don't know what you are missing, I love it. It's the highlight of my day. The other day I learnt that cats can make over a hundred different sounds, but dogs can only make about ten. I wouldn't mind learning cat language, if I could. I'd love to be able to communicate with Molly, my moggy."

"Talking about walking home from school the quickest way, we can do a mathematical formula for that you know."

"Come on, Lucy. You can't be serious? We are like chalk and cheese us two. Why on earth would I want to do more maths outside school?"

"I was just trying to help."

"You're still bonkers, you know. You're not like any other girl I know. You like making rockets in the back garden."

"The rockets were cool, though, weren't they?"

"I can't remember how you did it now. Wasn't it with a bottle of diet coke and a mint?"

"That's right, it was a Mentos mint, or several of them, but you have to warm the bottle of coke up in warm water first."

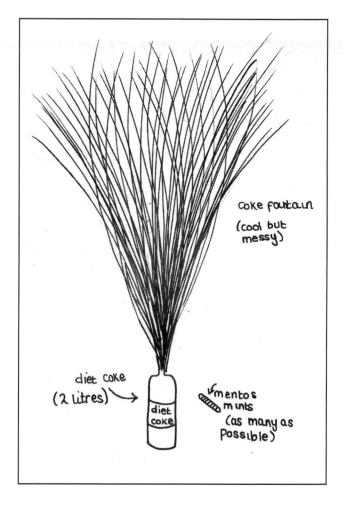

coke fountain
(cool but
messy)

diet coke
(2 litres) →

diet
coke

✓ mentos
mints
(as many as
possible)

"That was fun, but I'm worried that by the time we get to secondary school you won't want anything to do with stupid Jamie."

"I don't think that will ever be the case, we make a great team and, besides, Wocky will still need you. You are his best friend too. I just hope you don't get too fed up with all my investigations. It just interests me, that's all. Please don't call yourself stupid, because that's not the case."

"I'll always want to be your friend, Lucy. I still need someone to help me with my homework after all!"

"On the subject of Wocky, I've got an opportunity to explore some more right now, but I need your help, Jamie-Wan Kenobi.

"Can you come over here for an hour? Mum's going to wash the car and she takes ages. I don't want to go back down there again on my own."

"Sure, no probs. Should I bring a weapon?" He sounds serious.

"A weapon? What for?"

"What happens if the robot aliens have laser beams for eyes and they zap us?"

"I've got an idea. Bring your portable <u>Bluetooth</u> webcam and come as soon as you can."

"OK." We end the call.

I grab my compact mirror off the dressing table and slot it into the rucksack pocket.

"Lucy, do you want to help me with the car?" Mum shouts from downstairs.

I skip down as fast as I dare. "No, sorry Mum, Jamie's on his way over. We've got some research to do for school."

"Oh, what about?"

"Er... oh... robot aliens? For science, do they already exist anywhere?"

"Wow, that's sounds interesting. But you know nothing's been found anywhere in the universe to suggest that there is anything like that."

"Not yet! Me and J are working on a <u>theory</u>."

"Well, I'd love to know what you come up with. Is Jamie staying for lunch?"

"Not sure yet, I'll ask him when he comes."

"I'm just going to get the bucket out of the garage."

"OK, Mum." Once she has left the kitchen, I grab the first aid kit out of the bottom cupboard.

This is what I want. I remove the foil blanket and place the kit back in the cupboard. I'm upstairs adding this new item to my bag when it occurs to me that Mum may notice the ladder is missing when she goes into the garage. Just as I'm starting to worry the doorbell rings.

"I'll get it," shouts Mum.

It hasn't taken long for Jamie to get here. Mum opens the door, and he shoots straight upstairs when he sees me.

"Hi, Jenni," is his only comment as he whizzes past.

Mum doesn't even have time to respond. I can hear Pete apologising to Mum about Jamie's rudeness. I put my finger to my lips hoping he would be quiet for a minute whilst I listen in. Not that I'm nosey, of course, but I can sometimes find out more about what people say about you when they are talking to someone else.

"I'm feeling old too," complains Pete.

"You know you're old when you are filling a form out online and you have to scroll down to the bottom to find your age," laughs Mum.

"Too right," Jamie's dad agrees. "I was online last night, and I was asked to prove that I wasn't a robot, by my own computer! Can you believe the cheek of that?"

I hear Mum chuckling. There's nothing interesting here, just boring adult conversation. I usher Jamie into my room.

"What was all that about?" he asks.

"Just curious if they were talking about us or not."

"Were they?"

"No, but you know when people are talking it is sometimes what they don't say that's more important than what they do say," I try to explain.

"Well, what you've just said doesn't make any sense at all."

"For example," I continued, "if you asked someone if your dress looks nice…"

"I wouldn't ask that!" Jamie confirms, <u>indignantly</u>.

"Oh, right. Imagine you ask someone if your outfit looks nice; if they say yes, it looks OK, or it looks fine, do you take them at face value?" Jamie pulls a funny face and shrugs. "No, not always. They aren't saying you look fantastic or gorgeous are they? They probably don't want to lie to you and say you could look better, or it doesn't suit you. So, it's not always about what they say as much as what they refuse to say."

"I think I get you. So, what did, or didn't, our parents say?"

"Nothing. They weren't even talking about us this time. Come on, let's not waste any more time, our adventure awaits."

I usher him through the secret bookcase door, as Mum has already started washing the car. He's silent for a change, so maybe he's thinking about what to say or what he isn't saying and how I would interpret that.

We race down the three flights of stairs into the first room.

"Hold up, I'm out of breath." He leans against the table. "How do we know how long we have? Your mum could come in early."

I remove my phone from my pocket, type in the passcode and open up my webcam app.

"What are we looking at? Wait – that's your stairs?" He responds in amazement.

"Yep. I've moved my wireless webcam and placed it on the shelf outside my room looking down the

146

stairs. It fully charged too."

"That's brilliant. I wish I had thought of that. So, what's my camera for?"

"Ah, just you wait and see."

"Lucy?"

"Yeah?"

"Did you ever figure out what these numbers are on this other door?"

"Oh yes. It's the <u>Fibonacci</u> sequence."

"Fib-bon-archie what?"

"Fibonacci, he was a mathematician. He came up with this sequence. It's obvious now."

"Aren't you going to get your book out and tell me what the missing two numbers are?"

"I don't need to. Look at the sequence. 1+1=2, 1+2=3, 2+3=5, 3+5=8, 5+8=13, 8+13=…"

Jamie quickly interrupts, "21 and 13+21=34 and 21+34= er…"

"Equal 55."

"Yes," he agrees.

"And 34+55=89."

"So, the missing numbers are 55 and 89." He walks over to the door to type the code in.

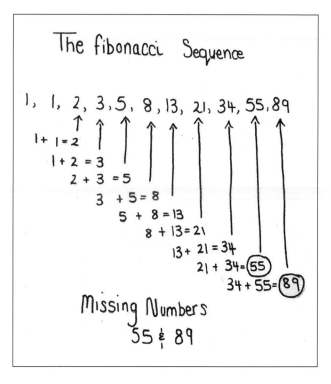

The fibonacci Sequence

1, 1, 2, 3, 5, 8, 13, 21, 34, 55, 89

1 + 1 = 2
1 + 2 = 3
2 + 3 = 5
3 + 5 = 8
5 + 8 = 13
8 + 13 = 21
13 + 21 = 34
21 + 34 = (55)
34 + 55 = (89)

Missing Numbers
55 & 89

"We haven't got time for this, Jamie. I need you upstairs with me."

"Have you looked in here already?" he asks.

"No. I haven't actually."

"But it could be another Wocky or clues to what's upstairs."

"OK then; a quick look."

At this point I regret not having a look earlier, as I'd worked out the code weeks ago. I can't believe I've overlooked this.

"I'm in." Jamie opens the door only to be immediately greeted with another one. "It's a metal door! Is this the same one as upstairs?"

"No this looks like a lift door," I suggest.

"It does, you're right."

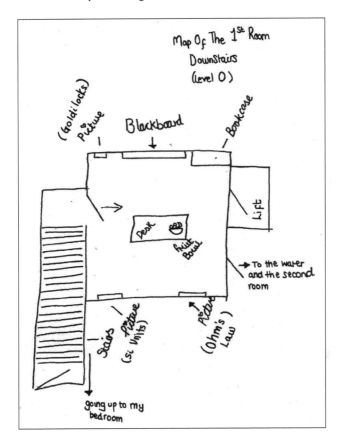

Map Of The 1st Room
Downstairs
(level 0)

(Goldilocks)
Picture

Blackboard

Bookcase

lift

Desk

Fruit Bowl

To the water
and the second
room

Stairs

Picture
(si Units)

Picture
(Ohm's Law)

going up to my
bedroom

We see the lift call button at the same time, but Jamie is quicker at pressing it.

"It could be like that lift in *Charlie and the Chocolate Factory* that can take you anywhere. It might fly. Where shall we go to?" Jamie asks.

Nothing seems to happen. He presses the button twice in <u>succession</u>.

"Maybe it's broken?" he decides.

I move over and pressed my thumb against the button. It lights up blue and I hear a whirring noise from above.

Jamie jumps back. "It's coming down."

"Down from where?" I vocalise my fear.

We both back away and stand near the other door ready to bolt. There are a couple of clunks then the door opens, but it's empty.

Jamie glances over, smiles and moves forward, without hesitation, into the lift.

Reluctantly, I follow. I check my phone. The webcam still on online and there's no sign of Mum.

"Look, 0, 1 and 2," he exclaims, as he points to the buttons. "It's not the <u>Willy Wonka</u> one, that's for sure."

The doors close. The display shows that we are currently on floor 0. I take a deep breath and press 1.

The lift jolts into life, and we travel upwards.

"Look," Jamie pointed to a nameplate on the buttons panel, "it's called <u>OTIS</u>."

I wonder why you would name a lift, or is it named after the person who owns the lift? I think back to when I visited our local fire station with Dad and all the fire engines had <u>DENNIS</u> on the front of them. I remember thinking that there are a lot of firemen called Dennis who work here! I enjoyed those days out together. It seems it's all the refuse collectors, who empty our bins, that are called Dennis now.

The lift jolts again, and I rock a little as I've forgot where I am for a moment.

The doors open...

Chapter 14
"It's going to remove our brains."

We look out into a corridor. It's the same clean, smooth surfaces as I'd seen before. We both listen, but we hear nothing.

"It smells so clean," remarks Jamie, "unlike downstairs!"

As we step out of the lift, the doors close behind us.

"Is this the spaceship?" he whispered.

"I think so."

I hear him gulp. We hold hands and this certainly helps both of us. My wrist is definitely getting better, as this would have been too painful to do last week.

I manage to remove my mirror from the side pocket of my bag and angle it round the corner. It opens out into a room, but I can't see any aliens or robots… yet.

"All clear." I move forward pulling Jamie along with me. This room has a very high table in the middle of the room, with a computer terminal on it. The screen is switched on. Someone has been using it recently. The table is made from stainless steel (I know this because Dad had a similar table to this in our garage), but there isn't a chair anywhere to be seen. How strange! The room is immaculately clean, and the <u>decor</u> is sparse. Along one of the walls there looks to be a row of drawers or filing cabinets built into the wall.

I let go of Jamie and I remove the foil blanket out of its packet.

"Are you cold? It's warmer up here than downstairs."

"No, I'm not cold. We're going to hide under here. The robots might be able to sense our body heat so this should make us invisible to them," I hope.

"I like it."

I notice we haven't made any marks on the floor. Our shoes are clean. Thinking back, the stone floor in that second room is much older and more damaged than the first room we have just come through. I'm going to have to think of another way to make a mess so as to encourage the robo-vac out.

"Get your webcam out and link it to your phone," I instruct Jamie. "Whilst you do that, I'll get a biscuit out."

"Great, I'll have one too."

"No, it's not to eat. It's to lure the robo-vacuum cleaner out. We'll leave some crumbs in front of the table and we can hide under here. As it passes, you stick the webcam on it."

"ME STICK IT ON?" Jamie's eyes bulge wide. I put my finger to my mouth, urging him to keep quiet.

"OK, I'll do it. Here, stick this Blu-Tack under the camera." I hand Jamie the Blu-Tack, as I start to move out from under the foil blanket.

"Where are you going?"

"I'm going to make a mess with these crumbs."

I move a couple of metres away and break the biscuit up whilst trailing crumbs around the corridor, into the room and near the table.

I look over to the computer screen, and my eyes quickly dart around the screen trying to make sense of all the information. It looks like some kind of spreadsheet labelled 'Blind Cave Fish'. It displays DNA tests and results against different dates.

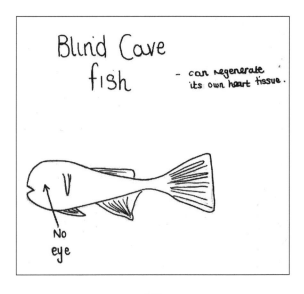

Beep, beep, beep.

I am suddenly aware that the robo-vac has powered up and is on its way.

Jamie hands over the camera; his hand is obviously shaking.

"I've got a bad feeling about this," he mumbles his favourite *Star Wars* reference.

We hide under the silver blanket and wait.

Sure enough, *beep, beep, beep*. The motor on the vacuum starts up as it begins sucking up the crumbs.

The red scanning laser has identified the rest of the crumbs with supreme accuracy.

Every house should have one of these, I conclude.

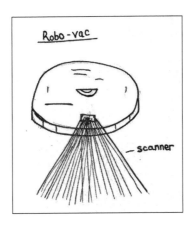

Jamie is clinging to my arm. He's going to need to let go if we are going to pull this off.

I see my chance. I pull away from Jamie, lean out from under the blanket and place the camera securely down on the top of the little robot. Jamie has probably used more Blu-Tack than I need, but at least the camera isn't going to fall off. The robot doesn't seem to notice, as it's facing the opposite way to us. There can't be any pressure sensors or nerve endings on its roof. But then again, why would there be?

I slip back under the foil effortlessly due to my thigh muscles, core strength and my balance. My dance training has certainly paid off!

Jamie reduces the brightness down on his phone, as it is nearly blinding us under here.

"This is cool. Now we can see where the little robot goes whilst we are safely hidden under here."

I can just about make out Jamie's big smile, as team LJ have pulled off another successful mission.

The robo-vac turns and faces us as it meticulously removes the last few crumbs.

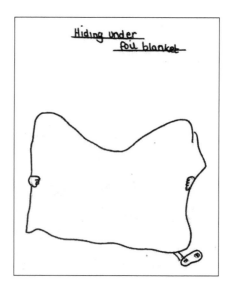

I'm now wondering if it can see us. We both keep deadly still, as the laser scans us up and down.

I hold my breath. Phew… it's turned away and squeaked back down the corridor. My mouth opens as I exhale, and both sets of our eyes are now glued to the phone screen.

A thought flashes before me. I grab my phone and check the webcam app to see if I can see Mum. Oh no! We're out of range of the Wi-Fi signal. I hadn't anticipated that it might not work down here.

"All good?" Jamie asks <u>inquisitively</u>.

I nod, not wanting to tell him now.

The robot moves up to a closed door. It emits a single beep, and the door opens by itself.

"In we go," Jamie commentates. This reminds me of a hospital operating theatre complete with an operating table and the overhead light. It doesn't seem that long ago since I was in one having my arm fixed up.

Jamie has the same thought and exclaims, "You could have had your arm done here. It's closer to home!"

We can't see much else though, as the camera is so close to the floor. The further it enters the room the less we can see. A robot is in here that we can see. It moves over to the table as if it were operating on something (or someone!).

"It's going to remove our brains if it catches us." Jamie seems genuinely concerned.

"That's a different robot to the one I've already seen. This one's got legs – not tracks."

"Soo, there's TWO of them?" Jamie's concern is rising.

"At least."

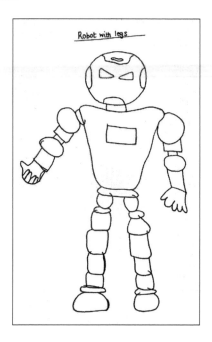

The vac turns around and leaves the room, as it has now finished scanning the, already clean, floor.

We watch as it crosses the hallway and enters another door, which also opens automatically as soon as it beeps.

"Do you think it's talking to the door?"

"No, but it must be sending some kind of a signal to it, so it unlocks."

"So, if any of the doors are locked, we could use the robo-vac to open them for us," Jamie suggests.

"But how?"

"We would have to hack into it. I could ask my brother?" he offers.

"No, I don't want to involve anyone else with this. If we have to, I will ask Maggie for her help."

"Yes, Maggie is a whizz with computers. She helped me when mine wasn't working at school last week."

"What did she do?"

"She switched it off and back on again."

"Jamie! Really?"

"Well, I know. I could have done that, but I didn't think. I know now though."

We return our attention back to the camera footage. The light is already on in this room and the other robot with tracks is in here too.

"I want one of those robots," Jamie remarks.

"Well let's hope it's not been sent from the future to terminate us!"

"Come on, Lucy, you're a scientist. You don't believe in that surely."

"What I do know is that just because no one on earth has proved it's possible, doesn't mean it's impossible!"

"You are scaring me now."

"Look," I point to the screen, changing the subject. "The robot is taking something out of a giant fridge."

"It looks like blood samples," Jamie squints, as he tries to make it out. "This room appears to be full of fridges and they all look the same. Maybe we could sneak in and grab some ice cream?"

"You are always thinking about your stomach, but we could go and have a look though," I smile at him.

The robot-vac isn't in this room long, as it appears to be in the way of the silver track robot, who seems to have what it went in there for and is about to leave the room.

The vac heads further down the corridor, but what concerns us most is that the silver track is coming our way.

We shuffle back under the foil blanket. After we finished rustling it, I listen. Silver track has stopped, turned, and entered another room. Once I hear the door close, I speak.

"I think it's gone into that operating theatre."

Jamie doesn't seem as worried as me.

"We're safe. Remember, it can't see us under here."

I nod but, if I'm honest, I'm less confident in my foil blanket idea than I actually let on.

"The vac's in another room now. This is like a robot junkyard," Jamie suggests.

"You could be right. It's full of spare robot parts. But it's not a junkyard, because all these parts look new. It looks like this is where they repair themselves."

"Yes. It looks like there are tools on that bench over there."

The vac turns and leaves the room.

"This was a great idea, Lucy. This is our reconnaissance op."

I'm really happy that this is working, and Jamie is super excited.

"I'm glad we are doing this together, J."

"I wouldn't want to be anywhere else," he smiles back. We watch as the vac enters another room.

This room seems to be very well lit. There appears to be charts on the wall, but we can't make out what they were. A series of microscopes and machines occupy the long desk and the floor area.

"What do you think is going on here, Lucy?"

"I don't know, but I'm very intrigued and a little frightened. If they are aliens, they could be investigating weaknesses in animal life here on earth."

"What if they are friendly aliens? They could be helping injured animals and maybe working out ways to stop them from becoming extinct. Or maybe a crazy, mad scientist is controlling these robots for their own self-interest."

"What? Like someone trying to take over the world using animals?"

"And kids?" Jamie adds looking horrified at his own suggestion.

"Look, it's passed a room and gone in the opposite one. It looks like our computer room at school."

"It does. The screens on these are far bigger than they are in school, though. Do you think Wocky is an alien?" Jamie asks, completely randomly.

I look at Jamie flabbergasted by what he has just asked. "No," I respond, shaking my head. But I'm questioning it all now.

"But what if he has been experimented on and he escaped? Or he could have been left downstairs to spy on us."

"No, surely not. Not Wocky! I can't believe any of that to be true. Why is downstairs completely different to up here? It's like two different worlds. I can't believe they're even connected."

"But they are. A door at one side and the lift at the other," he says, very logically.

"We will have to think about this another time. Let's just do one thing at once; my head is starting to hurt. Let's concentrate on this exploration. Then we can grab your webcam and get out of here."

"I agree. Look, look. Did you see that? There was some sort of model on the desk in this new room," Jamie points at the phone.

"Only just. It looked like…"

"A moon base," we say in unison.

"You don't think… they are from the moon, do you? Like extraterrestrials?" he asks, shuddering at the thought.

"No. But they might be planning on going there. Which room was that? I have lost track now. Wait. That's the robo-vac charging station opposite." We watch as the vac leaves the room and spins round before reversing on to the charging station. "I know where we are now. This is the same corridor that leads to the metal door that I came through before. I'll have to draw another map in my journal so I can get my head around this."

"I could do with one of these robo-vacs for walking the dog."

"Knowing your new dog, it would just sit on it and enjoy the ride," I giggle.

"You are right – it would. It's so idle. Has your mum finished washing the car yet?"

"Dang-it. I've lost track of the time."

"Check your phone," Jamie insists.

I try and reconnect to my webcam, but my phone still can't find it.

"I've lost connection." Jamie looks worried.

"We'd better be getting back then," he says, hurriedly starting to get up.

"Yeah, let's go."

"Can you get my webcam back?"

"Yes. You call the lift and I'll grab the cam. Wait in the lift and hold the door for me."

I sneak down the corridor as quickly as I can and stop opposite the charging station. This is the door the robo-vac didn't enter. A brass, tarnished sign simply reads 'The Study', and situated just below this sign is a second sign along with another coded lock.

THE STUDY

'**Enter your name here**' is written on the second sign. I glance over my shoulder at the vac which seems to have switched itself off and is just charging. I type in 'your name here' and try the lock. It doesn't work. I'm not going to be dumb and enter my own name as whoever's room this is will then be able to work out who has tried to get in, so I type 'Jack'. No, that doesn't work either. I can see Jamie, out of the corner of my eye, beckoning for me to hurry up. I turn around, lean over and carefully grab the camera from above the top of the robo-vac to avoid putting my arm in front of the sensor.

It's fortuitous that I'm using my right arm for this. There is still a blob of Blu-Tack stuck to the top of the vac, but I'm not going to tempt fate by trying to remove it. I race back down the corridor, too scared to look back behind me. As I dart round the corner, I nearly jump out of my skin.

Jamie is stood there still pressing the lift call button. He moves out of the way.

"You do it. It's not working." I pass him his webcam and push hard. The doors open immediately, and I glare at him in disbelief.

"I tried it. You saw me. It's <u>temperamental</u>."

Once we arrive back downstairs, I want to wait until the lift door closes before we walk away, just to make sure no one (or nothing) is following us.

"Come on. Let's go."

I hold up my hand, to gesture for him to stay quiet. After the lift doors close, I can't hear any sounds, which confirms to me that no one has recalled the lift. We head back upstairs, and I quietly close the doors behind us as we leave. The only sound we can hear is the foil blanket, which is so noisy. After all, it's just like one giant Kit Kat wrapper. When Jamie reaches the top of the stairs, he waits for me to catch him up.

"Check your phone again."

I have a look and this time it connects. No sign of Mum on the stairs. I give him a nod, and he unlatches the bookcase door and pulls it towards him.

"All clear," he whispers, and we enter my bedroom and close the bookcase door behind us.

After Jamie cleans the Blu-Tack off his camera, we try and fold the foil blanket, but it looks a mess.

"Great job," he says.

I'm not impressed. I knew it wouldn't fit back in the packet, but I can't complain, as I need his help due to my <u>handicap</u>.

"Do you want to stop for lunch?" I'm suddenly overcome with hunger and seeing as Jamie is nearly always thinking about food, I'm sure he will be too.

"Do I?"

"Silly question, I know. After lunch, I'll draw out level one and the new rooms we have discovered."

"You are going to have to tell your mum soon," Jamie offers.

"I know. But how do I bring up that conversation?" I really don't know how to talk about any of this with Mum.

We head down for lunch.

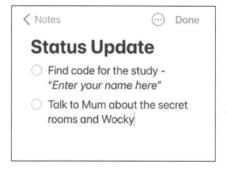

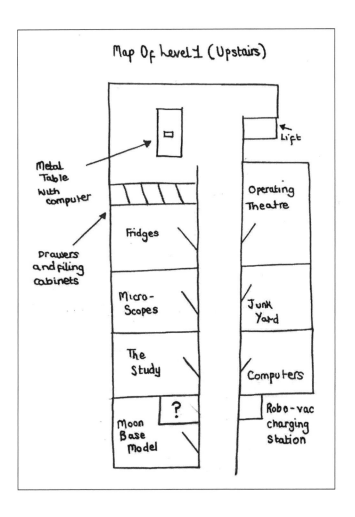

Map Of Level 1 (Upstairs)

Metal Table with computer

Lift

Operating Theatre

Drawers and filing cabinets

Fridges

Micro-Scopes

Junk Yard

The Study

Computers

?

Moon Base Model

Robo-vac charging Station

Chapter 15
The next party

"Good morning class."

"Good morning, Mrs Malikinski," half the class replies.

"I'm going to try something different today. I would like each of you to come up with a couple of examples of how you remember things."

Chris's hand shoots straight up. Before Mrs Malikinski can even acknowledge him, he blurts out, "I remember to put my underwear on 'cos it keeps my willy warm!" There are a few chuckles from around me.

"No, Chris, that's not the sort of comment we share with the class. I'll give you an example; if you can all write these down."

Everybody scrambles for their pens. Desks are slamming, drawers creaking and bags rustling for a few moments. Once everyone is poised, she begins to talk again.

"My example is <u>stalactites</u> and <u>stalagmites</u>. One points up and one points down. So, I remember it as follows. Tights on the washing line hang down, so stalactites hang downwards."

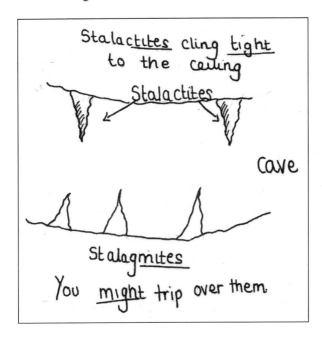

Stephanie's hand shoots up in a perfect straight line. "Yes, Stephanie?"

"That's a really good example, Miss, I'll remember that. I've got one for the class." Stephanie stands up, clears her throat and composes herself.

"Thirty days have September,

"April, June and November,

"All the rest have thirty-one.

"February has twenty-eight,

"But leap year coming one in four

"February then has one day more."

"That's great, Stephanie. I'll write it on the board and then the class can copy it down."

"Thanks, Miss." She smiles at the class as she holds her skirt and graciously sits back down.

"We're not going to top that," Jamie quips.

"Anyone else?"

Daisy speaks out, "It's not quite what you want, but my mum always says, measure twice, cut once. This is when she's sewing, and she doesn't want to cut the material too short and ruin it."

"That's good, Daisy. The same principle can be used in cooking and baking."

"My dad says the same. He's a joiner and measures wood twice before making the cut," Max agrees.

"Thanks, Daisy, for that, and thank you Max for joining in too."

Measure twice, cut once

"Jamie, you're sitting there very quietly. What have you thought of?"

Jamie starts to wriggle a bit in his seat, and he seems to shrivel up as if he's trying to hide under the table. I discreetly scribble *I, b4 E, ex C*. Jamie glances at it, as he's done many times before when he's not sure. A few awkward seconds pass then…

"I before E except after C."

r e<u>cei</u>pt   p<u>ie</u>ce

r e<u>cei</u>ve   bel<u>ie</u>ve

              f<u>ie</u>ld

"Good, Jamie. That can prove very handy in spellings. There are a few exceptions to this, but I won't go into them now. I'll give you another one myself: the fractions you are going to divide it by – turn it upside down and multiply. Don't worry, we will cover this later in the year."

There are a lot of groans and faces being pulled around the class whilst it's being written on the board.

I jot it down and start working through some examples to test the theory.

Dividing fractions

Turn the 2nd fraction upside down and multiply.

$$\frac{3}{4} \div \frac{1}{4}$$

$$\frac{3}{4} \times \frac{4}{1} = \frac{12}{4} = \frac{3}{1} = 3$$

$$\frac{1}{2} \div \frac{1}{4}$$

$$\frac{1}{2} \times \frac{4}{1} = \frac{4}{2} = \frac{2}{1} = 2$$

I put my hand up. "Miss?"

"Lucy."

"The <u>product</u> of two numbers is always even unless both numbers are odd."

"That's right, Lucy. Good job."

3 X 4 = 12
odd × even = even

4 X 4 = 16
even × even = even

3 × 3 = 9
odd × odd = odd

Products of two numbers is always even unless both numbers are odd.

"I've also got one for the order of the planets starting from the sun going further out."

The teacher nods for me to begin.

"My very excellent mum just served us noodles and pizza: Mercury, Venus, Earth, Mars, Jupiter, Saturn, Uranus, Neptune and Pluto."

"Great, Lucy. There are lots of <u>mnemonics</u> for the order of the planets and you can use Lucy's, which I'll write on the board, or you can make up your own, so you are more likely to remember it. We generally don't include Pluto now though, as it's only classed as a dwarf planet."

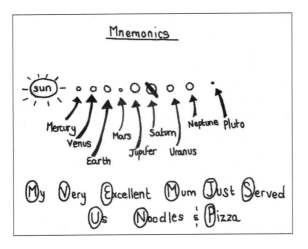

Mnemonics

Mercury Venus Earth Mars Jupiter Saturn Uranus Neptune Pluto

(M)y (V)ery (E)xcellent (M)um (J)ust (S)erved (U)s (N)oodles & (P)izza

"I know, Miss, but I don't like excluding it."

"That's fine, Lucy. Any more?" she says whilst looking around at the class.

I put my hand up again.

"Lucy, you're on fire today."

"I've got plenty of these, as this is how I remember a lot of stuff."

"Go on then, let's hear another then we will give someone else a turn."

Looking around me, I think nearly everyone is happy for me to keep going all lesson as they don't want to be picked on to answer, but Stephanie doesn't seem too pleased though.

"There are red and white blood cells in your blood. It's the white ones that fight off infections and protect you. To remember this, I think of the white blood cells as little doctors in my blood with their white coats on."

"Another good one, Lucy. It's not something you will learn about until secondary school but it's good you know. Now then, Harriet, you've normally got a lot to say." Everyone turns to face her. She stands and discreetly clears her throat.

"I would like to propose to the class that Lucy and I sing the 'Periodic Table Song'." I'm taken aback in astonishment. I love the song, and almost know it off by heart, but I've not prepared for this. The whole class abruptly turns to face me. I'm sure my mouth is still wide open.

"That sounds excellent, Harriet, but I don't think we have time for that today, and it's not something we are planning on covering this year. If we have time before the end of term, I would love to hear it though."

My heartbeat seems to be returning to normal. I look over at Harriet who appears very pleased with herself. She mouths, "You're welcome" at me. I'm just about to respond when Tom beats me to it.

"I've got one, Miss," indicates Tom from the back of the room. I don't spend much time with him, as he follows Jack around a lot, but last year we went on a school trip to a museum and he and I were partnered up. He was nice and pleasant company. It's a shame how the friends he hangs around with influence him in a bad way.

"A dessert (that you eat) has two S's in (as you always want more) and in a (sandy) desert, one S is enough."

Desert   Dessert

You would prefer more desserts than deserts so you use 2 's'.

"Excellent example, Tom. Write that down everybody."

I smile at him, and he smiles back.

Jamie nudges me. "Stop flirting with the enemy."

"I'm not, I'm just being friendly. Besides, he's not an enemy."

Theo raises his hand. "Yes, Theo."

"I've got a way I remember King Henry VIII's wives: divorced, beheaded, died, divorced, beheaded, survived. I learnt that from reading the *Horrible Histories* books."

"Great, Theo. I'll write it on the board." Mrs Malikinski's starting to run out of space on the whiteboard now.

"Yes, Charlotte."

"I know when to use 'a' or 'an' in a sentence. You can't use 'a' before a vowel: a, e, i, o or u. So, for example, it would be 'an' apple not 'a' apple and the opposite when it isn't a vowel. So again, 'a' phone not 'an' phone."

Jamie instinctively starts clapping. Everyone stares at him, and he stops abruptly, sinking into his chair whilst lowering his head to hide his glowing face. I give him a strange look, but he doesn't see.

Mrs Malikinski seems slightly befuddled by Jamie's outburst and turns back to face Charlotte.

"Very good, Charlotte. We will be covering this in the next term, but there are a few exceptions to be aware of. Copy this down class." She continues to write down Charlotte's example. "Some words *sound* like they begin with a vowel. In this case we use 'an' rather than 'a', for example, an hour. But some words sound like they begin with a consonant, like the word unicorn which sounds like you-ni-corn. This would be 'a' unicorn not 'an' unicorn. Don't worry too much about this right now, as we will cover this all later."

Henry 8th Wives

Catherine of Aragon   - Divorced

Anne Boleyn   - Beheaded

Jane Seymour   - Died

Anne of Cleves   - Divorced

Catherine Howard   - Beheaded

Katherine Parr   - Survived

(Thanks to horrible histories)

> A banana   An apple
> A pear   An orange

"Don't worry, Miss, we won't," Jack says, cheekily.

"Yes, Niall?"

"Red sky at night, shepherd's delight; red sky in the morning, shepherd's warning," Niall suggests. He'd had told me this before and it seems to work, most of the time.

"Nice one, Niall. If there's a red sky at night, it generally indicates that the weather will be nice the following day. However, if the sky is red in the morning, it suggests that we're in for not so nice weather that same day," Mrs Malikinski explains.

I carry on writing down some more ideas I have. I can see us getting this for homework, so this is an easy way to get ahead of it.

> Elephants have bigger ears in Africa than India as Africa is warmer, and the larger ear keeps them cooler due to its larger surface area.
>
> Eggs sink to the bottom of a cup of water if they are ok. They will float if they've gone bad (float to heaven).
>
> Clocks 'spring' forward and 'fall' back for British Summer time.

Maggie puts her hand up. "Yes, Maggie."

"I've got one, Miss. When we went to the Lake District last year, I remember that Keswick is higher up than Kendal because Keswick sounds like a kestrel, which would fly up high. Kendal is lower down because Kendal mint cake is very heavy. It's like eating a rock." I look up and nod in approval.

"A very good example, Maggie. Come on class, write in down."

"Do we have to, Miss? My hand hurts." I don't think she heard George moaning, because he's very quiet.

"Yes, Amelia."

"I remember that penguins live in Antarctica, at the bottom of the world, as they slide down, and polar bears live in the Arctic, as they can use their claws to climb up to the top of the world."

"Excellent example, Amelia," she says, as she writes it all down on the bottom of the whiteboard. "Your homework this week will be to come up with some more ideas like that." I smile, as I've nearly finished mine already.

It's close to break time. Jamie has a sneaky look under the table at what sandwiches he has today. He takes a quick bite. Obviously, his urge to eat overwhelms his willpower. We are all very aware of the punishment for eating in class. Mrs Malikinski starts reading out what she has already written on the board.

"Have you ever had green bread?" Jamie whispers.

"Er, yuk. That's mouldy bread. Don't eat that!"

"It doesn't taste very nice," he confirms. I think he's about to spit it out when... the bell sounds. We all instantly freeze and look up at Mrs Malikinski. She has a great rule that if anyone gets up and tries to leave before she dismisses us, we all have to wait and miss our break. I feel myself holding my breath – I don't know why though, it's a bit extreme.

"OK, class. Pens down. Break time. We will continue this when you get back," and with that she waves us out.

There is an instant stampede for the door.

"No running," comes her final plea.

That falls on deaf ears though. I look at Jamie, he has swallowed it. He looks back and just shrugs his shoulders. He must have got an iron stomach.

"How does anyone remember all that stuff? My brain's like fog now," Jamie complains.

"My dad taught me a trick using the 'Method of Loci'," I explain.

"Loci?"

"Yes, I remember the name as it's a Marvel character, even though in Marvel that's Loki with a 'K'. The idea is that you use pictures in your head to remind you of things. If you are trying to remember the order of something like pi, which starts off as 3.14159, I think of my journey to school." I can't tell if Jamie is taking any of this in or even listening any more, but I keep going. "As I walk down my drive – I

179

pass 3 hedges then, on the pavement, I walk past the 1st bus stop, Mr Taylor always leaves his 4 bins out, then I pass that really big oak tree on its own."

"I know which tree you mean, but what reminds you of 5?" he asks unpredictably.

"After the big oak, I turn the corner outside number 5 and the first house you then pass has that very large fence around it. There are 9 panels, which are easy to count, as the middle 3 are a different colour. Every time I want to recall pi to five decimal places, I remember my walk to school and visualise the route. Now, you have to come up with your own sequence for the things that you want to remember."

"Can't I just stay at your house, and I'll use yours?" he asks with his trademark cheesy grin.

"You can for me." I can't help but smile back.

During break, me and Jamie bump into Harriet by the benches. She looks like she is taking photos of herself.

"Photobomb," we both shout, as we dive into her picture.

"I'm not taking selfies, you know. It's the new app I've designed. In the app I can go to the designer stores' websites, pick what clothes I want to try on and it shows me a picture of me wearing them. It saves me hours of trying on clothes that other people may have already worn." She does a little shiver.

"Can I try?" I ask.

"Not yet. You need to scan your body into it a few times and create a personal profile before you can use it. I'm still trialling it. There are a few bugs to iron out, but it's nearly there. When it's done, I'll send everyone the link to download the app."

"Will it be free?" Jamie interjects. When he's not thinking of food, he's thinking of ways to save money.

"Do you think I'm running a charity here? Hello? Of course, it won't be free. I've got standards to maintain."

Theo walks by. Not wanting to miss out on the chance to say something, he joins in. "You should try putting yourself in other people's shoes for a change. See things from their point of view. Not everyone is a lucky as you, you know," he says, obviously talking to Harriet.

"Er, yuk. I can't even bear to think about wearing someone else's shoes." She looks at him in complete disgust.

Theo shakes his head and carries on walking by. I quickly think of something to say to try and change the subject.

"What are you doing for your next party, Harriet?" I ask, tentatively.

"I'm looking into a Virgin Galactic space flight. Tickets are hard to get, but my dad's going to have a word with Richard seeing as it's my birthday."

Virgin Galactic -
Suborbital Space Plane

HAPPY BIRTHDAY HARRIET

"Wow, that's amazing," Jamie blurts out. "That would look so cool on my application to astronaut training camp." His beautiful smile was wider than ever. I don't think I've ever seen him beam with so much happiness before.

"Is everyone invited? I thought those flights were incredibly expensive," I ask.

"Er, no! They don't allow germs in space," she retorts, looking directly at Jamie.

His face suddenly turns from joy to disgust and then to anger.

I raise the palm of my hand slowly, just so he could see, and mouth, "Stay cool, leave it with me".

"Can I help you with the invite list?"

"What makes you think you are going either?" she says rather abruptly.

"Well, you will need someone to follow you round with the sick bucket, won't you? It's not called the 'vomit comet' for nothing, you know."

"I suppose so. And you are very reliable. If you say you are going to do something, you always do."

I don't think my mum would always agree with Harriet's assessment, but at least I might be able to get Jamie an invite, even if I have to give up my place.

Harriet's watch beeps.

"You got a text?" I ask.

"No, it's just Obi telling me it's time for my insulin jab."

"Oh, are you diabetic? I didn't know."

"It's our little secret. I don't go bragging about everything, you know. This is a special club just for me."

"Tom's Type 1 as well, did you know?"

"I know; I've seen him at the hospital a few times. Not a word – OK? Not even to your boyfriend!"

I was about to correct her and confirm that Jamie's not my boyfriend, but she knew that already, it's just her way of being funny.

"Oh, Harriet. Anyway, why is your watch called Obi? Is it like in *Star Wars*?"

"No, don't be silly, Lucy. Obi is short for obedient one. It does exactly what I tell it to!"

Harriet disappears off to administer her injection.

"I know it's not my birthday yet, but I need to start thinking about what I would like to add to my present list," Jamie adds.

"It's a while yet, J, but have you already thought of anything?"

"I keep asking my dad for a cash machine for my bedroom, you know the ones that say free cash!"

"Good luck with that, but what about from me?"

"I would like a bottle of confidence!"

"Oh, I don't think even Etsy sells that, but I can definitely help you with your confidence."

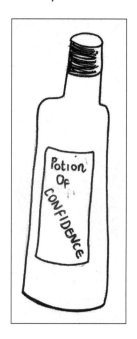

Chapter 16
The human solar system

"Right class, it's the big day today for our human solar system model. The weather is on our side, just as we had planned. Before we all go outside, we will just have five minutes going over everyone's places," Mrs Malikinski says, excitedly.

I overhear some of the boys talking about nominating Sarah to be the moon as she has a skin condition and, at the moment, it is very bad. Jack told the others her face just looks like the surface of the moon, all bumpy with huge craters. I don't like Jack very much, as he's a bully who is always putting people down. Jack is bigger than most of us, and he has four older brothers who bully him. He always wins fights at school as he is used to fighting with his brothers. He still picks on Jamie a lot, so we both keep our distance from him.

"Class, please open your notebooks and study everyone's positions on your diagrams."

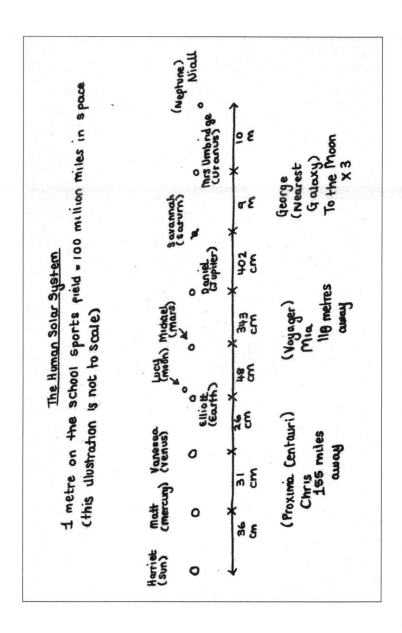

The Human Solar System

1 metre on the school sports field = 100 million miles in space
(this illustration is not to scale)

Harriet (Sun) — 36 cm
Matt (Mercury) — 31 cm
Vanessa (Venus)
Elliott (Earth) — 26 cm
Lucy (Moon)
Michael (Mars) — 48 cm — 343 cm
Daniel (Jupiter) — 402 cm
Savannah (Saturn) — 9 m
Mrs Umbridge (Uranus) — 10 m
Niall (Neptune)

Chris (Proxima Centauri) 155 miles away
Mia (Voyager) 110 metres away
George (Nearest Galaxy) To the Moon x3

The Human Solar System

		distance to each other	
		At school cm/m	in space (miles)
Sun	– Harriet	—	—
Mercury	– Matt	36cm	36 million
Venus	– Vanessa	31cm	31 million
Earth	– Elliott	26cm	26 million
Moon	– Lucy	Almost touching	238,000 miles
Mars	– Michael	48cm	48 million
Jupiter	– Daniel	343cm	343 million
Saturn	– Savannah	402cm	402 million
Uranus	– Mrs Umbridge	9m	914 million
Neptune	– Niall	10 m	1000 million
Voyager Space Probe – Mia		110 m	11 billion miles
Proxima Centauri – our nearest star (another sun) } Chris		250,000 m (155 miles)	25 trillion miles
(our nearest Galaxy) Canis major dwarf – George		over 3× to the moon	147,000 trillion or 25KLY

I open my notebook and smile; I am particularly proud of my drawing. I glance over at Jamie's, but he frowns.

"Mine's a mess," he whispers.

"As long as you understand it." I don't want to totally agree with him.

"We just need to pick someone to be our moon as Marty is off sick today," Mrs Malikinski adds.

I wasn't here when they picked who was going to be which planet, as I think I was auditioning for the school play in the main hall on that day.

Jack's hand shoots straight up. I know what he is about to say, so I stand up abruptly. I don't know why, but it gets everyone's attention.

"Lucy, are you OK?" asks a slightly concerned Mrs Malikinski.

"I would like to be the moon, Miss! I know my name doesn't begin with M, but I am very good at spinning round due to all the dancing I have done, so I think I would be perfect for this. I can rotate around the earth."

"Very well, Lucy. And Jack, do you also want to be the moon?"

Jack is taken aback by the little scene I have just made. It doesn't take much to confuse him. He starts to stutter.

I quickly interject, "I think if Jack wants to challenge me, we should have a dance-off!" I glance over to Jack with a confident smirk, and I give him a cheeky wink.

Jack looks very uncomfortable and sulks down in his chair. Some of the class giggle a little until he gives them the 'dead eye'.

"Right, that settles it then, Lucy, you are our moon today and, as your name begins with L, you may be interested to know that the Latin name for the moon is Luna."

"Thanks, Miss."

Jamie just looks at me, in awe, with his mouth open.

I don't know where that came from, and I have surprised myself, if I'm truthful. If I'd thought this through in advance, I don't think I would have dared do it, but I feel really happy now and incredibly confident, and this was only a by-product of what I had set out to achieve. Sarah is one of the nicest people I know. I'm glad I've saved her from ridicule, and she will never know. My good deed has been achieved for the day and it's only 9.30 a.m.; I might get another in before the day's out.

We all look down and study our solar system plans. Jamie notices the extra drawings and information I've also completed.

"Teacher's pet," he whispers as he flicks through my work. "You didn't need to do all this, you know?"

"I know, but I did some more research so I could try and understand it. It's quite mind-boggling all these numbers."

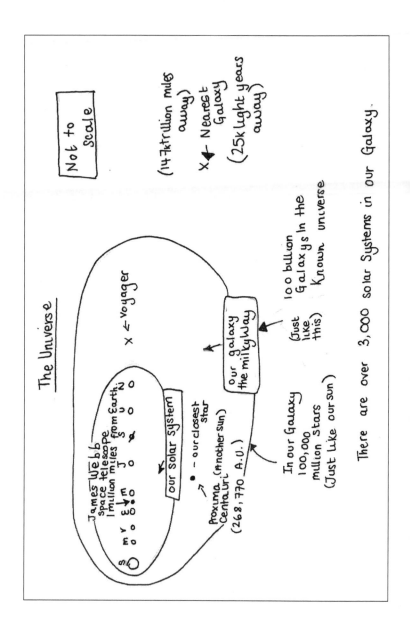

The Universe

Not to Scale

(147k trillion miles away)
x ← Nearest Galaxy
(25k light years away)

x ← voyager

Our galaxy the milkyway

100 billion Galaxys in the known universe
(just like this)

James Webb space telescope 1 million miles from Earth.

our Solar System

• ← our closest star

Proxima Centauri (Another Sun)
(268,770 A.U.)

In our Galaxy 100,000 million Stars (just like our sun)

There are over 3,000 solar Systems in our Galaxy.

Scientific Notation

Number name	Value	Scientific Notation	Metric prefix	Symbol
one	1	1×10^{0}		
ten	10	1×10^{1}		
One hundred	100	1×10^{2}		
One thousand	1,000	1×10^{3}	Kilo	k
ten thousand	10,000	1×10^{4}		
One hundred thousand	100,000	1×10^{5}		
One million	1,000,000	1×10^{6}	Mega	M
Ten million	10,000,000	1×10^{7}		
One hundred million	100,000,000	1×10^{8}		
One billion	1,000,000,000	1×10^{9}	Giga	G
Ten billion	10,000,000,000	1×10^{10}		
One hundred billion	100,000,000,000	1×10^{11}		
One trillion	1,000,000,000,000	1×10^{12}	Tera	T

Mrs Umbridge enters the room. "Are we ready in here?" she addresses Mrs Malikinski.

Mrs Umbridge is head of Year 6; I hope I'm not in her class next year. She shouts *a lot* at her class. We can hear the shouting even though her class is two rooms away from ours. Most of the naughty boys are in her class, as she seems to be the only Y6 teacher who can control them.

Today, Mrs Umbridge is going to be Uranus, as we couldn't find anyone else who had a name that started with a U! But I think Mrs Malikinski secretly wanted her to have a part as there would be less messing around with two <u>formidable</u> teachers keeping an eye on everyone.

"Yes, we are all ready, Mrs Umbridge. Class, close your books and follow Mrs Umbridge on to the sports field, please."

We are lucky at our school, as this is the only school in our town that still has a sports field in its grounds. All the other schools either never had a sports field to start with or have had houses built on them which means they have to walk 10 minutes to the park and hope it's empty if they want to use the space.

We walk out on to the playing field. It's massive; perfect for what we are about to do today but horrible to run round! The grass has been cut and, even if you can't see that, you can smell it. Probably no good for anyone with hay fever, though.

Mr Fix-It, our caretaker (I don't know his real name, it might be Morris, but I'm not sure), has marked out our positions with some circular markers that we sometimes use in the sports hall.

"He must have a very long tape measure," Jamie concludes.

"He might have just paced it out, one metre per step. It doesn't have to be that accurate with the distances we are talking about," I add.

Mrs Umbridge checks her clipboard, as we get near the centre of the field, and starts to shout out people's names and point to their positions.

"Harriet, you are the sun. You're here," she says pointing to the yellow circular disc on the ground.

Originally, Sarah was picked for the sun, but Harriet insisted it should be her as she would get dizzy being a planet. But it's not a secret why she wanted it, as she posts on her vlog all the time that she is the centre of our solar system and everything revolves around her. I have grown to tolerate her more this last year. I just accept how she is and, as long as she doesn't upset me or Jamie, she can behave as she likes.

"Next up, Matthew, you are Mercury."

He hates being called his full name. Matt takes his place. He smiles at Harriet as they are almost touching. She frowns, stands tall and tries to look down on him in disgust.

"Vanessa, here. Venus," commands Mrs Umbridge, and she sounds as if she is bored of this already.

"Elliot, here. Earth."

Mrs Umbridge looks up from her clipboard and, before the words come out of her mouth, I quickly take my place as the moon. "Bye, Jamie." I wave at him as I dash off.

"Michael, Mars, here. Come on, come on. Don't dilly-dally."

"Daniel, Jupiter? Here." She looks at Jamie, shakes her head, and carries on walking, ushering the other kids to follow her.

Jamie wanted to be Jupiter, but Daniel got it, not because of the huge red spot on his face but because he is the biggest out of all of us, and because Jupiter is our biggest planet. We agreed it made sense and would be easier to remember.

"Savannah, Saturn." Savannah's very pretty; all the boys keep reminding her, as if she needed reminding, so she was an obvious choice for the most beautiful planet. And if that wasn't enough, she has brought her hula hoop with her to simulate Saturn's rings. She is amazing at hula-hooping!

Mrs Umbridge takes her place as Uranus. As she told us last week, she is well suited as a large planet due to her size. She has the type of build that has its own gravity.

Mrs Malikinski takes Niall on to his disc, which I assume is blue for Neptune, not that I can see what colour it is, but Mr Fix-It has done a great job of colour-coding the discs to the planets. Elliot's spot had two discs overlapping for earth; a green one and blue one.

I start to rotate around Elliot, as I'm the moon, and he starts to rotate on the spot. Every time he faces Harriet, he says "Daytime" and when he faces away from her, he says "Night-time". Harriet isn't amused. She is playing with her watch as it's linked to her phone. Even though her phone is locked in the teacher's drawer, she can still link up with it and get the internet on her watch. I'm not going to snitch on her, but if she uses her watch to cheat in the SATs, that will be a different matter!

Every time I come between Elliot and Harriet – Elliot shouts "Eclipse".

I stop spinning after a couple of minutes, as I'm starting to get dizzy. I glance around. Harriet, Matt, Vanessa, Elliot, Michael and I are fairly close together. We could fit in the same space as one of the tables in the classroom. Elliot and Vanessa are so close they could hug if they wanted to. Not that they would! Would they?

The distance between Daniel and Michael is about the length of my bedroom. Savannah and Daniel are a similar distance again.

Mrs Umbridge looks like she is about two car lengths away from Savannah, and Niall looks like he is another two car lengths away from her.

It's amazing to think that me and Harriet are just over a metre away from each other and that's equivalent to about 93 <u>million</u> miles!

"Hey, Michael, just look at how close we are, only about half a metre on our model, and it would take a space rocket about a year to get there."

"That's mind-blowing," comes the reply.

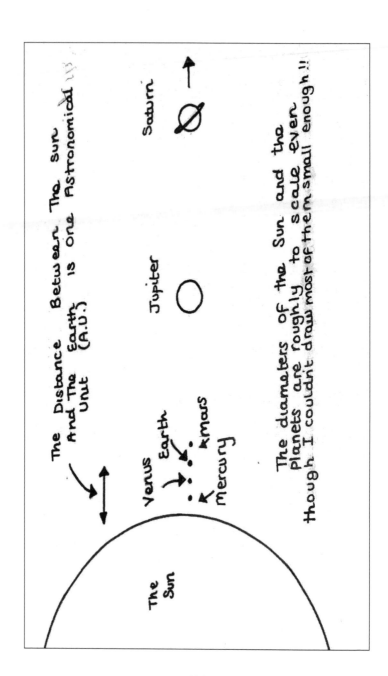

The Distance Between The Sun And The Earth is one Astronomical Unit (A.U.)

The Sun

Venus
Earth
Mars
Mercury

Jupiter

Saturn

The diameters of the Sun and the Planets are roughly to scale even though I couldn't draw most of them small enough !!

It takes light 8 mins to reach Earth from the sun. It takes over 4 hours to reach Neptune.

uranus

The distances between the planets are roughly to scale.

197

Neptune is 30 A. U. from the Sun.

Neptune

The scales used for distance and diameter is a 1000:1

Therefore, using the same scale as the diameter, the distances would be a thousand times longer. Instead of being over 3 pages, they would be over 3,000 pages. That's a lot of blank pages!

"Right class," Mrs Malikinski hollers from across the sports field. "Mia is going to be the space probe, *Voyager*. It took her 35 years to get to the edge of the solar system which is 11 <u>billion</u> miles away."

Mia looks so small now. She isn't tall anyway when compared to the rest of us. She is now at the furthest end of the field.

"The closest star to us is <u>Proxima Centauri</u>," Mrs Malikinski says, as she refers to her own notes. "That's approximately 25 <u>trillion</u> miles away, in its own solar system, but it's still in our <u>galaxy – the Milky Way</u>. We have picked Chris for this, as he is on holiday in London today, and that's where he would be on this scale. There are around <u>100 thousand million</u> stars in our galaxy just like Chris."

"Just what we want, more Chris's," Harriet blurts out.

"Miss, Miss," Stephanie shouts out. "I worked it out last night with my dad. If my bedroom was completely filled with sand, each grain of sand would represent one star and my bedroom would be our galaxy, the Milky Way. That's a lot of stars."

"You are right, Stephanie, it is a lot of stars," confirms Mrs Malikinski.

"No more numbers, it's blowing my mind," Jamie mutters. Some of the others <u>concur</u>.

"Shush," Stephanie chimes up with the authority of a teacher. "We're getting to the best bit."

Mrs Malikinski carries on. "The nearest galaxy is 147,000 trillion miles away. That's 147 thousand million billion miles which is why we use <u>light years</u> as a better measurement, as the numbers are getting way too big. So that distance would be the same as 25,000 light years away. And if we use George as an example of where that nearest galaxy would be on our scale, we would have to put him on the moon and then he would still only be a third of the way."

"That's exactly where he should be, as far away from me as possible," quips Harriet.

"I heard that, Harriet," George scolds.

"You were supposed to," comes her reply.

How Far?

Because the distances in space are vast, scientists use these two other units.

Astronomical Unit

1 A.U = 150 million Km
      = 93 million miles (93,000,000 miles)
      = Distance from the Sun to Earth

Light Year

1 LY = 9.46 trillion Km
     = 5.88 trillion miles (5,880,000,000,000 miles)
     = Distance Light can travel in one year

Light travels at 670,616,629 miles per hour.

"Rotate in your orbits," shouts Mrs Malikinski. All the planets start to rotate around Harriet – the sun. This is particularly difficult for me, as I still have to rotate around Elliot while he is walking around Harriet. It's all going surprising well, until there is a commotion at the end of the field where Mia is.

"Help, help!" she screams. Elliot stops abruptly and I collide with him.

"Hey, watch it!"

"Sorry." Daniel is in my line of sight. As I move over, I can make out that Mia is being chased by a sheep.

"Sheep attack," shouts someone. It sounds like Niall.

"Alien invasion more like," Daniel laughs. The lost sheep is charging towards Niall, led by a very panicked Mia. It's now complete bedlam on the field.

"No one panic. Stay in your orbits," commands Mrs Umbridge. I think it's a little late for that, as most of the planets have strayed out of the galaxy by this point and it's just mayhem. As I look around, Harriet seems to have made a sly exit back into school. Perhaps she doesn't want to smell of sheep? Niall looks at ease as the ferocious beast circles him. I can see his longish hair blowing in the wind; it looks amazing – I'll have to try and find out what conditioner he uses! He confidently leads the sheep back to the field at the end of the sports ground; well he does live on a farm after all. We all start clapping and head back to class. I think that's the human solar system done for now.

When you turn a light off, it appears to go off instantly.

If you could switch off the sun it would take 8 minutes to go dark.

$$\frac{(\text{Light M.P.H})}{(\text{minutes in an hour})} = \frac{670,616,629}{60} = 11,176,943.8 \text{ miles per minute}$$

$$\frac{\text{Distance to sun in miles}}{\text{Light-miles per minute}} = \frac{93,000,000}{11,176,943.8} = 8.3 \text{ minutes}$$

It takes over 4 hours for light from the sun to reach Neptune!

We are going to need a faster rocket

If you borrowed a plane which does 2000 miles per hour.

It would only take 15 minutes to travel the length of the UK

OR 2 hours from UK to America.

But it would take 154 years to get to Neptune!

Chapter 17
Codes

"Lucy, what have you been doing today at school?" Mum quizzes.

"Oh, we had a cool practical science lesson today."

"You know when you get to secondary school you get to pick which sciences you want to do. There's physics, which is about how things move, chemistry which is about <u>elements</u> and chemicals and biology which is more to do with life, animals and our bodies."

"Can you do all three? I don't think Jamie will want to do any, if he has a choice."

"I think you probably can. Well, I think it's important to do a general science, even if you are not that interested in them, as that will include a bit of everything. And Dad always said it's important for everyone to know a bit of basic science."

"Will we make potions in chemistry? I'm looking forward to that."

"Yes, I'm sure you will."

"Do you think there is such a thing as a love potion, Mum?"

"I know there is, it's called gin!"

"Mum!"

"Ah, that reminds me. Jamie's mum, Alison, phoned. She wants a girls' night out. We haven't arranged anything yet, but you can stay at Jamie's if you want."

"Er, good idea, but I think he'd prefer to come here, as his brother is annoying him at the minute."

"OK, but that means getting a sitter, and you don't get on with Michaela, do you?"

"I think we'll be fine. If me and Jamie are together, she'll leave us be."

"Right, I'll message Alison back later and arrange something. Ah… I know what I was going to ask you. I was talking to Sarah, Grace's mum…"

"I know. You don't have to keep telling me who everyone is, Mum!"

"She saw a message on Grace's phone, and it just said can't make it PPPE as usual. What does that mean?"

"She uses it a lot. I think she makes new acronyms up every week. That one is 'parents pooh-poohing everything.'"

"Oh, OK. I won't tell Sarah that."

Before I know it, I have eaten my tea, done my homework and I'm at a loose end. I hate being bored. I'm just going to message Jamie to see if he wanted to play online, when Mum shouts up from downstairs.

"Lucy, I'm going to do the ironing now. Have you got anything that needs pressing?"

I look around, but I can't see anything. I've just had an idea though. I run downstairs.

"No, Mum, nothing else."

"Well, it's a good job as I've got this mountain to do," she says pointing to a stack of clothes, that's nearly as tall as me, on the chair.

"That's a lot of ironing. How long will that take?"

"Put it this way, I'm going to watch a film while I do it!"

"Isn't that dangerous? I don't want you to get distracted and burn yourself!"

"Don't worry, Lucy. I've had years of practice."

"Well, I'm going to finish my homework and then read until bedtime. I'll come down for a kiss before I go to bed, though."

"OK. I'll still be here."

I race back upstairs. Time for more exploring. I've got a good hour, I think. I grab my stuff and dash down into the secret rooms.

After the precarious crossing of the ladder, I greet Wocky.

He looks up at me and tilts his head to the right. His eyes get wider and his lips part. I know exactly what he wants, so I reach into the pocket in my bag for the digestives. I place a few on the floor and give him a stroke. He isn't interested in me now he's eating. I move on, type in the code for the left-hand door and then walk down the corridor to the middle door and read the sign again.

Do not enter. Those who do will not return…

I try the handle, but it's locked. I will have to work out the combination code, but I don't have much to go on. There are only numbers on the lock, no letters, so I need to try and work out the code.

I try pressing 9 as there are nine words in the sentence on the sign.

I then try 2, 3, 5, 5, 3, 2, 4, 3, 6, as this represents the number of letters in each word. Still no luck. I wish I'd brought that _Secret Coding for Beginners_ book down with me now. I try to recall the different codes I've learnt.

I wonder…? I wonder if I convert all the individual letters into numbers, just like the number code on the blackboard for the names on there.

I take out my trusty notebook and write out the alphabet in two columns.

A to M are the 13 in the first column and N to Z are the second column of 13 letters. I always find this easier to work out as M and N are similar letters and they are exactly in the middle of the alphabet. On the next page, I write out each of the words from the sentence on its own line.

I work through the code. The first letter is D and numerically D is 4. The second letter is O and O is 15.

Do   = 4 , 15
Not   = 14 , 15 , 20
Enter = 5 , 14 , 20 , 5 , 18
Those = 20 , 8 , 15 , 19 , 5
Who   = 23 , 8 , 15
Do   = 4 , 15
Will   = 23 , 9 , 12 , 12
Not   = 14 , 15 , 20
Return = 18 , 5 , 20 , 21 , 18 , 14

As I work through this code I realise 'Do' and 'Not' appear twice so that makes it a little easier as I can just copy them.

I look at the page now I've worked out the numbers that represent each of the letters, and that's a lot of numbers. I double-check each one, as I regularly get some numbers or letters mixed up, and with this it would be easy to make a mistake.

All correct. I slowly and meticulously type in each number; all 33 of them. The lock makes a 'clunk' noise and I'm in. It's a miracle!

I open the door and walk in. I glance up at the wall, and I remember the safe behind the rainbow painting which hangs there. I smile because rainbows always make me happy. I'm excited too. I hope the password I figured out earlier (thanks to Google which informed me it was binary code) works and lets me access the computer. But I can do it. I feel as if I can do anything now. Well, anything except my German spelling test which is next week. That reminds me, I still need to practise for that, but not today. Today I have a new mission. I switch on the computer using the huge button. I wonder how old is this computer? I hope it still works. The whirring starts and I jump back. I don't know why, as I'm expecting these awful noises, so it must have just been my natural instinct. The noises get more annoying and screechy (certainly worse than Jamie playing the violin and that's one of the worst sounds I've ever heard!), followed by some beeping and then a flash from the screen. Is this normal? It almost feels like there are gremlins inside it beating it into life with hammers. I look around the room. It's very bare apart from the desk where the computer is and the picture on the wall – there's nothing else here; nothing at all. What a lot of wasted space. I think about how cluttered my bedroom is. Maybe I can move some of my things down here. Maybe...

The computer makes another loud beep and then the green password screen flashes up.

I type in the four-letter name from the binary code that I'd looked up online.

L I L Y

The screen changes, so it must be correct. I do a little hop with excitement and fling my arms in the air. It looks like something is loading... I'm dancing around on my tiptoes in anticipation. If anyone was watching they would think I was barefoot on a hot sandy beach. I look round. Thankfully, no one is watching.

Your name here:
G3P6G14P2G3P5

Another code? What does this mean? I take a photo with my phone. I will copy it into my notebook later. What I don't understand, though, is that there doesn't appear to be anywhere for me to type an answer into. I try typing my name, but nothing comes up. This appears to be an answer rather than a question. Maybe there is nothing else on here but this code?

There's no back button, no Windows icon and no apps on here, just a green screen. How did anyone get anything done on these things? To think, this technology got astronauts to the moon. They must have been very brave! I think back to what I learnt in school last month in the computer workshop we did. Think, Lucy, think! I try to clear my mind and visualise the lesson. That's it – Control, Alt and Delete.

I look down at the keyboard. Found them. I press and hold Ctrl and Alt together, then press Delete. I was expecting a help window to pop up. Then... *BEEEEEEEPPPP*!

Fatal error occurred

Then it all goes dead. No sound, no screen. Oh no! It's <u>kaput</u>, I've killed it. It's a good job I'm not in a spaceship right now, trying to look on the bright side of the situation.

"England, we have a problem," I say out loud copying Tom Hanks from the <u>Apollo 13</u> film.

Daydream over. I'm alright and I have the code, but what good it is I still don't know yet.

I head back to my bedroom but not until after giving Wocky a big cuddle. Oh, I wish I could keep you. I would need to give you a good bath first though, you are looking rather <u>bedraggled</u>. He opens his mouth and starts panting. I leave him one more biscuit before I make my way back upstairs.

"I'm going to have to bring a comb down here and sort your fur out, aren't I?" He doesn't answer.

I quietly close the bookcase door and sneak downstairs to check on Mum without her knowing. She is still ironing and watching something funny on the TV, so I sneak back into my room and crash on to the bed to carry on studying the *Secret Coding for Beginners* book. I keep reading until I'm too tired to take it in.

‹ Notes   ⋯   Done

Status Update

○ On the study door it says "Enter your name here" – is the code from that big old computer (G3P6G14P2G3P5) the code we're looking for? It's worth a try!

Chapter 18
Grandad

Me and Jamie call in to see my grandad on the way home from school. I try and do this at least once a week, as he's the only grandparent I have left. I wish I had known my other grandparents. Mum says I would have loved spending time with them all and they would have loved me equally as much. Grandad is my dad's dad, so he is especially important to me. Jamie thinks he is cool too, and we love listening to all his stories and eating his chocolate.

"You know I told you about Harry's wife, Margaret?" Before we can answer, he carries on anyway. "She only went to one of those fortune tellers, didn't she?"

"Do you believe in that, Grandad?" I ask, surprised.

"Certainly not. It's all nonsense. People just hear the bits that they can relate to, and the fortune tellers can pick up on that and exploit it."

"So, what did Margaret find out?" I ask.

"Oh yes. I forgot what I was saying then! She was told all the usual stuff. She'll find good fortune on a sunny day and an animal will cross paths with her, love will find her if it hasn't already. But she said something very unusual… 'BUBBLE WITH A HAIRDRESSER!' What on earth does that mean?"

"I don't know, Grandad."

"Maybe the fortune teller was crazy," Jamie comments.

"Did I tell you about the time my mum avoided a bomb in the war? I was so close to never having been born."

He has told us several times before, but I know not to interrupt him, as he likes telling his stories and we both like listening to them, so we make ourselves comfortable.

"She was late leaving the factory where she worked, so she ran across the road trying to catch up with the number six tram which would take her home. It was the last one running that evening."

"Did she catch up with it?" Jamie enquires politely, although I'm sure he must remember the story from last time we were here.

"No, she could see it in the distance, but she knew even if she had run through the park to the Four Lane Ends stop, she still wouldn't make it. She had done that before and only once caught up with it. The air raid sirens started."

Me and Jamie start making loud whirring noises like a police car siren but underwater. Grandad continues so we stop and listen.

"She knew she had to try and get home as soon as she could because the neighbour had a reinforced cellar that half the street packed into when the bombing raids started."

"Was it exciting?" Jamie asks.

"I couldn't really say; I wasn't born until later that year. But everyone was terrified. Mum said she could hear the planes coming over from several miles away, and she knew that they were heading for the factories, which is exactly where she was! She ran for miles, trying to keep off the main roads. The German planes were overhead now, and bombs were starting to fall.

"*BOOM. BOOM!*" Grandad yells. He gets us every time with this, and we jump out of our skins. I don't know if he keeps changing the story every time he tells it or if he purposely alters when the bombs land to add to the intensity of his story.

"When she got through the park, she was at the most dangerous part of the journey home; Four Lane Ends. This is the crossroads of two major roads that leads to all of the factories. The sirens were still sounding, and it was hard to hear the planes now as the explosions were so loud, especially when a weapons factory was hit. It was really <u>eerie</u> now on these main roads. No trams running. No cars. No people. All the lights were out or covered up. There was just the flicker of flames from buildings on fire in the distance. She sprinted across the road holding on to her tummy with me inside it. She turned the corner on to <u>Infirmary</u> Road when the unmistakeable sound of bombs being dropped whistled above her. The bomb landed on the butcher's shop, smashing through the whole building before it bounced out on to the road in front of her. She was frozen with fear. A fireman ran up behind her and escorted her quickly to the nearest shelter. He explained it must have been a dud, a faulty bomb, but it still presented a danger. She hid all night in the shelter with dozens of others, all strangers, but they were united by the need to carry on and to be strong for each other. The next morning the devastation was evident. She needed to get home. She needed to see Mam – which was her mum. As she waited at the tram stop, the friendly fireman, Keith, approached and informed her there wouldn't be any trams running that day as the number six was hit last night; no one survived. When I was born, I was named Keith after the fireman who saved us."

Even though I've heard this a thousand times, it still brings a tear to my eyes.

"Did she get home in the end?" Jamie asks not wanting the story to end.

"Yes. She eventually walked back. Mam was overjoyed to see her, as she had also heard about the tram."

"She should have sent a DM," Jamie suggests.

"DM?" Grandad's a little confused.

"It's a text, Grandad, or a direct message. But Jamie's forgetting there were no mobile phones back then. But I suppose she could have used a phone box."

"That was no use either, as we didn't have a phone in the house!" Grandad pauses for a moment as if he was reliving the past.

"It's a shame not everyone is born into the family or era they would like, to get the best out of life," Jamie remarks, as I know he wanted to be a soldier in the war. I think he likes the idea but would be too scared if it came to it. Grandad snaps out of his trance.

"It's the way you live YOUR life and the choices YOU make that determines who YOU ARE, not which family you are born into!"

Jamie doesn't speak up much in case he is shot back down or ridiculed by someone. I can see he is a little taken aback by that, but it was worth it, as we both have learnt something that might have taken us years to figure out by ourselves.

Grandad stands up, removes his pocketbook and checks his reminders list. A smile materialises on his face.

"Hey, you two, look at this." Grandad ushers us out of the room into the hallway. We find ourselves shuffling behind him.

"Sorry I'm so slow. These feet aren't what they used to be. I could give Bobby Charlton a run for his money in my day, you know."

Me and J just look at each other and shrug.

"Do you want a hand, Grandad?" I ask politely.

"No, I'm nearly there. I've got to keep moving myself otherwise my legs will give up altogether."

"Where are we going?"

"I'm showing you my new stairlift," he says ever so proudly.

"I thought you already had one."

"I did but it was USELESS! It was slower than me. What's the point in that!"

"This one's quicker, is it?" enquires Jamie.

"By Jove, boy, it certainly is. I've had it supercharged. It dries my hair on the way back down from the shower." We both look at him. He doesn't really have any hair now so that's a strange thing for him to say.

"You two ever been to Alton Towers?"

"Yes, yes," we both reply.

"What's your favourite ride? Wait... don't tell me... the Corkscrew."

"They've not had the Corkscrew there for years, Grandad. Mine's Rita: Queen of Speed."

"Mine's Th13teen," offers Jamie.

"Is it fast?"

"Fast enough for me. I'm not tall enough for Rita," he says, wistfully.

Grandad looks perplexed as he looks us both up and down.

"Well, are YOU in for a treat! Tickets please. Tickets."

I hand him a pretend ticket and Jamie copies me. We still have no idea what is going on.

"All aboard. All aboard." He puts the seat down and instructs us to climb on.

"Both of us?" asks Jamie, apprehensively. "Won't it break?"

"No. This thing could carry an elephant. My mate George, you know who I mean, the one from the engineering firm I used to work for…" Grandad trails off and loses his train of thought. "That place hasn't been the same since I left. Really gone downhill, you know."

"George. Yes. I remember." I gently remind him without wanting to seem rude.

"Yes, George. He's modified it me for. Go on, fasten your seat belts."

Jamie now looks worried. "It, it, has a seat belt! How fast does this thing go?"

We squeeze on together. I'm glad I showered this morning, as we are a little close for comfort.

"Ready?" Grandad says with a wink of his eye. "Hold on." He picks up a remote control and Jamie grabs my hand. I can see his bottom lip is starting to wobble, but I'm not sure what there is to worry about.

"Five, four, three, two, one… To infinity and beyond!" Grandad shouts, as we stare at him in disbelief.

The stairlift nearly flings us out of its seat with a <u>breakneck</u> speed which will rival the acceleration of

Rita's – I'm sure. Before we know it, we are whizzing round the bend at the top of Grandad's stairs before coming to an abrupt halt. I think my stomach is still downstairs. I don't look at Jamie, as he's not keen on rides, so I dread to think about his stomach, but he's gripping my hand so tight I think I might need a pot on again!

"Time to come down," Grandad announces.

Before we have time to brace ourselves, we are pinned back into the seat, as it races back around the bend again. A memory flashes before me of when I used to play Scalextric with my dad. If the cars were going too fast round a corner, they would fly off the track. Fortunately, we're still attached to the track on the stairlift. The ride back down is utterly terrifying – just like a rollercoaster but we WEREN'T expecting this. We come to a more relaxed stop than expected, but I still can't find my tummy. I thought I had left it just here when we set off.

"What do you think? It's marvellous, isn't it?" Grandad announces, proudly.

Jamie has unbuckled the seat belt and is almost off it before the thing has stopped.

"It's great, Grandad. It's a good job we haven't just eaten."

"Good idea, let's eat."

"You OK, J?" I ask.

"I'm just going to the toilet."

"It's back upstairs. Are you going to take the stairlift?" I jest.

"No. I'll walk thanks."

The Stair Lift

"What's this, Grandad?" I ask pointing to a pile of notes and DVDs.

"Oh, I'm doing an <u>Open University</u> course. Got to keep busy, you know."

"What's it about?"

"How to be a super student."

"But… why? Why do you need to learn that now, at your age?"

"You've got to keep learning, Lucy. I never stop. I keep up with the news, watch lots of documentaries and read lots of books."

"But you're so wise, Grandad, surely you know everything!"

"No, I certainly don't. What I do know is that no one knows everything. It doesn't matter how much you study or how clever you are, there is always more to learn."

"That's depressing," sulks Jamie, re-entering the room.

"Shh, Jamie." I give him a nudge.

"I'm more aware now of what I don't know than I ever used to be. I know what I don't know."

"That doesn't make sense, does it?" says a puzzled Jamie.

"Even someone who dedicates their whole life to working and studying just one subject will never know everything there is to know and they will constantly be trying to keep up, but they will be very aware of what they don't know. The exception to this is my best friend, Bert. He was a PE teacher, you know. He said he knew everything about PE. He learned all the rules to the games, and that's it. He said there was no homework. No coursework. He had nothing else to learn or to do so his teaching career was easy."

"Oh, it's not like that any more, Grandad. We get PE homework. We have to learn about different parts of the body and how it moves and how to exercise, don't we, Jamie?"

"Yeah, I hate PE. It's really hard."

"Good job Bert's retired now then. I used to get beaten a lot at school." Me and Jamie look at each other in disbelief.

"Really, couldn't you tell the teachers?"

"No, it was by the teachers. You put one foot out of place and whack. Your handwriting was messy, whack. Shoes weren't clean…"

"Whack!" we all say in unison.

"If you spoke back to the teacher or lied…"

"Whack," me and Jamie interject.

"No. Not for that. If you lied, you had to wash your mouth out with soap in the toilets with the teacher watching. You only did that once, I can tell you. It was utterly revolting."

"That's awful, Grandad."

"Don't they do that now?" he sounds surprised.

"Er, no, because that's cruel. All the teachers are nice, even the head teacher."

"Oh, the headmaster, everybody feared him. If you had to go to the headmaster… he could shout. In our lessons, we could hear him yelling at someone from time to time. All the teachers feared him too."

"Did you ever get sent to him, Grandad?"

"No. No, fortunately not. I got enough beating with the long wooden ruler to behave."

"They hit you with a ruler?" Jamie asks incredulously.

"Several times a week. It did keep most of us in line, mind you. We were always relieved when someone else got picked on by the teacher and dragged to the front, but when the metre-long, wooden ruler came out, every one of us watching felt every hit. Some of us cried just watching."

"That's dreadful. Couldn't you tell your parents or the police?"

"All the parents knew it was part of how they disciplined you at school. They just told you stop being naughty and it wouldn't happen. And the police... well, the police would hit you too if they thought you were up to no good."

"The police hit you?"

"No, not me, but some of my friends got a clip round the ear for being cheeky."

"Well, if that happened now, I'd ring <u>ChildLine</u>. When that policeman came to school last year, Lucy, remember, he was nice."

"Yeah, he was very <u>approachable</u>. We asked him loads of questions."

"It's a different world now. For the better, no doubt," Grandad says to neither of us in particular.

"Dad said his teacher used to make him write out the dictionary during breaks and at dinner time."

"Yes, I remember. You would have thought that that would have made him good at spelling, wouldn't you?" Grandad laughed. "But, it didn't. He was better at words beginning with 'A' though. That reminds me, if you find an old combination padlock in your dad's things it's mine. I'll have it back now; it reminds me of the war."

"OK, Grandad. I'll keep an eye out for it."

"Thank you for your kindness."

Jamie's tummy rumbles. "Do you want some food, laddie?"

"Yes please," Jamie replies, a little too enthusiastically.

We head to the kitchen. Jamie looks around to see what food is on offer.

"Er, what has your Grandad been eating? That looks like a bowl of worms."

"Grandad, what have you had for breakfast?"

"Sorry, it takes me a while to walk these days. You ought to have seen me in my youth."

We are both just pointing at the bowl.

"That's All-Bran. I had it for my breakfast. It helps my bowels."

J and I pull a funny face at each other. "We don't want to know, Grandad," I say, as we shake our heads.

"You want to know? Well, OK then. I had to go to the hospital and have a camera up my bum…"

"WHAT?" we shriek in unison.

"Couldn't you just do a bum selfie? A bumfie?" injects Jamie. I give Jamie a horrified look whilst trying to hold back a smirk.

Horrified Emoji

"Knowing me, I'd poo on my phone," Grandad laughs.

J takes out his phone. "Hey, Siri, set reminder. Fit screen protector to phone."

"OK, reminder set. Fit screen protector before pooing on phone!" Siri confirms.

"NO SIRI!"

"It's cleverer than you think," Grandad concludes.

He pauses <u>momentarily</u> as if he is trying to remember something else. He removes his notebook from his right back pocket and opens it up. I notice it says 'phone' in big letters on it.

"You know, you've got to keep evolving and keep up with the times. Otherwise, you will be just like the dinosaurs and go extinct. I'm going to get some applications like you both have."

"They are just called apps, Grandad," I correct.

"Yes, some apps. Like 'What's Up' and that talking clock one, 'Tick-Tock'." Me and J look at each other and try not to giggle.

"How about Instagram?" Jamie adds.

"Insta Gran? Is that a dating app for grandparents? I'll have that." He makes a note.

"Not quite, Grandad, but your phone's too old for apps anyway."

He reaches behind him. "Look, I've just bought a new iPhone 13. Isn't it lovely?"

"Wow, Grandad. It's fantastic."

"Now, show me how to turn the damn thing on will you!"

Chapter 19
Outsmarting the babysitter

I keep checking my watch. Not long to go now. I can't wait for school to finish and to get home and put the plan into motion.

Mrs Malikinski addresses the class, "Right class, next week we will be making a cake. Please bring the ingredients with you. You should have all written them down by now, but I'll leave them on the board anyway. Homework for next week is to calculate how much icing we will need to cover the top of the cake and how much ribbon you need for the <u>circumference</u> of the cake."

George's hand shoots up. "Yes, George."

"What's the circumference, Miss?"

"The circumference is the outer <u>perimeter</u> of the cake." She draws a circle on the board. "This is what the cake looks like from above, a bird's-eye view of it."

"None of my cakes look like that," Jamie whispers.

"So, anything inside this circle will be covered with icing and that is the area of the circle. This is calculated by using π x r2." She writes it on the board. "Pi is a letter in the Greek alphabet."

"What is that funny shape before the r squared, Miss?"

"Good question, Elliot. The symbol for pi looks like two letter Ts next to each other. We will use an approximation of pi so as not to overcomplicate our calculation. Pi runs to lots of decimal places so, for ease, we use pi = 3.14." Miss Malikinski writes this on the board next to the circle, so I copy this down in my book.

"To calculate the area we need to multiply the radius squared by 3.14." She draws a dot in the centre of the circle, which I add to my circle. "If you draw a line from the centre of the circle to edge of the cake, this is your radius. The radius of our cake is 10cm." I can see Jamie frantically trying to scribble all this down and make sense of it.

Miss Malikinski continues. "To work out the circumference, in this case the length of our ribbon, we use pi multiplied by the diameter."

George's hand shoots straight up again. Stephanie sees this and immediately puts her hand up as well.

"The diameter, George, is…" George's hand drops down, followed quickly by Stephanie's, "any line from one side of the circle to the other that goes through the centre of the circle." I draw the diameter on my cake picture. "So, because the radius is 10cm, which takes you to the centre of the cake, the diameter is the same as double the radius. Therefore, the diameter will be 20cm."

I quickly do the calculations.

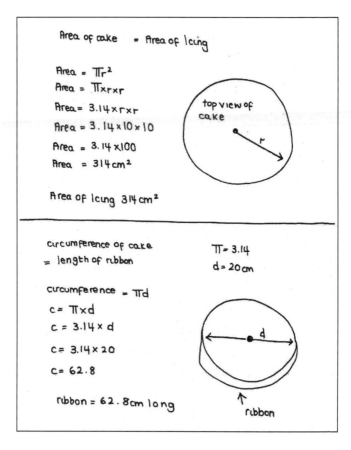

I double-check my answers. They look like what I would expect. Excellent. Homework done, and I haven't even left school yet! I glance at Jamie who is scribbling away, copying my work.

"Nearly done, just checking you've got it right," he smirks.

"Miss?"

"Yes, Lucy."

"Isn't pi r squared just for working the area out on flat surfaces? Because the cake will rise, so it will be domed on top not flat."

"You are right, Lucy, but for our example we will keep it simple and assume the cake will be flat, just like it would be if it was a layered cake, and you were icing the middle."

"Our cakes are always flat on top. My dad says it's because there's something wrong with our oven," Chris jokes.

"Well, I'm sure your cake will be just fine, Chris."

A large beep comes from somewhere around me. All the class go quiet and stare. I look around.

"*Beep.*" An embarrassed Jamie takes his phone out of his pocket.

"Jamie, this is your reminder…"

"No, Siri, no…" he shrieks, desperately.

"Fit screen protector before pooing on your phone!" Siri announces.

The class go berserk, everyone seems to be laughing and pointing at Jamie. Mrs Malikinski is just about to comment when the bell rings.

"OK class, off you go. Have a nice weekend."

With his head bowed, Jamie sneaks out as quickly as humanly possible. I try and keep up.

"Think positively, J, this could have happened at the start of the lesson and then you would have had to sit there embarrassed for the whole time."

"Yes, I suppose that would have been far worse," he agrees.

"All set for tonight? See you later. Don't forget your bag," I remind him. With that, we say our goodbyes.

I race home to prepare; have my tea, get my bag ready and I go over the plan in my head whilst I wait for Jamie to arrive, which seems like forever, so I start pacing up and down.

"Lucy, stand still. You will wear the carpet out," Mum points out.

"I'm just excited, Mum."

"Excited I'm leaving you? Great."

"No, of course not. I'm just excited to see Jamie again."

"You only saw him three hours ago," she jokes. "How do I look?" she says, doing a twirl.

"You look absolutely fabulous, Mum. But... you have bags under your eyes. Let me help. I've got a great make-up tip." Michaela, the babysitter, who arrived a little while ago, looks up from her phone but doesn't comment.

"Sorry, Lucy, no make-up tip will sort these out. These are bags for life!" Mum laughs.

Ding-dong, the doorbell chimes.

"Ding-dong, the witch is dead! Which old witch? The wicked witch! Ding-dong, the wicked witch is dead," Mum and I sing in unison, as I skip to the front door.

I open the door to greet Jamie. "Ding-dong, the witch is dead…"

"No! Stop singing *The Wizard of Oz*. I could hear you outside," remarks Jamie.

"We watched *The Wizard of Oz* yesterday. I bet you wouldn't have guessed."

"Nothing surprises me with you, Lucy." He looks up at Mum and says, "My mum's waiting in the car."

Mum grabs her bag. "Bye Michaela. Bye Jamie." She gives me a kiss as she walks out of the door. "Don't stay up too late, you two."

"We won't, Mum. Have a good night with Alison."

We close and lock the door. I had been worried that Michaela might have forgotten that she was babysitting for us tonight and my whole plan would be foiled before it had even begun. Michaela's a teenager and she seems to do what she wants, when she wants (I can't wait until I'm a teenager!). I know Mum was a bit worried about using her again, as once she fell asleep and forgot to give me any supper and, if that wasn't bad enough, she left a film playing about vampires and zombies. I didn't watch it, as it looked too scary, but it shouldn't have been on anyway.

Mum knows I can look after myself now, so having Michaela round is just a <u>formality</u> really, especially seeing as Jamie is here too. We can make ourselves a sandwich and drinks, and Michaela will be getting paid for effectively doing nothing.

"Right, Jamie, we'll go over the plan again."

"Do we have to? You know what we are doing. I'll just follow you."

"I don't want any mistakes. I've been planning this for weeks. You know with my broken wrist I have been limited to what I can do without you. This is the perfect time. You said your mum is planning on keeping everyone out late and going to a nightclub. I know my mum won't be interested in that but, as it's Friday and we have nothing on tomorrow, she will probably be convinced to stay out, which means we've got as long as we need tonight."

We quickly arrange our beds and backpacks. It doesn't take long, as I'd done most of this before Jamie arrived. His airbed is fully inflated and the extra teddies and pillow for our deception plan are under the bed ready. My rucksack is fully stocked, and I've got a whole packet of digestives for Wocky. I'd also put new batteries in my torch. Jamie isn't as prepared, though. He, somehow, has still left his school books in his bag!

"WHY…? JAMIE, WHY?"

"I forgot to take them out," he says, sheepishly.

"We just have to wait now until Michaela sits down to eat and starts watching a DVD. She always brings some films with her. She thinks our movies are rubbish!"

Just as the words leave my mouth, we hear her talking loudly on the phone to someone. "Yep, all clear. They've gone now."

I look at Jamie quizzically. "What's she up to?"

The doorbell rings.

"I think we are about to find out."

Michaela races to the door and opens it, to let a very tall, dark-haired boy in. He looks a bit dopey. Jamie and I hide at the top of the stairs, watching secretly whilst she sneaks him in. How very <u>surreptitious</u> of her. I'm debating whether to text Mum, but I think better of it.

"This is the distraction we need," I announce to Jamie.

Chapter 20
I've brought Top Trumps

"Right, what are we going to do before our secret mission? I've brought my Top Trumps *Star Wars* cards again," Jamie says, excitedly.

"Actually, I've got a new Top Trumps for my birthday, but we'll play it later."

Jamie starts looking round my room for anything new. "Ooh, a joke book!" he says, as he takes it off my bookshelf for a closer look.

"Go on then."

Jamie flicks through the pages and picks one.

"Why can't you hear a pterodactyl go to the toilet?"

"I don't know, why can't you hear a pterodactyl go to the toilet?"

"Because they have a silent 'P.'"

"I like it," I giggle.

"OK, here's another one. Which word contains three syllables and all 26 letters?"

I think for a moment. "No idea. It must be a long one."

"The alphabet!"

I groan. "Oh, I've got one for you now," I interject whilst Jamie is still turning the pages. "Why can't you trust atoms?"

"Trust you to do a science one, Lucy. You know I can't do science. Go on then, why can't you trust atoms?"

"Because they make up everything."

"That's actually quite good," Jamie says, reluctantly. "Listen to this that my brother told me, why did the toilet paper cross the road?"

"Because it was in a shopping bag?" I hazard a guess.

"No, because it was stuck in the crack!" he laughs at this one.

"Er, that's gross, Jamie."

Jamie looks at the new picture frame I got for my birthday. "Who sends you a picture frame with themselves in it?" he asks. "They've got to be quite <u>vain</u> haven't they! Is this your auntie and uncle that you hardly ever see?"

"No, that's the picture that comes with this frame, silly. You take that picture out and put your own in. I just can't decide which one to use yet."

"I think if it was mine, I would keep their picture. It looks better than any I've got!" he decides.

"Right, come on then, we'll play my Top Trumps."

"Which one is it?"

"Elements!"

"Really? Lucy! Really?"

"My uncle bought it for my birthday, and I've only played it once before with my mum."

He caves in. "OK, just for a little bit."

I shuffle out the cards. "I'll go first." Jamie nods in agreement.

"<u>Mercury</u>, Hg, <u>density</u> 13,546 kg/m3," I read the card.

"You win. I've got <u>hydrogen</u>, H, density 0.1 kg/m3. What is density though?" Jamie asks.

"Let me just check the instructions." I read it out, "The density of a substance is its mass per unit volume. The values are measured at room temperature. One cubic metre of water weighs 1,000kg, so the density of water is 1,000 kg/m3."

"I still don't get it. So, it's just a measure of how heavy it is?"

"No, not quite. It's how heavy something of the same size is. So, you couldn't say Daniel is denser than me. He is definitely heavier, but he is over a foot taller than me. But a piece of paper would be less dense than a piece of metal if they were both the same size."

"OK. So, it's like the Dead Sea where the water's far denser due to the large amount of salt in it compared to water everywhere else."

"That's exactly right. I forgot, Maggie went there in the holidays, didn't she, and she told us how she just floated on the surface due to how dense the water is. Anyway, just read the explanation on your card, Jamie."

"This will take forever," he groans, but reluctantly agrees. "Hydrogen is a colourless, odourless gas that can form an explosive mixture with air. It's the most common element in the universe and is the fuel that powers the sun. Hydrogen is also an essential element for life."

"Wow, I didn't know any of that," I say, with interest.

"Go on, read yours. I can see you're dying to," he smirks.

"Mercury is the only metallic element that is liquid at room temperature. It has been used in thermometers, dental fillings and batteries but, as it is very poisonous, scientists have been looking for alternatives."

"That is quite cool. It's the only metallic element that is liquid at room temperature."

"I did know that 'cos it's on my periodic table."

I've barely finished my sentence when Michaela bursts in. "WHAT ARE YOU TWO UP TO?"

I nearly wet myself she has made me jump that much, and Jamie has dropped all his cards.

"N… n… nothing," I stutter.

"Only joking, I thought you'd be on <u>Fortnite</u> or whatever kids your age are playing. I didn't need to worry, though, you've not changed at all. If you want anything from the kitchen, come and get it now, as I'm going to watch a film and I don't want to be disturbed."

"Don't you mean WE don't want to be disturbed? I know your boyfriend is here," I challenge.

"Yes, Andy's here. So, if you want a drink before bed, you'd better come and get it now."

Me and Jamie look at each other. He doesn't need any convincing to eat. We follow Michaela back down the stairs and into the kitchen. I pour Jamie a glass of water and myself a glass of milk.

"Milk! You kids are so strange. Why don't you drink pop? You're so health conscious," Michaela scoffs.

"Milk is full of calcium and so good for your bones," I reply.

"Does Andy want a drink; I could take it to him?" Jamie strikes up the courage to talk directly to her.

"No, you stay here. Andy's a bit shy, and I don't want you scaring him away. When you're done you can go back upstairs and don't come back down. Your mum's left some food in the slow cooker for me, but we're not going to eat it all so you can have some of that.

"You don't need me to tuck you in any more – do you?"

I shake my head a bit too enthusiastically. Jamie has a big smile on his face and starts to nod. I give him a little kick. His nod reluctantly turns into a feeble shake of the head.

"Right, I'm going back in the lounge now. In ten minutes, I want you back upstairs. I'll know if you come back down 'cos of your squeaky stairs." We both look at each other our mouths wide open.

As she heads back into the lounge, Jamie mumbles, "I'm shy as well."

"Jamie, she's eight years older than you!" He blushes a little and then heads towards the slow cooker. "What's for supper? I didn't realise you had one of these. My dad says we have a slow cooker – it takes DAYS before anything is cooked in our kitchen!"

"Your dad's funny," I chuckle.

"Funny to you. I have to live with him telling his 'dad jokes' all the time!"

I open the fridge and remove two plates with sandwiches on them. "This is what I prepared earlier. Like it?"

"You've been watching *Blue Peter* again, haven't you? No wonder you've got so many of their badges!"

"There is nothing wrong with being organised. Anyway, I knew you'd be hungry, and I didn't want to waste any time."

We take our drinks and plates upstairs. "We are going upstairs now, Michaela," I announce loudly as we pass the lounge door.

"Night then," comes a half-hearted reply; she's obviously distracted talking to Andy.

I purposely make the stairs squeak as we make our way up to my bedroom.

"Did you hear? She knows about the squeaky stairs. We'll never be able to sneak down now," Jamie whispers loudly.

"I know, but do you think she knows that we know exactly which one it is?"

"Err… we don't know if she knows that we know," Jamie scratches his head.

We sit down eating our sandwiches whilst we ponder that one.

"These are scrumdiddlyumptious," remarks Jamie.

"Aren't you having all of your drink, J?"

"I was just thinking there are no toilets down there though, are there?"

"That's a good point, actually. No, I haven't seen any." I put the rest of my milk on one side for later.

"There might be some in the alien spaceship? Unless aliens don't need to wee?" he says, pensively.

"If they are robots, they won't need a toilet, but if they are alive, they will need to eat and drink and therefore will need a toilet."

"Let's look for a toilet when we're down there and we'll know the answer to that question, won't we?"

Jamie is playing with his ice in his glass, and he looks puzzled. "This water is getting colder even though it's a lot warmer in your bedroom right now. I would have thought as soon as you took the water out of the fridge it would start to warm up until it got to room temperature – just like that experiment we did at school."

"Yes, but you are forgetting one thing," I suggest.

"What's that?"

"The ice in your glass. The temperature of the water can't get any warmer until all the ice has melted. The heat from my bedroom is melting the ice. Didn't you do that optional piece of homework we were given?" I knew the answer to that question, so I don't wait for a response. "It was all about <u>thermodynamics</u>."

"Oh, I get it now." I can see he doesn't want to talk about that any more.

He looks round at my bedroom as if he is trying to <u>envisage</u> something.

"What are you thinking?"

"Shall we build a den like the one we built at mine? Have you got any sheets or blankets?"

I open up my bottom drawer and grab three sheets. "Here, you grab that end and put it over the chair."

Jamie grabs a few books and that helps keep the sheet in place. I place my end over the end of the bed and weigh it down with a few teddies.

"I've got some pegs in my toy box over there." I point Jamie in the right direction. We then use the pegs to attach the other sheets, so we have a door.

"Looks good." Jamie stands back to admire our creation.

"We're amazing at den building. All we need now is a sing-song. Let me put some music on."

"I haven't got a musical bone in me!"

"I beg to differ." I start playing on his musical ribs whilst he squirms around making all kind of obscure sounds.

"Stop it. Stop it! It's not fair. You caught me off guard!" He tries to catch his breath.

I stop instantly and look for my phone to put a song on, but I'm taken by surprise and I can't stop giggling. *I'm* now the piano!

"Stop. Stop, you are hurting now." Jamie stops tickling me immediately. "Let's brush our teeth and wash our faces before we forget."

"OK, you go first."

After I've done mine, Jamie goes into the bathroom, but he isn't in there for very long.

"Have you brushed your teeth properly?" I realise I sound like Mum.

"Yes, of course," he says, a little sheepishly.

"And washed your face with the facecloth?"

"Oh. It's a facecloth? I thought it was a bum cloth!"

"What! I'll have to throw that away now!"

"Only messing," he laughs, but I'm not sure whether he is. I make a mental note to wash it tomorrow.

Jamie checks his phone, as it has started pinging a lot. Then mine starts too.

"Daniel's started a group chat. I've added you in." I grab my phone. *Ping, ping, ping.* Before I consider joining in, I check who is in the group, so I know who I'm talking to.

There's a lot of the class in it: Daniel, Savannah, Harriet, Theo, Max, Amelia, Kitty, Maggie, Billy, Chris, Hannah, Matt, Jamie and me.

Class Chat

Daniel posts Crazy Frog ringtone by Axel F

Amelia

That's so annoying!! My parents have banned me from listening to it!!

Maggie

I agree

Max

Love it! Any more, Dan?

Are you at the seaside, Kitty?

Kitty

Yep, I'm in our new static caravan

Maggie

Surely your dad bought an anti-static caravan. Otherwise doesn't your hair stand on end when you touch it?

Class Chat

Kitty
Very funny! It's static because it's 2 big 2 move!

Daniel
My dad pulls ours with the car!

Does any1 want 2 play Fortnite?

Billy
I'm not playing anything with Chris. HE CHEATS!!

Max
Yea! I agree. Cheater cheater bogie eater!

Kitty
Please stop being gross and stop being nasty 2 each other

Lucy
I'm with Kitty on this

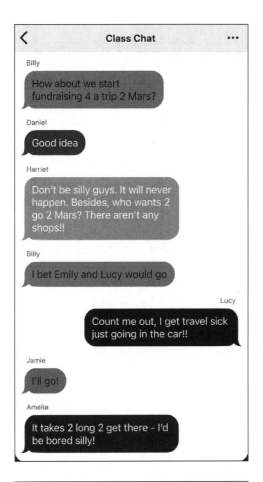

Billy
How about we start fundraising 4 a trip 2 Mars?

Daniel
Good idea

Harriet
Don't be silly guys. It will never happen. Besides, who wants 2 go 2 Mars? There aren't any shops!!

Billy
I bet Emily and Lucy would go

Lucy
Count me out, I get travel sick just going in the car!!

Jamie
I'll go!

Amelia
It takes 2 long 2 get there – I'd be bored silly!

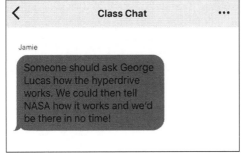

Jamie
Someone should ask George Lucas how the hyperdrive works. We could then tell NASA how it works and we'd be there in no time!

I look up at Jamie. "REALLY?"
"WHAT? It's just an idea," he replies.

I think for a minute and then ask Jamie, "Does Billy not change his pants at all in February?"

Jamie looks up and pulls a funny face.

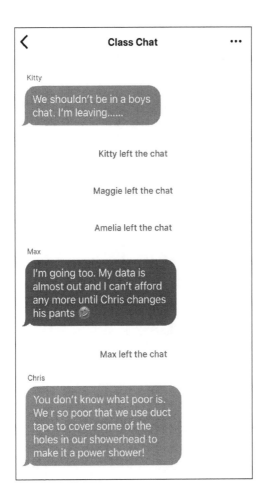

Class Chat

Kitty

We shouldn't be in a boys chat. I'm leaving......

Kitty left the chat

Maggie left the chat

Amelia left the chat

Max

I'm going too. My data is almost out and I can't afford any more until Chris changes his pants 💩

Max left the chat

Chris

You don't know what poor is. We r so poor that we use duct tape to cover some of the holes in our showerhead to make it a power shower!

"That's actually a good idea," I say to Jamie, "it will increase the pressure."

"If you say so," he says, not seeming to care.

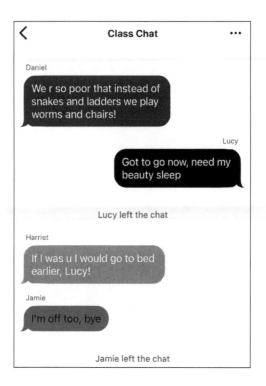

Class Chat

Daniel
We r so poor that instead of snakes and ladders we play worms and chairs!

Lucy
Got to go now, need my beauty sleep

Lucy left the chat

Harriet
If I was u I would go to bed earlier, Lucy!

Jamie
I'm off too, bye

Jamie left the chat

"I was enjoying that."

"It's all a bit silly, J."

"I won't tell you what Harriet just said then."

"It's alright, I don't want to know," I sigh.

"With Daniel and Chris talking about being poor, it's reminded me that I forgot to tell you about what happened last week."

I put my phone down and look up at him, intrigued, as he continues.

"It was a nice day, so me and my dad walked to Tesco's and we sat down by the door while he was finishing his drink. A minute later, a lady veered towards us. I looked up as she got closer. She bent down in front of Dad and said, 'I hope this helps' and threw a pound coin into his cup. I know he had his gardening clothes on, but I'm sure we didn't look homeless."

"What did your dad say?"

"He said, 'We will just sit here a while longer'!"

"I like your dad," I smile.

Enough time seems to have passed now, so we decide it's now or never.

We study the map one last time.

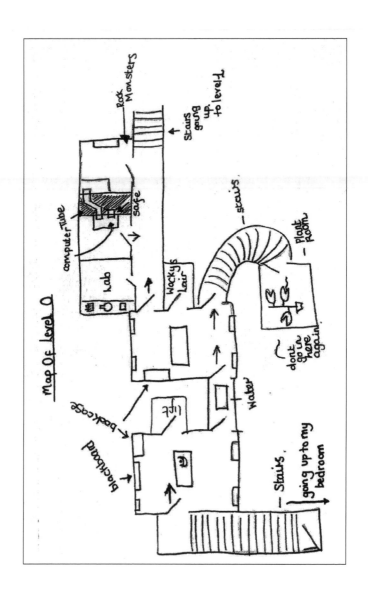

Map Of level 0

Rock Monsters

Stairs going up

Tread of the going

computer Tube

safe

Lab

Wackys Lair

stairs

Plant Room

dont go in here again

bookcase

lift

blackboard

Water

Stairs

going up to my bedroom

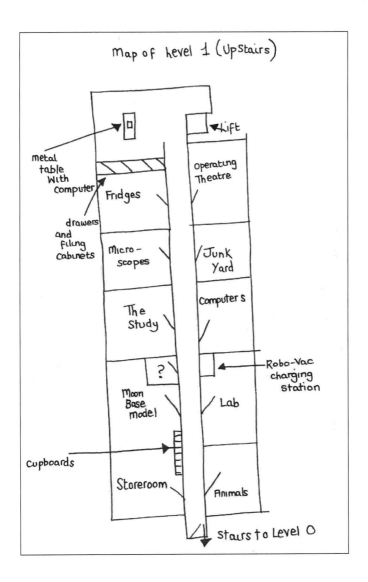

Map of level 1 (Upstairs)

metal table with computer

drawers and filing cabinets

Fridges

Micro-scopes

The Study

?

Moon Base model

Cupboards

Storeroom

Lift

Operating Theatre

Junk Yard

Computers

Robo-Vac charging station

Lab

Animals

Stairs to Level 0

253

Chapter 21
The secret room

I creep to the top of the stairs. I can hear the film on downstairs and a little bit of giggling. It sounds like a bit of <u>canoodling</u> is going on, so I know we won't get disturbed. When I re-enter my bedroom, I close the door silently behind me and give Jamie the thumbs up.

We quickly arrange the teddies and pillows under the bed sheets to make it look like we are fast asleep in bed (just in case Michaela comes in to check on us), and we stand back to check if it gives the desired effect.

"Yours is better than mine," Jamie comments.

"I think they are equally as good," I reply. We grab our bags and open the secret bookcase door as quietly as we can. I regret not oiling the hinges, so I type a little reminder for myself on my phone – oil door. Jamie is halfway down the stairs though now.

"Come on slowcoach," he calls.

"I'm coming." I quickly follow him. We enter the first room, then over the ladder bridge and through into the second room. Wocky <u>dramatically</u> bounds over to greet us.

"Oh, I've missed you," Jamie says whilst giving him a big hug.

"I brought some dog treats with me. I'm going to see if he likes them." As soon as I open the packet the <u>distinctive</u> smell fills the room.

"Wow, that's <u>potent</u>," remarks Jamie.

Wocky pauses and looks up at me whilst inhaling deeply. His long tongue unravels, as if it was absorbing as much of this new smell as possible, and a smile appears on his face which shows all of his surprisingly sharp, but very gross, teeth.

"Wow, his breath is worse than that food," Jamie blurts out moving away from him.

In an instant, Wocky darts in my direction, but I'm ready though. I have already grabbed a handful of these doggy treats, and I quickly throw them into the air. Wocky is ferocious in his actions, like a lion with its prey.

"Get some more out, quickly, quickly," shouts Jamie. In a flash, Wocky has <u>lassoed</u> all the treats with his tongue. It was very impressive, and, for a moment, I was mesmerised.

"Now Lucy, now," J shouts. I throw some more just in time. I've just realised though that I've <u>made a rod for my own back</u>. I only have half a bag of treats left, and he's eating them as fast as I can throw them. He's not going to want any more digestives now, or flies for that matter. I'm going to have to buy more dog treats!

Jamie has already opened the other door, using

the code MALI and is standing in the passageway.

"Let's go," he yells with hint of panic in his voice. I throw another handful towards the other end of the room and make a dash for the exit with Jamie slamming the door behind me.

"You've started something there. He loves them. Did you see how fast he moves?" I pause and take a deep breath to compose myself.

"Yes, I agree. For a moment there, I felt like I'd fallen into the bear enclosure at the zoo!"

"Don't forget, we don't really know that much about Wocky. He could be dangerous. I hope you've got some more treats left for our way back out."

I take a look. Not as many as I would like, but I say, "Yeah, it'll be fine. He might be full now," I say, trying to be optimistic.

"Maybe running out of a room from a hungry Wocky should be an Olympic sport," he muses.

I look at him strangely. "You do come out with some very odd things you know, Jamie."

"What? There are so many of them. Have you ever counted how many different sports there are? If there was one for picking your nose, though, George would definitely get gold."

"Yeah, Stephanie would get gold for being the smartest in the class; she is such an egghead. And Jack, well he would get gold for being the most annoying."

"What would I get?" Jamie asks hopefully.

"You'd get gold for being the nicest and most

genuine person." His mesmerizing smile beams once again.

"You could get gold for anything you wanted to do, Lucy. When you put your mind to it you can achieve anything."

"Thanks, J." That's put a smile on my face now too.

We make our way along the corridor and up the stairs. I make it to the door first. I type in the code, Goldilocks, then press my hand on the large button and the door unlocks immediately. I look back at Jamie.

"Ready?"

"Ready, I think."

We remove our shoes, as planned, then he holds my hand as we enter the sparkling clean corridor. As I look back, I see the door automatically close behind us. I knew it would, but I still wasn't sure whether I should be pleased or scared. I opt to remain positive, as we don't have a spare hand to close it ourselves anyway. We sneak past the robo-vac which is charging on its station. Its front scanner is off which affords us the opportunity to continue.

We arrive at the study door. Jamie reluctantly lets go of my hand long enough for me to remove my phone and look up the code. I hope it's the right one, because we don't have any other options.

"Here goes nothing," Jamie whispers in his Han Solo voice. I would have commented, but I'm too focused on trying to input the correct sequence.

I type in the code: G3P6G14P2G3P5.

Incredibly, it works, and the door opens.

"We're getting good at this, aren't we?" suggests Jamie.

"I think we are," I reply, feeling rather smug. I didn't really think this would work at all, but I'd kept that to myself.

The room smells fusty and unused. It's dark in here and this room doesn't appear to have automatic light sensors. I look round for a light switch and flick it.

A large chandelier lights up the room. The bulbs are the old <u>filament</u> ones, the same as Grandad still has as I know he can't get on with <u>LED</u> bulbs.

"Wow, this is an amazing study," Jamie says with his mouth slightly open in awe.

It really is. The room is probably twice the size of my bedroom, but this one has a really high ceiling. It's got very <u>elaborate</u> wooden mouldings and carvings around the door and on the ceiling. Jamie closes the door quickly behind him and that creates a little dust storm which causes us to both cough.

"I bet nothing's been touched in here for years," Jamie remarks, whilst leaving footprints on the dusty wooden floor, as he walks around taking a closer look.

"Look Jamie." I point to a window which is hiding behind thick curtains.

"Well spotted, Luce. You found a window."

"Don't be sarcastic. Seriously, this is the only room we've been in that's had a window."

"Is it?" he scratches his head.

As I pull the curtains back, I'm met with streaks of moonlight shining through, as it appears to be boarded up on the outside.

This extra light only highlights the amount of dust floating in the air. I stand by the window and survey the room.

There is a painting hung on the wall to the right of me. It is The Hay Wain by John Constable. I recognise it as Grandad has the same one. Below it is row upon row of metal filing cabinets, which look a little out of place given the decor in this room. To both sides of the only door are chests of drawers and, to my left, is a ladder on rails attached to a wall-to-wall bookshelf where Jamie is stood, randomly pulling books out.

"I bet robo-vac would have a field day in here," he comments.

"Yes. There must be a reason why this is all locked up and kept intact when all the other rooms are perfectly clean," I suggest.

"I can't find any more secret passageways though, Lucy."

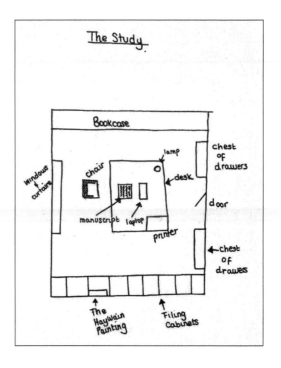

The Study

There is something very special about this room. I can't quite put my finger on what it is, but it is a lovely room. Well, it will be when it's clean! I'm in half a mind as to whether to open the door and let the little robo-vac in, but that can wait for now. Over on the desk is a very large reading lamp, so I switch it on.

"Wooow, that's bright. I had my back turned to that and it shone through me," chirps up Jamie.

There are some reading glasses on the desk. I open the case and try them on. They're a bit big for me, but I can still see through them, so I <u>deduce</u> that they are for an adult and it's someone whose eyesight had only just started to deteriorate as they are mainly magnifying everything. I remove them and place them back as I found them. There's a small photo frame with just a quote in it: 'We are all stardust'. I like that, so I copy into my notebook. There is also a letter opener on the desk, a magnifying glass, a jotter pad and a pot of Sharpies in front of a HP printer, but what dominates the desk is a huge manuscript.

"What have you found, Luce? I've got nothing."

"I think this is a man's study."

"I think you're right. It's so messy."

"It's not really messy, just dusty," I reply. "The glasses on here look like a man's size and style, not a woman's. At first, I thought this was a room that had been untouched for decades."

"What's a <u>decade</u>?"

"One decade is ten years. But look, this printer can't be more than five years old and..."

"I bet the ink's gone in that then," interrupts Jamie.

"But there are Sharpies on the desk that still work," I say whilst trying them on the jotter pad.

"So, someone could be coming back here? Do you think that they might just be on holiday?"

"I don't know, it still doesn't add up. There must be something in here that's secret which is why it doesn't get cleaned."

"What does it say on the paperwork?"

"It appears to be a book or a <u>thesis</u>."

"Thesis? What?"

"Someone's research, I think." There is a laptop hiding underneath, but I leave that for now and study ream of papers.

I look at the contents page.

1. Overpopulation
2. Global warming
3. Climate change

4. The trouble with plastic
5. Volcanos
6. Earthquakes
7. Tsunamis
8. Hurricanes and tornadoes
9. Extreme weather
10. Asteroid attack
11. The reliance on technology
12. The unexplored oceans and cave systems
13. Nanotechnology
14. The rich – poor divide and the companies which run the world
15. The lunar base
16. The Martian home from home
17. Viruses and how to control them
18. Global nations working together for the common goal
19. Genetic engineering and biotechnology
20. Evolution
21. The future and how we get there.

I flick through to section two. "Global warming," I read out loud.

"Isn't global warming a good thing?" Jamie questions. "It would save us going on holiday to warmer places."

"I've always wanted a banana tree. With global warming it might be possible! But look what it says here," I point to some concerns highlighted in the document, "higher sea levels, more severe flooding, melting ice caps and more extreme weather like hurricanes, storms and <u>tsunamis</u>. These new conditions would wipe out huge populations of animal life on land and in the sea which we depend on. It would be devastating to farming. That is far more serious than I imagined."

I look up at Jamie, but he's nodding as if he isn't really listening.

"You are surprisingly quiet," I comment. He had his mouth almost wide open.

"We could sell this. There must be hundreds of pages here. We'll be billionaires," he finally says, whilst jumping in the air.

"It's not ours to sell. This is someone's research, and they could have been working on it for years." I look at the initial pages and then to the last two pages; nothing, no names or signatures. "This is why the door was locked," I guess.

"Try the desk drawers, Lucy, there might be some clues as to whose paper it is."

I pull the first drawer out. "There's just stationery in here. The other drawer has a padlock with a combination code on; it's locked. We need the code."

"What's the clue?"

"There isn't one this time," I say, a little frustrated.

"Let me have a look. It looks just like my brother's bike lock." Jamie moves closer.

"Do you think they all have the same combination?"

"No, but I'll try it – 2313. No. But I can crack it. I opened my brother's when I wanted to use his bike."

"I bet he was pleased with that!"

"He still doesn't know," Jamie chuckles, clearly proud of himself.

"How can you crack it? Can you show me?"

Jamie starts to explain. "You have to listen very hard to the clicks inside the lock whilst you are turning the dial and then you pull on it as if you were trying to force it open. First pass me your screwdriver."

I fish it out of my bag and hand it over to Jamie, still confused as to what will come next.

He puts the handle of the metal screwdriver to his ear and the other end on the lock.

"I get it. The sound will travel up the screwdriver so you can hear the click."

"Yeah, something like that. Pull," he instructs.

I pull on the lock as requested.

Jamie slowly turns the dial forward, then back again. "Got one," he says triumphantly. "Three."

"Hang on. I'll write it in my notebook." I jot it down and then resume my position. He turns the dial again. "Nine."

I feel the lock move a little. It's still locked, but it's working.

"Great work, J." I jot that down and we carry on. This time it's taking longer. He slows down so it actually looks like he is turning it in slow motion. My hand is starting to hurt, as I'm pulling the lock quite hard.

"Got it! Four," he says, with a confident smile.

"Are you sure? I didn't feel anything?"

"No, but I heard it."

Once again, I write the number down and we continue. "Five."

There's a clunking sound and the padlock pulls open.

"I knew there was a reason I brought you along," I say, knowing he wouldn't take offence from that.

We high-five. "Teamwork."

"Master Burglar Jamie in da house."

"I wouldn't brag about that, or you'll have the police knocking at your door," I giggle.

"Look at the code – 3945."

"That easy to remember, it's World War II; 1939-1945."

"Don't dilly-dally, Luce. Open the draw."

I pull it open to reveal its contents.

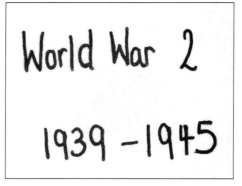

Chapter 22
The secret room part 2

Within the drawer, I'm surprised to see the only content is a metal lockbox. Jamie laughs. I look over confused.

"It looks likes James's lunch box. Just without the dinosaur stickers," he comments.

"So it does. He is the only person who brings his sandwiches to school in what could only be described as a moneybox. I don't think he wants anyone to pinch his banana!"

"We need a key," Jamie says, deflated.

I shake the box gently. "It sounds like there's something inside."

"Wait," Jamie almost shouts at me, as he points to the underside of the box.

"What?"

"There is something on the bottom. Look."

As I turn over the box, I read out the typed note taped to the metal base.

" 'Reach for the stars' for answers."

We both look up at the ceiling.

"No stars here," Jamie confirms rather despondently.

"Reach for the stars sounds familiar. It can't be a code, as we need a key. This must be a clue as to where to find the key."

Jamie walks over to *The Hay Wain* and moves the picture. "No keys here, either. Have you checked under the desk? It could be stuck under the drawer with chewing gum."

"Oh, I hope not!" I look and thankfully it's not.

As Jamie starts opening up the filing cabinets and rummaging through them, I move the manuscript so I can open up the laptop and switch it on. There is a sticky note stuck on the edge of the screen as I open it up. I take a picture of it, as it might be another clue for us to work out. An image of a memory stick equals a fish, and an image of a computer equals a monkey.

'*Enter password*' flashes up.

I type in 'monkey'.

A large '*X*' flashes up followed by an ear-shattering sound. I jump back and Jamie falls backwards.

"What was that? What have you done?" He looks rather panicked.

"I typed in the wrong password. It sounds like Simon Cowell's just pressed the buzzer on *Britain's Got Talent!*"

"Don't get it wrong again. I nearly had a heart attack." He feels his pulse.

"I'm going to leave it for now. It's obviously not worth guessing, so I'll come back to that."

I notice a small notepad that must have been hiding under the laptop. As I flick through it, there are a lot of handwritten notes and ideas, but the writing isn't very legible. This is definitely a man's writing, I decide – it looks just like Dad's writing did.

This is all I can make out:

269

What to do with waste – put it in black holes?

Use drones for policing the streets and to help the fire service survey damage and put out fires.

Use magnets to move space junk into the atmosphere so it can burn up? Or use lasers to zap it?

Use caves on Mars to protect astronauts from UV radiation.

Use plutonium for power on Mars?

Harness the sun's power with solar panels. Beam energy back down to earth?

Put OAPs in a low gravity nursing home as they won't need as much strength to move around. Their heart won't need to work as hard.

Giant solar filter following our orbit around the sun to block some of the sun's harmful radiation out. This could reduce the Earth's temperature and counteract global warming.

This isn't helping us right now, so I close it up and place it back on the desk.

"What's in the filing cabinets?" I ask.

"Loads of boring stuff. Papers, papers, and more papers. Who writes all this stuff? How can anyone amass this much paper?" he seems genuinely perplexed as he gestures to all of the filing cabinets.

"Anything on stars?"

"No idea. It's mainly focusing on animals. Some files on proteins, some on stem cell research. Oh, what's this?" he says whilst flicking through some folders.

"Don't get any of them mixed up, they are probably in an order," I warn.

"I wonder if there is any information on inventions in here."

"Why, do you want to invent something?"

"Too right. You know my dad keeps complaining that I watch too much TV."

"Yes, he says you'll get square eyes," I giggle.

"Precisely. Well, I want to invent the first oval TV to avoid that issue. Then I can play Xbox all day long!"

"That's cool."

"Listen to this. There are over 50 <u>trillion microplastic particles</u> in the oceans." He continues reading using his finger to keep his place. "That's 500 times more than the stars in our Milky Way galaxy!"

"Wow. I'm struggling to visualise that."

"I thought I felt sorry for the person who wrote all this stuff, but that's nothing compared to whoever counted all the microplastic particles in the oceans! Where would you start? I lose count when I count the pennies in my penny jar!"

"That's blown my mind," I agree.

"Here, something else. On these papers it's talking about burning methane in oxygen which produces carbon dioxide because there is carbon in methane and therefore carbon in carbon dioxide. It goes on to say if hydrogen burns in oxygen, it only produces water so it will help with climate change. And... and... listen to this; hydrogen is the most abundant element in the universe, and it could be used on the moon or Mars base of the future!"

I can't believe how excited Jamie is over this. He seems to actually understand it all, and he usually hates science.

"I'll take some pictures of these equations, Luce, and I'll send them you. It then goes on to talk about making water and rocket fuel from hydrogen in space."

Burning methane in oxygen

$$CH_4 + 2O_2 = 2H_2O + CO_2$$

methane + oxygen = water + carbon dioxide

Burning Hydrogen in Oxygen

$$2H_2 + O_2 = 2H_2O$$

hydrogen + oxygen = Water

No carbon dioxide
or carbon.
The future?

(H) Hydrogen needed for fuel
(O_2) Oxygen needed for breathing
(H_2O) Water needed for life
You can make H_2O from H & O
You can make H & O from H_2O

Hydrogen is the most abundant
element in the universe. We
just need oxygen; we can make
(O_2) oxygen from (CO_2) carbon
dioxide and we have too much
of this, we also breathe this
out.

273

"Wow, that's very interesting, but I still don't think it helps us in reaching for the stars." As I say it, I reach in the air and the wall of books is just visible in my <u>peripheral vision</u>. I turn to face the books and start looking at the top shelf.

I don't know what I'm looking for but hope I might know once I see it. I start working my way down; row by row.

"Hey, listen to this." I don't turn round to face Jamie; I'm not being rude, I just don't want to lose my place looking through these book titles. He doesn't wait for me to reply. "It says here that mushrooms are being used to break down plastics."

"I wonder how many mushrooms you'll need or how big they have to be?" I answer, still keeping my focus on the rows of books.

"I think this research is also about how they can use DNA from mushrooms to recreate this on a larger scale."

"That's interesting," I'm referring to both Jamie's findings and his interest in it; I'm pleasantly surprised.

I stare at the fourth row of books down. My eyes are starting to feel strained, and I have neck ache looking up so high.

"J, let me know if you see an index for these books. It will be easier than trying to read all these spines. Found it," I rejoice.

"What?"

"*Cosmology – Reach for the Stars*. It's the same as the book on my bookshelf."

"Oh yeah, the one you pull to activate the secret door."

"Come and give me a hand." I slide the ladder along its runners and realise it needs some oil. As I line it up, Jamie takes hold of it and keeps it steady for me.

"It's very steep. It doesn't feel natural climbing this."

"Don't worry, I've got the ladder. You just hold on. You've got this, Luce."

Once I'm high enough, I take my right arm and wrap it around the next rung up to hold me tight. I steady my feet and lean into the ladder, because I'm conscious that if my centre of gravity is wrong I'm more likely to topple off. I'm now able to reach out and grab the large book with my left hand. I pass it down to J. "Grab this," I ask.

"Got it. It's not as heavy as it looks, it's just hard to hold. I hope we don't have to read it."

I carefully make my way down and relax again. That was a little <u>nerve-racking</u>.

We open the book together not knowing what to expect.

"You did it, Luce. You're a superstar."

The book is hollowed out on the inside and a key is stuck inside the void.

"That is one cool hiding place. This is the sort of book I love."

"I'm gobsmacked."

"You're so clever, Lucy. How did you…? Sherlock Holmes eat your heart out. You are the best detective ever. I bet one day NASA will name a space mission after you."

"Well, if they do, I will want it to investigate Jupiter and its moons," I decide.

"I'll pass that message on for you."

I try the key in the lockbox, and it works. The metal box opens. Inside, there is another key.

"What's that for?" Jamie asks.

"We've been searching for this key for months. It's for the safe behind the rainbow picture downstairs."

"Oh yeah. How do you know?"

"Look at the key ring. It's a picture of a rainbow."

"Well, it's obvious now you've said that. Come on, let's go. I'm dying to know what's in that safe. I've never opened a real safe before."

I stare at the key for a while. I still don't know what to make of this place. I feel like I'm trespassing and looking at things that are private but, strangely enough, I feel like I belong here; like it was meant to be. None of this makes any sense.

"Come on… come on. You're holding the next part of the puzzle. No time to waste. Unless of course, you want to grow old in here reading everything in those cabinets," Jamie jokes.

"You're right, let's explore some more."

Chapter 23
"STOP RIGHT THERE"

After putting everything back to how we found it and placing the key in the zipped pocket in my rucksack, I head over to the door and slowly open it.

"All clear."

Jamie closes the filing cabinet, switches off the light and stands behind me.

He taps me on the back. "Ready when you are."

"I'll move out and check it's clear. You stay in the doorway until I wave you on. Don't let the door lock until we know it's safe."

Still holding my shoes, I head out. Without thinking, I turn left and move, without hesitation, along the corridor. I hear some screams and squawks coming from one of the rooms which stops me dead in my tracks. I hold my hand up to Jamie to indicate for him to stay still. It sounds like someone is being tortured in there. We have got to make sure we don't get captured. Listening intently, I move swiftly and silently along the corridor. No robots in sight. I peer around the corner to the lift entrance. It's all clear.

After pressing the call button, I look back at Jamie who looks eager to move, obviously not wanting to be left behind in here.

After what feels like a lifetime, the clunk followed by a beep from the lift confirms it has arrived. The doors open, and I wave Jamie on. He doesn't waste any time in pulling the door closed behind him and running towards me.

Suddenly, the door opens to the operating theatre where all the screaming had come from. The 6-foot tall robot walks out into the hallway between me and Jamie, separating us from each other!

"STOP RIGHT THERE," it commands, as it holds both arms up with its palms facing each of us.

We both freeze. I squeeze my legs together as tight as I can. Out of the corner of my eye, I can see the lift door is still open. If it was anyone else except Jamie, I think I would have bolted and left them, but there is no way I am leaving Jamie behind.

Are we next for the operating table? Could we be imprisoned down here? Thoughts are running through my head at a thousand miles per hour. We have no phone service down here. No one knows where we are. No one would be able to hear our screams. We are both too scared to scream as we stand <u>petrified</u> almost as if <u>Medusa</u> has turned us to stone. Is this where we get our <u>comeuppance</u> for sneaking around?

"DON'T MOVE," comes the monotone voice of the robot once again. His vision is zigzagging across the floor.

Maybe it's malfunctioned? I wonder if Jamie could shine his torch and dazzle it enough for us to get to the lift. *Bing. Clunk.* The lift doors close. We are done for now. I try to control my breathing to calm myself down. I can feel my heart racing – it must be 200 beats per minute right now – and a wave of sickness floods me.

The robot starts moving towards me.

"STAY WHERE YOU ARE."

It's very convincing, just the same as Mrs Umbridge when she does the school assembly.

"No need to panic, just stay perfectly still for now," says the robot, still scouring the floor as if it has lost an earring.

I can see Jamie better now. He looks as white as a sheet.

"It's alright, J. I've got a plan." I haven't, but it's the best I can do to reassure him. I still have no idea what's happening. Then the robot speaks again:

"A thousand nanobots have escaped. I'm trying to track them all. I don't want you to tread on them," he says to me.

"I can't see anything," I pluck up the courage to reply.

Nanobot?

You can fit about 40,000 nanobots on a full stop.

"They are too small for the human eye to see. I will have to suck them up with AVB." As soon as the robot has finished speaking, the robo-vac beeps and comes to life, squeaking all the way over.

"What's AVB?" I ask, still unsure about the fact that I am actually talking to this alien robot.

Its eyes dart left and then right, just like someone trying to keep track of a frightened spider racing across the floor.

"AVB stands for Automated Vacuum Bot," it replies.

"Oh, it's the robo-vac." The AVB shines its red laser across the floor and moves forward, sucking as it goes.

"Come." The robot waves Jamie closer, but he doesn't move.

"It's OK, J."

"Come now." It sounds like the Terminator (not that I've seen the film, of course, as I think it's a 15, but maybe I could've watched nearly a half of it seeing as I'm older than 7 and a half!).

Jamie swiftly moves towards us until…

"STOP. They are on your feet. DO NOT MOVE. They are looking for a host."

"What's a <u>host</u>, Lucy?" Jamie sounds terrified.

"Us!" I reply <u>anxiously</u>.

"I don't like entertaining," he responds, nervously.

I'm panicking for him not even knowing what these things are. I don't know what's worse – seeing what's on your foot or knowing something's on there but not knowing where it is.

"They won't hurt you. Stay still and AVB will suck them off you."

Jamie starts to cry, which makes my eyes water, but I know I need to stay strong for the both of us. After all, it is me who has put us both in this <u>predicament</u> in the first place.

The robo-vac zooms over to Jamie. A hatch opens on its side and a little nozzle extends. <u>Ingenious</u>, I think to myself. The little vac cleans Jamie's feet and ankles. Normally he would be ticklish, but tonight he manages to resist.

The robo-vac stops and heads back to its charging station.

"Panic over. You can move freely again," says

the <u>gargantuan</u>, shiny robot which is towering over us. "Sorry about that inconvenience. This hasn't happened before."

"What… what… are they?" asks Jamie, visibly very shaken by the whole experience.

"Nanobots. They won't hurt you. We use them in humans and animals to repair damaged cells. They can be programmed to move through your blood to exactly where we want them to. Unfortunately, tonight there was a little power surge and the system crashed, so they were free to escape."

My mind is completely blown. "So, they are little robot doctors that repair you from the inside," I paraphrase, still in shock.

"Yes. That is kind of right."

"SHUT UP!" says Jamie in total disbelief. "I don't want any of those in me. No thank you," he continues whilst still scratching his ankles.

"How small are they?" I wonder out loud.

"Our nanobots are 14.5482 nanometres."

"I've no idea how small that is. Can you tell us approximately? For example, how small are they compared to an ant?"

"Yes, certainly. A nanometre is 10-9. That's a millionth of a millimetre," confirms the robot. "Most of them are about a thousand times smaller than an ant, but some of them are over a hundred thousand times smaller."

		Scientific Notation	Metric Prefix	symbol
One billionth	0.000000001	1×10^{-9}	Nano	n
One hundred-millionth	0.00000001	1×10^{-8}		
One ten-millionth	0.0000001	1×10^{-7}		
One millionth	0.000001	1×10^{-6}	Micro	m
One hundred-thousandth	0.00001	1×10^{-5}		
One ten-thousandth	0.0001	1×10^{-4}		
One thousandth	0.001	1×10^{-3}	Milli	m
One hundreth	0.01	1×10^{-2}	Centi	c
One tenth	0.1	1×10^{-1}	Deci	d
One	1	1×10^{-0}		

"Wow, that's teeny-tiny. No wonder you lost them." I'm feeling more relaxed now.

"I wouldn't like to change the batteries in them," jokes Jamie, who also seems to be calming down a little now too.

"No, you don't need to…"

"He was joking," I explain.

"Ha… ha… ha… very funny," says the robot, although its laugh is very monotone and not very convincing.

"How do you know you have got them all?" asks Jamie, still scratching.

"I can scan for them. I can see in several wavelengths. There is no escape from me. Ha… ha… ha…"

Me and Jamie don't laugh; we actually find this prospect a little terrifying.

"Right, Jamie. It's time we leave now, because Mum's expecting us outside. Come on, let's go."

Jamie looks confused, but then he realises this is my escape plan.

"Oh yes. Must go. Bye." He gives a little wave to the robot.

As I turn around, I can't help but notice a giant ray and pufferfish suspended from the ceiling. I jump back as it startles me.

"Do you like our robot ray and robot pufferfish that I've just put up?" the robot asks. I look a little closer. They look real but, on closer inspection, they are mechanical.

"Why... why robot fish?" I'm baffled.

pufferfish

Ray Fish

"They have been designed to blend in with the other fish whilst scanning the oceans. There is so much of the ocean that hasn't been explored yet. The robot ray is used for scanning the upper layers and the pufferfish can go much deeper. Due to its spherical shape, it can withstand the pressures better. We've just been carrying out some modifications to them before they are sent back out again," the robot explains.

I'm still not sure what to make of this, so I simply thank the robot and head to the lift.

"Wait… Let me show you the plans for our moon base. It won't be long now before it's a reality," the robot shouts after us.

Jamie shrugs, but I'm very apprehensive. We're trespassing after all, but the robot hasn't zapped us with his laser eyes. My instincts tell me to be careful; after all he is a stranger.

I think on it before replying, "OK, but we only have a minute, though."

"Follow me." The robot heads back down the corridor, passes the study and the robo-vac, and stops at the door on the right-hand side. Me and Jamie follow holding hands (although he is squeezing a little too tightly).

As we follow the robot, I notice he can walk surprising smoothly. He is certainly very high-tech, and I begin to wonder if he's… from the future?

"Let's stay in the doorway. I don't want to get locked in a room." Jamie nods in agreement.

"Here we go. This is a scale model of our planned lunar base. We are very proud of it," the robot says, in its very monotone voice.

We stand in the doorway and I'm amazed. I didn't know what to expect, really. I was thinking of models I had made with Dad out of cardboard boxes, plastic bottles and cereal packets. This wasn't a *Blue Peter* badge moment.

"It's amazing," Jamie blurts out.

"How did you make it?" I'm now very inquisitive.

"We have our own 3D printer in the corner of the room. We also have a 3D bioprinter in another room. The designs are created using software on a terminal and the printer prints exactly what we want. We have a control room here and the rocket launch pad here." He shows us on the model.

This makes Grandad's model railway look ancient, I must admit.

"These are the laboratories here and these are the habitats."

"So, you are planning to go to the moon?"

"Not me. Robots and drones will most likely be sent first to initiate the building work. I am just helping here with the designs and research. We do lots of scientific research on curing diseases, cancers and many other conditions. We are heading the research into the, still unexplored, deep oceans and establishing a colony on Mars."

I'm starting to get the heebie-jeebies. "You have been busy. Thank you, that's been very interesting, but I think we need to go now."

"Talking of going, do you have a toilet here?" Jamie asks.

"Yes, it is next door. It has a sign on it which says WC." Jamie and I obviously look mystified by this, so the robot offers an explanation. "WC means water closet." I look at Jamie in astonishment and tug on his arm.

"It's OK, we need to go now. Thanks for the tour. Bye." We race back down the corridor to the lift hoping nothing gets in our way.

"Nice to meet you. Bye for now," replies the robot.

I press the lift call button. It lights up and beeps and the doors open instantly. We dive into the lift not even looking to see if there is anyone in there. Fortunately, there isn't.

We hear another door open, and a screaming kind of squeal suddenly intensifies – far worse than when I accidently stood on Emily's cat.

"QUICK THEY'RE COMING," Jamie tries to say with a shaky voice.

Chapter 24
The safe

I look down at the control panel and press the 0 but nothing happens. Focusing my thumb precisely on the button, I try again. It lights up and the doors close. We both stare at the narrowing gap both hoping that we don't see anything appear at the doors.

The doors close and we feel the lift jolt and move in a downwards direction.

Jamie gathers his breath and raises his hand looking for a high five. I allow myself to smile now we're safely in the lift and we high-five.

"We did it," he says, sounding relieved. "And now we know that there is a toilet, so maybe they aren't just robots after all."

"But does that mean that they are aliens disguised as robots, or is there someone else up there as well as robots?" We both shudder at the thought that we still have more questions than answers.

We put our shoes back on while we're in the lift. As the doors open and we exit, I realise we have come the wrong way.

"What's wrong?" Jamie asks.

"We should have turned right out of the study and gone down the stairs. This way we have to cross the water again and Wocky will expect more treats."

"We just needed to get out of there, so don't beat yourself up, Luce. I know you generally think these things through, so you rarely make mistakes, but at least we're out of danger. We've crossed the ladder before, so we can relax now."

"You're right."

I notice Jamie looking puzzled. "What's on your mind?" I ask.

"I was just thinking of all those flags on that moon base model. I saw NASA and what looked like the British flag and ESA flag, but what were all those others?" He sounds rather <u>flummoxed</u>.

"Yeah, I noticed that as well. I know Amazon's space programme is called Blue Origin and their flag has a feather on it."

"Oh, and I saw... that other billionaire's flag... You know... <u>Whatchamacallit</u>... Virgin Galactic."

"Yes, and Elon Musk's SpaceX had a flag, and there were also flags for India, China, Russia and, I think, United Arab Emirates, Japan and Korea."

"It seems everyone is in a race to get to the moon," Jamie observes.

"My grandad says it's not a bad thing, though. Before we were born, the first space race was between Russia and America. If they hadn't been trying to beat each other, they would have probably given up. Besides, with all the troubles in the world, it's nice when all the countries work together; they forget about their differences and work towards a common goal in the name of science."

"It sounds like you thought that last bit up, but I remember your grandad saying that as well."

"You're right, he did."

We've gone through the other door and slowly cross the ladder. We're getting used to doing it now, so it doesn't seem half as daunting this time and we're also distracted by chatting, which helps. As we open the door into the next room, Wocky jumps up to us both.

"Do you think he's missed us or the treats?" Jamie laughs.

"He's liking you; maybe he can smell those nanobots!" I giggle.

"Don't go there. I'm still itching just thinking about them."

"I'll get some treats out of my bag for him while you fuss him."

As I rummage through my backpack, I watch the reunion between Wocky and Jamie which makes me immensely happy. You'd have thought they were long-lost brothers separated at birth. If only I could show Wocky to Mum and then have him as a pet in our house.

Unexpectedly, I'm hit with the force of a juggernaut and knocked over, as Wocky can smell the dog treats and clearly doesn't want to wait any longer. My daydream quickly dissolves, as I throw a couple of treats into the middle of the room. Jamie offers his hand, and he pulls me back up and on to my feet.

"You OK there? Did he take you by surprise?"

"Just a bit." I dust myself off. "Let's check out that safe now."

Jamie races over to the left-hand door and enters the code.

"It's…" but before I can speak, he's entered it.

"I remember it!" He sounds surprised. "I can't remember to take my lunch to school or brush my teeth, but I remembered this! I'm not as dumb as people say."

"You're not dumb at all, J."

I don't think he's listening, as he has already moved along the corridor to the middle door whilst the lights are still trying to flicker into life.

"What's the code for this again?" he asks.

I open my notebook and show him whilst he types in the code and opens the door. I take the opportunity to update the map of upstairs.

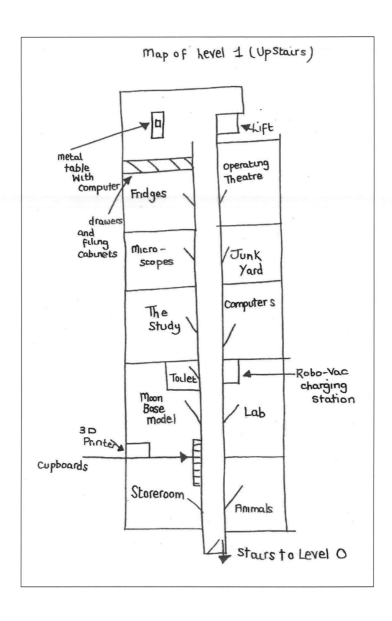

Map of Level 1 (Upstairs)

metal table with computer

Lift

Fridges

Operating Theatre

drawers and filing cabinets

Micro-scopes

Junk Yard

Computers

The Study

Toilet

Robo-Vac charging station

Moon Base model

Lab

3D Printer

Cupboards

Storeroom

Animals

Stairs to Level 0

"Wow, that's the longest code yet." He runs over to the table and leaps on to it like he was going for gold in the Olympics.

"I've never seen you move as fast, J. Are you having a sugar rush or something?"

"Can't wait. Can't wait. Very exciting," he replies, as he takes the rainbow picture down from off the wall. "We haven't got all night; we'll have to get back soon." He places the picture carefully on to the table. "Hand me the key," he demands.

I was going to climb up and join him, but I find myself anchored down, as Wocky seems to have grabbed hold of my leg. I lean over and pass him the key which is attached to the rainbow key ring.

I can feel myself getting a little giddy now, as he turns the key and opens the safe.

"What's in there?" I ask, straining up to try and see.

"I can't see yet." He switches on his torch and shines it in the safe. "Oh, it's a memory stick," he replies pulling it out with his other hand.

"I wonder what's on it?"

"I'm not sure, but I bet it's password-protected. It must be important to be locked away like this." He passes it down to me. I turn it around in my hand looking for anything on it.

"It says 6PB and Goldilocks on it?" I confirm.

"Come on, you are going to have to explain that," Jamie says.

"Goldilocks. Don't you get it? The answer to the universe. This could be the answer to everything!"

"We are going to be rich. Yippee," Jamie squeals.

"No, it's more than that. This information could solve all the world's problems. Besides, it's not ours, so we wouldn't get rich off it and the people who do this sort of work don't do it for the money; they want to make a difference."

"But it might have next week's bingo ball numbers on," he says with a straight face.

I glare at him just before he lets out a little chuckle.

"What's the 6PB for though? On mine for school, it's 2MB for <u>megabytes</u>."

"I've got a <u>gigabyte</u> memory stick and my computer's hard drive is one <u>terabyte</u>. It must be six <u>petabytes</u>."

"What's a petabyte? I've never heard that one before," he says shaking his head.

"A peta equals 1000 tera."

"Wow, just think of all the information that could be on that memory stick!"

I place it in the zip pocket within my rucksack.

"Can't you try it in this computer," he stares at the <u>humongous</u> machine on the desk next to him.

"No, I've already looked. It doesn't have any <u>USB</u> <u>ports</u> on it that I can see. We will have to try it on my laptop when we get back home."

I'm about to leave when Jamie says, "Wait, there's something else in here." He's moving his torch around with his left hand. "I think there is another cupboard within the safe."

I'm intrigued. "Go on then, open it up," I say rather shirtily.

He reaches in. "A light has come on in the safe. It's a fridge. A fridge in a safe? What a great idea to protect your sandwiches."

"A fridge? Are you sure?" I'm not sure if he's being serious or joking at this point.

"I can feel the cold coming off it!" he announces.

"Well, I suspect anything in there will be well out of date, so don't touch it if looks mouldy!"

I can see him removing something.

"What have you found?" I can't possibly think what on earth could be in there.

"It's a test tube with a red solution in it. It might be <u>Ribena</u>," he says, with a smile. "Shall I try it?"

"Probably best not to try. I think that's highly unlikely to be Ribena. Does it say anything on the test tube?"

"It does say something. Hang on." He tries to rub the frost off the label whilst holding it in his right hand.

"Just put the torch down or pass the test tube to me," I suggest.

"It's OK. I can look. Don't be eager." He points the torch to the writing.

"AB negative. Pure sample."

"It's a blood sample," I yell out. "But of what? Is it Wocky's? If it's Wocky's DNA we could make another one; his twin." All sorts of ideas are running through my mind.

"We'd be rich. Everybody would want a Wocky. We could start a 'build a bear workshop' – but for real!" Jamie's so giddy with the prospect.

He carries on rubbing the test tube label.

"I'm trying to make out the name." A couple of drops hit the table below. "It's leaking," he squeals.

"No, it's just water. The frost on it is melting and turning to water as the warmer air in here is touching the cold tube and forming <u>condensation</u>," I explain.

"What are you talking about, Lucy?"

"Remember from school? The warm air cools and turns from a gas to a liquid forming condensation."

"Whatever. I can see the name. Wait, it's your name; Castleton!"

"What?" I exclaim. "My blood? But… how? Why?"

"No, it says Michael Castleton."

"That's, that's… my dad! Are you sure?"

"Why would your dad's blood be in here? Do you think the robots were experimenting on your dad?"

"It might be a cure for my dad's illness, but maybe he didn't get it in time. Right, put it back, Jamie. It obviously needs to be in the fridge. I don't know what to do with this information so for now, it's best we put it back in there while we think about this. Please, put it back, Jamie."

"I think it says something else on here," he says trying to turn the tube round in his fingers.

"This contains my dad's DNA, Jamie. I've…"

I see the test tube slip out of his hand. He tries to grab it with his left hand but, as he's holding his torch as well, he just knocks it causing the tube to go into a spin.

I lunge forward, as if I'm saving a goal in a penalty shoot-out, with no regard to any injuries I might sustain as a result. I'm just completely focusing on the catch, but it's not meant to be. Wocky is holding on tight, and I don't have the momentum to reach. The test tube hits the edge of the wooden table. It looks intact. It hasn't broken. Then it rolls off the end. I bash into the table and my arm takes most of the impact. Jamie wobbles but holds on to the edge of the safe to stop himself falling on to me. There appears to be a perpetual silence, as we wait for the inevitable to happen.

SMASH!

"NOOO," I scream louder than I think I've ever done before.

Wocky takes evasive action and runs out of the room.

As I look down, I can see shards of the glass test tube scattered on the stone floor and the red liquid seeping into the stone.

"Jamie, you clumsy fool," I yell. "I told you to put your torch down."

"I'm so sorry, Lucy. I didn't mean to. It was an accident."

"It shouldn't have happened. You should have passed it to me. You were rushing."

"I'm sorry. I'm really, really sorry."

"Close the fridge door and the safe and come down."

I collapse on to the floor with my head in my hands. It's like watching my dad disappear again.

Jamie hangs the picture back up and climbs down.

"Don't worry, Lucy. It was only old blood. We still have the memory stick, remember."

"That's my dad," I snap back at him.

"We don't know what it was, but it's probably no good seeing as your dad passed away a couple of years ago."

"That was his DNA. It's the only living thing I had left of him. And it's gone now, because of you!" I spit my words out.

Jamie is deadly quiet. He knows when it's best to listen than to talk.

"This memory stick could contain all the information I needed to clone my dad using the DNA from his own blood. My only chance of getting him back is gone." I can't hold the tears back any more, and quite frankly I don't want to.

Jamie starts to cry as well. "I'm so sorry. I didn't realise," he blubbers out.

I storm out of the room and head back home. Jamie follows me at a distance, and I can hear him closing the doors behind me.

I climb straight into bed. I can't even look at him. Sorry teeth you are not getting brushed tonight. I grab every teddy I can find and cuddle them all tightly. I can feel my pillow getting wetter by the minute as the tears stream down my face. It all seems <u>insurmountable</u>. This is probably the worst night ever! The hope of getting my dad back has been dashed and banished into eternity. The worst thing is I have also lost my best friend, and I can't even talk to Mum about it.

IF YOU CRY
IN THE SHOWER -
DOES IT REALLY
COUNT?

Chapter 25
The fabulous encounter

A few days have passed without me answering Jamie's calls or messages. We still sit next to each other in class which is difficult for me even though he's being incredibly <u>sympathetic</u>. Even break times are hard. Jamie keeps his distance, as he knows he can't do any more.

Alone, I sit on the bench. I see Harriet nearby and, to my surprise, she walks over.

"Where's your boyfriend?" she asks.

"Me and Jamie aren't talking."

"I know. Daisy told me. Has he broken your heart?"

"He is NOT my boyfriend, Harriet. You know that."

<u>Uncharacteristically</u>, she sits down next to me and it takes me by surprise.

"Come, spill the <u>caviar</u>. What HAS he done?"

I look at her puzzled. "The saying is spill the beans!"

"Not in my house," she exclaims. "Beans? How very common. Come on, let me help you, as you look positively <u>ghastly</u> right now."

"He broke something that was important to me," I explain.

"Oh, your heart. I'm so sorry to hear that. Don't worry, there are plenty of other nobodies out there," she says with a chuckle. Even though she can be quite mean at times, I know she's trying to cheer me up. "What did he break?" she asks sounding a little more concerned now, as she can see I'm not laughing.

"It was something of my dad's. It was precious to me and now it's gone," I fight back the tears.

"I don't think he would have meant to break it, Lucy. You know how clumsy he is. Remember that time when he used to follow that dinner lady around and she asked him to help carry all of those boxes of eggs into the kitchen?"

I do remember that. I wasn't there, but I saw the aftermath. He must have tripped and there were eggs everywhere; all down his clothes and spread across the hall. It was like an ice rink in there for days. My frown begins to falter. It's almost turned into a smile recalling the incident.

"You do remember," she says, smiling. "We couldn't have an assembly for two days after that, as it was still too slippery. The whole school started the joke, why did the chicken cross the road? To get away from Jamie, obviously. He didn't like it, did he?"

"No, he was terribly upset. It was just an accident after all."

"And whatever he broke of your dad's was probably just an accident as well."

"It was. He didn't mean to do it, and he was devastated at the time," I agree.

"So, it could have happened to anyone. You shouldn't blame Jamie. You're both so sad when you fall out."

"It's just that he shouldn't have been touching it in the first place. Especially because it was so important," I interject.

"Well, I'm sure he feels worse now than he did when he broke all of those eggs."

I remember back to how depressed he was at that time. He felt he couldn't do anything right.

"He had you as a friend back then. He doesn't have anyone now. Not even George is talking to him."

"Thanks, Harriet, I feel really bad now. I might have overreacted. My friendship with Jamie is too important to lose."

"Glad I could help. I'm fabulous at these things, you know. Just remember if there was no darkness, we wouldn't be able to see the stars! These things sometimes happen for a reason."

I'm a little taken back by her <u>insightfulness</u>, but I'm ready to change the subject now, so I reply, "I'm surprised YOU haven't got a boyfriend."

"No way! They are all so smelly and immature," she says, screwing up her nose.

"Even Billy?" I suggest. "I thought you liked him."

"Billy's alright, I suppose. But I'm going to date someone from secondary school, if anyone. Anyway, speak of the devil," she says, as Jamie walks over. "Jamie, come over here, your girlfriend wants a word."

He skips over in a heartbeat.

Harriet grabs his hand, pulls him close and before anyone could guess what was happening, she gives him a quick kiss on his cheek.

A big smile starts to automatically appear before his brain has had time to register what has just happened.

"Jealous yet?" she smirks at me.

"I've told you before we are NOT dating." I emphasise the word 'not' to try and make her listen.

"I know, I know. I just like winding you both up," she giggles. "Go on then, make up the pair of you. I didn't do that for the good of my health."

I open my arms, and he rushes in for a hug. "I'm sorry I overreacted, Jamie. It was just an accident, I know that. You know how important that was for me. I hate it when we're not talking."

"I'm really sorry, Lucy. I shouldn't have touched it, like you said. I was just so excited, and it just slipped out of my hand. I'm so sorry. Will you ever forgive me?"

"Already done. Best friends forever," I confirm.

"And ever and ever." I feel a tear in the corner of my eye. I look at Jamie, and his eyes are watering too.

I glance over at Harriet, and she's looking at herself in her compact mirror, wiping her lips with a face wipe.

"Fabulous again," she confirms, as she closes the mirror and puts it back in her bag. "Don't you ever tell anyone about that kiss, Jamie, or you're history," she threatens.

"Oh, I think the whole school will know that we are dating shortly," Jamie teases.

"We certainly aren't."

"I've got your DNA on my cheek to prove otherwise," he winks.

"Well, I wouldn't have put you two together, but I'm happy for you both," I smile for the first time today.

"Don't you start. I try and do a good thing and what do I get in return? If anyone says anything, I will tell them you fainted at my <u>awesomeness</u>, and I had to give you CPR, the kiss of life, to bring you back," Harriet says, assertively.

Jamie starts rubbing his cheek. "I've got a bit of your fabulousness on me now. My precious. Mine. My precious," he says, trying to imitate Gollum from *The Lord of the Rings*.

"You do look a lot like Gollum now you mention it," retorts Harriet.

"I didn't think you were a Tolkien fan." I'm a little surprised.

"I haven't read or watched *The Lord of the Rings*, but I know what you are talking about."

"I am the chosen one. The claw is my master. I HAVE BEEN CHOSEN," Jamie says in a funny voice.

"Yes, I know the alien from *Toy Story*. But I haven't *chosen* you." Harriet is starting to get a little exasperated now.

"Oh, but *you* did. I saw that kiss. It was passionate." I try hard to contain my giggles.

"Shall I call round at your house tonight? I can introduce myself to your family," he asks.

"Certainly not. We will call the police."

"Tomorrow night then. In fact, every night, my sweetheart. I could shout up to you whilst you look out from your balcony, it would be like *Romeo and Juliet*." He bursts out laughing.

"Don't you dare, you stalker. My dad would shoot you and feed you to the dogs."

"Then every time you look at the dogs you would remember me. That's sweet."

We all burst out laughing. I've never known Jamie to be so confident in his quips before. He's on fire today, especially as very few people usually challenge Harriet.

"All friends again?" I ask.

"Er… you two are. I was only passing," Harriet confirms.

Jamie rubs his cheek again. "I'm never going to wash this side of my face again and if anyone asks,

308

I'll tell them to smell it as it's the essence of Harriet I'm wearing."

"I'll give you the kiss of death if you carry on," she scolds.

"Hey, talking of smells, smell this." Jamie lifts his arms and wafts his deodorant towards us. "It's designer. You will appreciate it, Harriet. It's Jack Wills."

"No! Please stop, and that's not designer!"

"It is. My brother said so."

"Well, Jamie, let me tell you. There's designer and designer."

"Which one is mine?"

"Whichever is the cheaper version. If you want to see designer, look no further than my new Louboutin shoes."

Harriet lifts her leg up to flaunt her new black shoes with the red sole.

"You'll get in trouble for wearing those. They are not compliant with school policy," I comment, although I will admit, they're pretty.

"Oh please, as if the school will say anything to me." She flicks her hair back confidently.

"They are the same as Molly's. She's got some ''Booton's' as well," Jamie offers.

"It's Louboutin's. Get it right. And I've seen Molly's shoes. She's just got a red sharpie and coloured the sole on her Primark shoes. It's not the same."

"But they look the same," Jamie challenges.

"Oh, sweetie, it really isn't. I picked these up from Paris last weekend when my dad went to visit Christian. I got a personal fitting, you know."

"Christian?" I ask, trying to join in the conversation.

"Christian Louboutin. Don't you know anything? I thought you were clever, Lucy."

"Where is your <u>entourage</u> today? I've not seen them around," I try to change the subject.

"On-too-rarge?" Jamie repeats. "What does that mean?"

"Her backup; Clara and Hannah, who always follow her around."

"Oh yeah. Have they deserted you now you have me?" Jamie winks.

"Eww. Yuk. Please don't do that again. Clara has chickenpox and Hannah is going out with Max, so she's been spending EVERY WAKING MINUTE with him."

"You're a bit lonely then. You can hang with us," I offer.

"No. I've been in your company now far too long. I don't want anyone to get the wrong idea about us. My work here is done. Peace in the universe is restored."

"Thanks, Harriet," I say meaningfully.

"Thanks, Harriet," Jamie says touching his cheek.

"Not a word about that, Jamie," she warns, whilst pulling her finger across her lips implying that Jamie needs to keep his mouth tightly shut.

Jamie copies her. "It's our little secret," he says, adding a wink for good measure.

Alice walks by us.

"That smells gorgeous," remarks Jamie. "What is it?"

"It smells like doughnuts." I agree, it does smell good.

"Oh, it is. Emily said Alice has put her hair up in a bun – literally! She's used a doughnut. She keeps taking it out to have a bite."

"Er, gross," I retch.

"Ingenious," says Jamie.

"You are always thinking of your tummy, J." I shudder thinking about how sticky that would make my hair and how hard it would be to wash the sugar and glaze out.

We can see Alice now running in the distance, screaming, while seemingly being chased by some very hungry wasps!

"OH NO," we say in unison.

Status Update
- Talk to Mum
- Dad's DNA
- Computer = monkey?
- Memory stick = fish?

Chapter 26
AMSED-6.7

It's time to talk to Mum.

I'm in over my head and there are so many links here to Dad, but I can't make sense of any of them. My palms start to sweat as I think about how I'm going to broach the subject.

I've kept it a secret for so long but now I wish I had told her about this straight away, as we don't keep any secrets from each other. I'm getting more worked up and <u>anxious</u> every minute. I stare at the 'O' on the periodic table. It's my sanctuary in times like these because we all need Oxygen to breathe. I take several deep breaths, but this reminds me, I haven't done my exercises and stretching routine today. I'll just work through these then I'll talk to Mum, I decide.

I vary my routine from week to week and, about 10 minutes in, I bend over with my legs straight to touch my toes. I do this once every day and, although it hurts down the back of my legs as I increase the stretch, I can tell I'm getting closer. I can just about touch my toes now, whereas I was nowhere near last year and I'm out of practice since I stopped dance lessons! I think in another few weeks, I'll be able to grab them properly. I'm pleased with that progress and now I feel more energised. I look around the room. What can I do now? I'm still full of trepidation.

I decide I can't put this off any longer. No excuses will make up for the fact I've kept it to myself (well, excluding Jamie who I obviously did tell) for so long. I count myself in; three... two... one...

I march down the stairs like a naughty pupil being led to the head teacher's office. Time to come clean, I remind myself as I enter the kitchen.

"Oh, there you are, Lucy. Do you want to do some baking this afternoon?" Mum asks with a cheery smile.

"Mum, can you sit down, please. There's something I've got tell you."

"Oh, this sounds serious. Have you had a fight with Jamie?" Mum frowns.

"Er... no. It's a bit strange really. Well very strange, actually, so it might be best if I show you. I've got a secret room in my bedroom, and it leads into lots of other rooms. And there are robots and laboratories and animals as well as strange creatures and, somehow, I think it's connected to Dad," I ramble. When I was trying to plan what I was going to say while I was upstairs, I couldn't think of what to say, so now I just blurt it all out. I haven't paid any attention to my mum's reaction up to now.

She's listening with a slight smile. She isn't shocked, upset or angry. She isn't even questioning what I'm saying. Does she think I'm making it all up? She probably assumes it's all been a dream.

"Mum? Are you listening to me? I've got robot aliens and monsters in another room!" If she believes me, surely, she should be pulling me out of the house by now and phoning 999 and asking for the men in black!

But no... she just smiles and says, "I've been waiting such a long time for you to tell me. You and Jamie have had quite a little adventure haven't you? Dad didn't want me to tell you until you were ready, but you've discovered it out for yourself."

"Ready for what? And how does Dad know about this?" I ask, completely confused.

"Well, it's a long story."

"Please tell me everything. I mean everything."

Mum walks over to put the kettle on. "Many years ago, before you were born, your dad and I bought that old, creepy haunted house round the corner. Our plan was to renovate it and live in it. It's got great potential with three floors and a basement, not to mention that huge garden."

"So that's our house? I remember Dad use to always point out the <u>Gothic architecture</u> on it."

"Yes, that's right." The kettle boils and Mum pours out two cups of tea. "We never really had the time or the money to finish it, but we bought it for a steal..."

"You stole it?" I interject.

"No, we bought it cheaply, as no one else wanted it. It was apparently haunted, don't forget. That's worked in our favour ever since, as no one ever goes near it."

"So, what's that got to do with the secret rooms I can get to from my bedroom?"

"Everything." Mum removes the teabags and adds the milk. "That house is the upstairs to your downstairs."

"Ah? I don't understand." I try and process what Mum has just said, but it doesn't make sense.

"The rooms and levels you've been exploring are in the basement to that house. They're Dad's secret labs and workshop."

"But... but Dad's passed away. So how? I'm so confused."

Mum brings the drinks over and sits down opposite me. "Dad was working with several universities and large manufacturing companies to help with all kinds of research. He wanted to get help and funding from Amazon, Google and Elon Musk, but they were too busy with their own very similar research projects."

I want to have my tea as my mouth is so dry but, as I touch the cup, I nearly burn myself.

"It's too hot to drink now, so leave it a minute to cool down. Dad was doing all this research years before he died," Mum explains.

"And who's doing it now?"

"The robots do most of it. Occasionally, one of the engineers or scientists comes over to see for themselves, but it's mainly automated. I have to pop in and help from time to time."

"You've been down there and seen it all?"

"Oh yes," Mum says with a big grin, nodding her head like the Churchill dog.

"You kept this a secret from me! And I was worried about me keeping it a secret from you. Mum!" I'm flabbergasted.

"Well, I didn't want to burden you with it all while you're still a child."

"I'm so grown-up, Mum. I could help out."

"Dad was right, you are a lot older than your years. Maybe it's time you get involved as well. As long as it doesn't affect your schoolwork, though."

"No, it won't, Mum. You know I can do it. I can show my teachers what I'm doing."

"Sorry, Lucy, this is a secret project. The manufacturers we are working with can't afford for this research to come out. They've invested too much money in it. So, what do you think to AMSED-6.7?"

"What's that?"

"That's the robot alien, as you called it, although he's not an alien. He was sent over from a Japanese company. Dad built him and programmed him to carry out this work. He does just about everything down there."

"Why is he called AMSED-6.7?"

"I think it stands for Advanced Multifunctional Surgical Engineering Droid – model 6.7."

"Wow – that's a mouthful. What about the other robot, what is that one called?"

"Oh, the silver track, as you call him. That's Dave," Mum smirks.

"What's Dave stand for?"

"It doesn't stand for anything. It just seemed like a more normal name and easier for us to remember. AMSED-6.7 even put Dave together. Dave does all the heavy lifting and the manual labour whilst AMSED-6.7 does all the testing and research."

"Are they internet enabled?"

"Of course, isn't everything these days?"

"So how do you know if they are working and not just playing *Roblox* in their head," I ask.

"That's a good question, Lucy."

"This is why 'I' need to be in charge now." I suddenly remember Wocky. "What about Wocky?"

"Well, that was one of Dad's earlier creations. I call him Scruffy."

"Mum, that's not nice. Well, I suppose his hair could do with comb."

"Dad named him KLDC4."

"What? What kind of a name is that?"

"It's the different animals he's made from. Dad used genes from a koala bear, a lizard, a dog and a camel, I think."

"And 4?"

Mum sighs. "There were three others before him that didn't survive."

"Did you have to bury them?"

"No. They were microscopic. Their cells didn't multiple, so they just weren't viable."

"So, Dad grew Wocky from cells?" I start getting incredibly giddy, just like when I've had too many Haribo.

"Yes. He was trying to <u>genetically engineer</u> him as a kind of sniffer 'dog' that could detect cancer."

"So Wocky can smell if someone's got cancer and let them know?"

"That was the idea, but we gave up on that project, as we didn't think Scruffy could be trained to do it. So, he was the last of that experiment. Wocky was a mistake."

"WHAT A WONDERFUL MISTAKE. So, why doesn't he look more like a sniffer dog?" I ask.

"That's also a good question. We believe the bear genes are more dominant than the dog genes, hence why he looks more like a bear than a dog."

"Why a bear?"

"Dad's thinking was bears are quite slow, not giddy, and sleep a lot so it wouldn't need a lot of looking after. It's not an exact science though, and you never really know how things will turn out."

"And they do hibernate in winter," I add.

"I recall we also added camel genes, hence the humps on Scruffy, so it could store fat and therefore

319

could go long periods of time without food. As you can see, he is quite an <u>amalgamation</u> of animals."

"What about the lizard tongue?" I enquire.

"Yes, Dad was very excited when he got the DNA right for that. It makes an excellent fly catcher, but the main reason is some reptiles can heal themselves and we believe Scruffy can too."

"Don't call him Scruffy, Mum. It's Wocky."

"I've been calling him Scruffy for years, but I do like the name Wocky, so we can go with that from now on. Just remember, in Dad's notes he's referred to by KLDC4."

"Great name, Dad! It just rolls off the tongue," I roll my eyes.

"It's a good job we agreed on your name together," Mum giggles.

"Too right. It's a good job Dad didn't try and make a Cerberus or a chimera. Even though a Pegasus would have been nice! He loved his <u>Greek mythology</u>."

"Just remind me again, what are those first two creatures? I remember that a Pegasus is a winged horse," Mum asks, inquisitively.

"Yes, and a chimera is a fire-breathing monster that's a combination of a lion, goat and a snake. And the Cerberus is a three-headed hound or beast."

"Oh, like that dog in Harry Potter?"

"Similar. Maybe that's where the idea came from. She called it Fluffy."

Suddenly a veil of sadness descends over me.

"Couldn't Dad find a cure for himself?"

"He was working on lots of projects, but the research done today will benefit the next generation, like you. I did ask if he wanted to be <u>cryogenically frozen</u> and brought back to life when the science had more answers."

"Frozen? Like the <u>tree frog</u> that can be frozen and it's still alive because it produces its own antifreeze."

"Similar," Mum agrees.

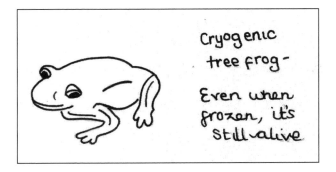

Cryogenic tree frog -

Even when frozen, it's still alive

"So why, why didn't he do it?"

"It's not that simple, Lucy. It costs thousands of pounds and it's not a perfect science, at the moment. There's no guarantee that people can be 'thawed' out safely and if they can, we're not sure that they will even be the same. What if it's a hundred years from now? We would be dead by then, anyway."

"Unless we get frozen too? Anyway, I'm going to get some of Wocky's DNA and have some of that <u>regeneration</u> so I can heal myself," I say. My mind is racing with ideas.

"Don't get ahead of yourself, Lucy. It's very dangerous. Some of the top scientists have been working on this for years but haven't got very far with it."

"That's because I've not started yet," I say with a smirk.

"I like your optimism and your enthusiasm, Lucy. You just remind me of him."

My heart sinks, as I remember the broken vial containing Dad's blood sample.

"Mum, I've also got some very bad news." I sink down in the chair and drop my head, ashamed of what I had let happen.

Chapter 27
Dad's immortal

"What is it you want to tell me?" Mum asks.

"Dad's blood sample, all his DNA, it's gone. We dropped it." I try and hold back my tears.

"I know, but accidents happen."

"BUT... BUT it was the only way I could recreate Dad again."

"It isn't the only way," Mum reassures me. "We have plenty of Dad's DNA stored, and he even printed off all of his and our full DNA code. There are hundreds of folders full of it."

"SO, WE CAN STILL DO IT?" I suddenly see a ray of hope.

Mum takes a sip of her tea and pauses for a moment.

"MUM, CAN WE, CAN WE?"

"It's not that easy, Lucy, and even if it could be done all you would have is someone that looks and sounds like Dad. It wouldn't be him, and he wouldn't have any memories of us."

"Wait, if we made him now as a baby, I'd be ten years older than my dad!" I'm puzzled by my own conclusion.

"Yes, it's debatable if it's morally right to do such a thing too. This is all theoretical, don't forget. Many cell mutations could take effect during his growth, and we might not even recognise him anyway. You've only got to look at twins for example. External influences affect how they turn out and how their personalities evolve."

"YOU ARE BLOWING MY MIND, MUM. I know how Jamie feels now. I can <u>empathise</u> with him." I stop in my tracks, as I register Mum's response to me telling her about Dad's blood sample. "Wait a minute, how did you know we had dropped Dad's blood? You didn't sound surprised."

"For security reasons, we have sensors and cameras throughout all the rooms. I can access them all through an app on my phone. So, I always knew where you were and what you were up to," Mum reveals, much to my astonishment.

"So, you knew every time I snuck down there at night and about the ladders we snuck in and what about when Wocky got into my bedroom?"

"Yes, all of it. I did find it hard to keep a straight face with his <u>impromptu</u> visit, running <u>amok</u> in your bedroom. I had to leave the room before Scruffy, sorry, I mean Wocky, realised it was me and came for a hug. I always knew you were safe, though, at all times. AMSED-6.7 was monitoring your movements as well."

"What about those little, angry rock monsters we <u>encountered</u> last year? Me and Jamie nearly lost our legs!"

"Oh, I know what you mean. I don't know what they are. Dad experimented with mixing different DNAs. You will have to ask AMSED-6.7 and read Dad's research."

"BUT WE NEARLY DIED IN THERE!" I exclaim.

"No, you were fine. They might have eaten your shoes, but they don't eat meat. They are even repelled by blood. Once they have eaten and are full, they are very playful. We did get concerned when you got stuck in the vent tube, though. We didn't anticipate that! But you were fine."

"We didn't feel like it at the time," I recall.

"Just see it as character-building, Lucy. You are better off from that experience."

"I don't fully agree with that, Mum. But I can see the funny side of it now."

"Time has a way of healing all wounds, even though you don't realise it at the time," Mum says <u>philosophically</u>.

"So, what's with all the codes on the doors?" I ask, still with a million questions whizzing around my head.

"The codes were Dad's idea. He somehow knew you would find that place, and he didn't want to make it too easy for you. He wanted you to want to know more and work for it."

"What about the names on the blackboard, in the first room?"

"They're the names of the engineers and scientists that are helping with the research."

"And all the pictures on the walls?" I enquire.

"Some are for reference, for you, and some are clues to the door codes. I especially like the eye test one."

"The eye test, I ignored that. My eyes are fine."

"It's a code. I won't spoil it for you, though. Have another look at EVERY OTHER letter. Look for your name and work from there. Oh, and if you take it off the wall and look on the other side, it says – '*Daddy loves you*'," Mum smiles.

"Wow, how did I miss that? I will defo check that out later. And the binary code on the old computer, what's all that about?"

"Oh, that's what Dad wanted to call you before we eventually decided on Lucy."

"Yeah, I remember him telling me that now… but… but… what about the monkey and fish clue from the office?"

"Slow down and take a breath, Lucy. It's a lot to take in," reassures Mum. My brain is going faster than my mouth. Come on mouth keep up with my hippocampus.

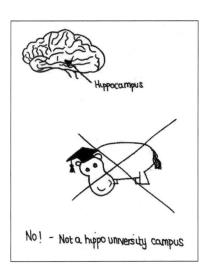

Hippocampus

No! - Not a hippo university campus

"What fish and monkey have you had forever, Lucy?"

"Charlie my fish and Lucas, my little monkey teddy, and Dad knew that."

"You don't need my help at all. You can work all these clues out yourself," Mum says reassuringly.

"Well, what would have happened if someone found out about all this and broke in and destroyed the lab?" I ask.

"It couldn't happen. Even if Jamie had sneaked down himself, he couldn't have got up to the next level, as the security door and the lift are both fingerprint and palm entry only. Only our hands will open the doors."

"Oh, that's clever. That explains it now. I just thought Jamie wasn't pressing hard enough. But I still don't get how it's all possible."

"It's going to take you a long time to process all this, Lucy, and there's no rush. I will always be here to help and support you in every way possible."

"I understand that Dad built the lab and wanted me to find it by myself, but how did he know we would buy this place and my bedroom has the secret door in it."

"Well, that's a whole other story… this was your dad's uncle's house – Uncle Alan. You won't remember him though. He lived here alone, and when we bought the haunted house, he helped Dad to build the secret bookcase door, the first room you go into and the tunnel to link them."

"Tunnel?"

"It was a tunnel to start with, but eventually they converted it to stairs. This way Dad could visit his Uncle Alan and carry on his work in the lab without anyone knowing. So, from the outside the haunted house just looked empty and abandoned. All the packages that he had delivered came to this house. They would take them down the stairs and use the lift up to the lab."

"Were you not afraid of kids messing in the grounds or people trying to break in and live there… what are they called, squats or something?"

"You mean squatters. No, we weren't worried. Security measures have been put in place to keep people away. Remember when Jack dared George to run up to the door and knock?"

"Yes, but that was a few years ago now. George got scared and wouldn't do it, so Jack did it instead."

"But Jack never made it to the door, he got scared off and ran back," Mum winks.

"That's not what he told everyone. He said he knocked, and the house was obviously empty, so it bored him." I recall the story Jack told us.

"I know what he told everyone, but the sensors in the garden alerted AMSED and he started playing animal noises out of the speakers and then a scratching sound from behind the door. As Jack got closer, he said, 'I know where you live, Jack' and that made him run away. He then played dogs barking through the speakers, so Jack thought he was being chased."

"Wait until I tell everyone. I wish I had known that at the time," I smile.

"You can't tell anyone, Lucy, that's the whole point. This story works well as a cover story to keep everyone away."

I'm still thinking through what Mum has just shared with me. "How did AMSED know Jack's name?"

"He's very clever. He used facial recognition and found Jack's profile on social media. So, by the time Jack reached the door, AMSED knew everything about him; what he did for his birthday, who his friends were, where he'd been on holiday and what he'd had for breakfast!"

"That's scary," I pull a face.

"It certainly is," Mum agrees.

"Can AMSED help me with my homework?"

"I think he's a little busy for that, but if you work together and help him, I think you'll get top marks in science!"

"Did Uncle Alan pass away?" I ask.

"Yes. It was a few years ago now. He left this house to you in his will, as we wanted it to stay in the family, for obvious reasons, which is why when we had to sell our big house it made sense to move into here."

I finish my cup of tea. I've just learnt a lot of information, and this is harder than being at school. My mind flips back to Dad.

"Dad always said he wanted to be immortal. I now get why freezing him might not have worked and growing him again from cells would take too long. But surely, with all the DNA information we have, we can implant it into someone else or perfect the regeneration genes to bring his body back to life," I pause for a moment as I think. "That's it; he's buried so we still have his body. We just need to get it to regenerate. We can do this."

"It is best not to get attached to that idea, Lucy. If there was anything that could have been done at the time it would have been done. Sometimes, we just have to accept that there are some things that we have no control over."

"But Dad had control over everything," I protest. "Everything was done for a reason; even his mistakes were on purpose to teach me lessons."

"He didn't plan or anticipate his illness, though. Very few people do and that's how life goes sometimes. We have to enjoy every minute we have with each other because life is so precious."

"But Dad wanted to be immortal," I repeat.

"You don't see it, do you, Lucy? DAD IS IMMORTAL!"

"WHAT! What do you mean?"

"YOUR DAD LIVES ON IN YOU! You share his DNA and his genes and, even though he would have wished to have had more time to spend with you, he has shaped you into who you are. You have learnt enough from him that you know what you need to do, and learn, in order to get to where you want to go in life and which direction you need to take."

"So, Dad is inside me?"

"Kind of, he will always be part of you. Just like I will always be part of you too."

"I want to carry on his research. I know I can do it. I want to help the world and help with exploring the universe."

"They're very bold plans, Lucy, so let's take one step at a time. Even small steps can make an enormous difference if a lot of people do the same. Let's focus on school first!"

"I can do both, Mum."

"How about we work on these things together? Dad shared a lot of his work with me; he was very passionate about it. Besides, what we can't work out from his research we can just ask AMSED."

"That's sounds awesome, Mum. Can we really do this together? I thought you hated science?"

"I just find science hard; it doesn't mean I hate it. I appreciate the importance of it and how society needs it to secure our future. I would learn more about it for you. I would love us to work on this together. Dad would be so proud of you. Are you ready for the next chapter in your life, Lucy?"

"I can't wait, especially as you are part of it, Mum," I say with the biggest smile on my face I think I've ever had. Mum's smile beams back as she wipes tears from her eyes.

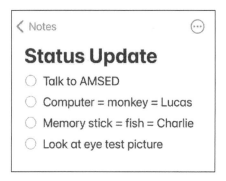

Chapter 28
When in doubt always start at the beginning

I wake up early the next morning. Fortunately, it's Sunday, so I have no school, but I do have some questions on my mind that I wanted answering.

I quickly get dressed and write Mum a little note – '*Just going downstairs to talk to AMSED*'. Not that I needed to tell her, as she'll know where I am, but it feels good that I can tell her myself now.

I venture through the bookcase door and, for the first time, I'm not at all concerned about making any noise.

As I reach the bottom of the stairs, I glance back up. I could really do with a slide here. And one of those bags to sit in just like you have at a <u>helter-skelter</u>. I take out my phone and write this down under the heading – Improvements to Lucy's Secret Lair (LSL).

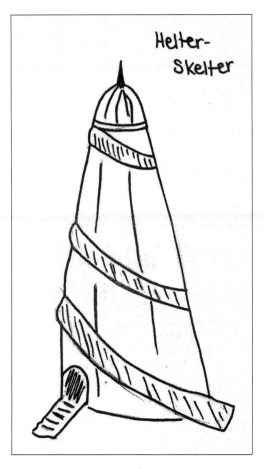

Coming down here feels different now. Rather than it being a secret, I can now explore freely. I feel more confident now and I've got a new sense of direction, a new purpose. All those ideas of being a hairdresser or a shop assistant have faded away. I'm going to save humanity. It seems quite a big ask, but what a challenge to set myself. After all, Mrs Malikinski says 'Always aim high'.

I reach the lift and enter the Fibonacci code. I don't even need to look it up any more, as I have memorised most of the codes now. The doors open and, as I press the first-floor button, I notice the button scans my fingerprint. How did I not see that before? I stare at the number 2. I'm going to have a busy day, I think to myself. I'll need to know every inch of this place now I'm in charge!

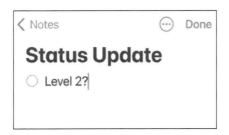

The door opens. WOWSERS! I jump back. AMSED is standing to attention outside the lift.

"You startled me," I exclaim.

"Sorry, Lucy, I didn't mean to. Your mum messaged me last night and filled me in, so I wanted to be here to greet you."

"That's so kind of you. So, AMSED, you can receive text messages?"

"Yes, and email, and I've also got all the social media accounts. Bet you can't guess how many followers I have?" he challenges.

"Two hundred?" I guess.

"No, just one and that is Dave. I programmed him to do it as well! I hope that counts."

My phone pings. "That's me. I've sent you, my number," AMSED confirms.

"I didn't think we had any service down here?"

"I'm like a giant aerial. I've always got service."

"You're as fast as our fibre broadband," I giggle.

"That's too slow for me. I get information beamed to me directly from space satellites."

I have no idea what he is on about, so I just say, "Oh, that's cool."

"So, Lucy, how can I be of service now you're the boss?"

"I like the sound of that. Say it again," I laugh.

"So, Lucy, how can I be of service now you're the boss?"

"I didn't mean literally say it again, but never mind. I could do with a map of this level for starters, AMSED."

Ping, ping, ping, comes the familiar sound from my phone.

"I have sent the floor plan and inventory along with details of the experiments we are currently conducting."

"I like how efficient you are. What else can you do?"

"My main programmes are companion droid and..."

"What's that?" I interrupt.

"I'm programmed to talk to people and keep them

336

company. Look after them, if you like. I can make tea and make their bed and even dress people."

"I won't tell Grandad, or I'll never get you back." I take out my phone and add to my notes – '*Make companion droid for Grandad*'. "Sorry, please carry on."

"I can also carry out surgeries and operations. Also, surgeons can remotely access me and use my hands and eyes to carry out operations more safely and with more precision than a human surgeon could."

"That's cool, so you're a doctor?"

"Yes, that is correct, Lucy. I am also a protocol droid."

"I know, like C-3PO, in *Star Wars*."

"I don't know *Star Wars*, but I have heard that reference before and it is correct. However, I can only speak 24 languages as this is all I need to carry out my work here."

"You need to speak that many languages to work here?" I say, surprised.

"I have read research papers from many different countries, and we have shipments coming in from all over the world," AMSED explains.

"How long did it take to learn all that?" I ask.

"Oh, it takes about three seconds to upload to the memory chip."

"Wow, I wish I could do that," I sigh.

"It is so nice having someone to talk to again. Dave isn't very talkative. He is really just the hired muscle."

"Jamie can help out," I offer.

"Sure, we could start him off on some simple jobs like tidying up and poo duty."

"POO DUTY?"

"Someone has got to pick up Wocky's poos. He doesn't do it himself. We will give Jamie some doggy poo bags and when he has done that, he can do the rock monsters' poos. That is a bit trickier though."

"I think he might be busy that day," I giggle.

"Shame."

"Wait a minute, you have never watched *Stars Wars*, but you can speak 24 languages? You've got your priorities all wrong, AMSED."

"I don't understand."

"You and I are going to sit down one weekend and watch them all," I demand.

"I do like watching films, it helps me relax, but you'll have to eat the popcorn!"

"Don't worry about the popcorn, I can certainly eat that. I love watching films too. You can definitely relax, escape your troubles and the world around you."

"I don't really relax, you know. It was a joke. I never switch off," AMSED clarifies.

"What about when your batteries run down?"

"They never do. My main core is radioactive and will power me for hundreds of years and…"

"WAIT. HOLD ON." I jump back and keep stepping backwards. "YOU ARE RADIOACTIVE?"

"Don't worry, Lucy. You are perfectly safe. My core is all shielded."

"Are you sure?" I'm not convinced that he can be entirely safe.

"Trust me, I'm a doctor."

"Wait, was that a joke?"

"Your dad told me to stop telling jokes as they are not funny," AMSED says.

"You can't be as bad as him. Dad jokes are the worst. So now I know what you can do..."

"I have only just started. I have many programmes – I have the Terminator chip. I have been sent from the future..."

"You're joking again, right?" I ask, sceptically.

"EXTERMINATE, EXTERMINATE."

I don't know whether to laugh or cry at this stage. I'm just frozen to the spot. Is he <u>malfunctioning</u>?

"Joking, Lucy," AMSED confirms.

"I thought so, you can't fool me. You're very funny. So, you've watched *The Terminator* and *Doctor Who*?"

"No, I haven't watched them, but I know the references."

"Have you not watched any films?" I ask in surprise.

"I have watched *The Sound of Music*. The hills… are alive… with the sound… of mu..sic."

"No stop it, you can't sing. I don't feel as inferior now I've found something you can't do," I laugh. "I'll have to teach you some of MY songs."

"Is this a requirement for us to work together?" he asks.

"It sure is." I start thinking about what songs to begin with, as I look him up and down. "You're a bit like Iron Man, aren't you?" I decide.

"Yes, but I am not made of iron, I can't fly, I don't have missiles up my sleeve and I don't have a person inside me. Apart from that, I'm exactly like Iron Man," he says with what looks like a smirk on his face.

"I think we are going to get on just fine, me and you. You've got a great personality, for a robot."

"It is my <u>artificial intelligence</u>. I constantly learn and evolve a thousand times a second, not to brag of course. I spent a lot of time with your dad. We learned a lot from each other. Your dad could achieve anything if he put his mind to it. You remind me of him."

"I've got so many questions I want answering I

don't know where to begin," I explain.

"As your dad always used to say – when in doubt, always start at the beginning. You can ask me anything you like. What do you want to know?"

Mum was right. This is a new chapter in my life and the future belongs to us. I'm going to strive to be the best I can… I'm going to 'Reach for the stars'.

The end

All we have to decide is what to do with the time that is given us.
– Gandalf

A note from the author and illustrator

Thank you so much for reading our book. We hope you have enjoyed it.

As we have independently published this we don't have the same support and help as most other books on sale, so we rely on word-of-mouth recommendations and, most importantly, reviews.

We would be incredibly grateful if you could go out of your way and leave us a review with Amazon or the online retailer where you purchased our book.

We love to hear feedback from readers, and we try our best to reply to everyone. Our contact details are on our website and the web address is printed on the back cover.

Every book purchased helps the charities we are supporting.

GLOSSARY

Chapter 1

Emphasises – Makes Wocky's three humps more clearly defined.

Bewildered – Confused or very puzzled.

Literally – Taking words exactly as they are spoken or written. If you were to literally bite someone's head off, they would no longer have a head!

Referee – The act of watching and overseeing a match to ensure fair play.

Interrogate – Ask questions to obtain the information you are after.

Tentatively – Without certainty, not definitely.

Ancient – Belonging to the very distant past or having existed for a very long time. Very old (not parents!).

Mani-pedi – Manicure (cosmetic treatment of the hands) and pedicure (cosmetic treatment of the feet). Painting of nails etc.

Chapter 2

FaceTime – This is a video call system developed by Apple Inc.

Unconventionally – Non-conforming or out of the ordinary.

Sheepishly – In an embarrassed manner or lacking in self-confidence.

Enthusiastically – Showing eager enjoyment, interest, or approval.

Formulating – Creating or devising.

Reality – In actual fact.

Millimetres – A unit of measurement equal to 1/10 of a centimetre (or one thousandth of a metre). Depicted by the little lines between centimetres on a ruler.

Sarcastically – In a rude or ridiculing kind of way.

Fumbling – Doing or handling something clumsily.

Cosmology – The science of the origin and development of the universe.

Apprehensively – Viewing the future with anxiety. Showing fear about what is about to happen.

Anticipate – Predict the outcome.

Paralympics – A series of international contests for athletes with disabilities following the Olympics.

Anchored – Well and truly stuck. Secured firmly.

Hypotenuse – The longest side of a right-angled triangle, opposite the right angle. Not to be mistaken for a hippopotamus, that's something entirely different!

Pythagoras – The Pythagoras theorem is a mathematical formula that states the square of the hypotenuse (of a right-angled triangle) is equal to the sum of the squares of the other two sides. $C2 = A2 + B2$. (This comes in handy from time to time.)

Squared – A mathematical term for multiplying a number by itself. $32 = 3 \times 3 = 9$.

Square root – A mathematical term which is the opposite of squaring a number. The square root of 9 ($\sqrt{9}$) = 3.

Triumphantly – Great happiness and joy with an achievement.

Pi – (π) Is a mathematical term defined as the ratio of a circle's circumference to its diameter. It is a never-ending number. To keep it simple it is 3.142 to three decimal places. 'Pi' isn't that bad, if you add an 'e' you could always eat it!

Chapter 3

Assertively – In a confident way that shows you are not frightened.

Claustrophobia – An extreme or irrational fear of confined places. Not the fear of Santa Claus.

Latin – Latin is a classical language still in use today but very rarely used in everyday communications. Modern-day English does have Latin influences. There are a lot of scientific names including medicines and botany (study of plants) that also use Latin.

Chapter 4

Numerous – Many. A great number.

Fossilised – Becomes a fossil.

Gibberish gobbledegook – Unintelligible writing. Excessive use of technical terms.

Conundrum – A difficult problem.

Physics, biology, chemistry – The three main sciences. Physics studies matter and energy and how they interact. Biology is the study of life. Chemistry is the study of the elements in everything and their properties.

Oceanography, robotics, astronomy – Oceanography is an earth science that studies the oceans. Robotics mixes computer science with engineering in developing robots. Astronomy is a natural science that studies celestial objects like planets in the universe.

Flabbergasted – Greatly surprised or astonished.

Tele-pathetic – Tele- means over a distance. Like calls using a tele-phone. Pathetic implies low standards or inadequate, or to cause pity. Telepathetic is an old word that was used in the late 19th century instead of telepathic, but Jamie wouldn't have known this. For the purposes of the story, Jamie is making a mistake by saying tele-pathetic instead of telepathic which is what he meant to say.

Telepathic – The supposed ability of knowing other people's thoughts and the capability of being able to transmit thoughts to others. I know you know what I mean!

Roblox – An online game platform with 100 million active monthly players and a collection of more than 50 million games created by its users.

Goldilocks theory – Is based on the children's story of things being not too hot or not too cold. This idea can be applied to a multitude of concepts in life. In astrobiology, it relates to a planet's orbit around its star. The earth is in our sun's Goldilocks zone so the temperature here is just right for us.

Scarce – Insufficient for demand. Limited availability and hard to find.

SI units – A standard International System of Units. It is the modern form of the metric measurement widely used throughout the world.

Metre – An SI base unit of length using the metric system. 1m = 100cm = 1000mm in metric. (Approximately 39.37 inches, or 3 foot 3 inches in imperial.)

Ohm's law – A law describing the relationship between voltage (V), current (I) and resistance (R) in electrical circuits. This law is named after the German physicist Georg Simon Ohm (surprisingly).

Chapter 5

DM – Stands for direct message.

FYI – For your information (just like this glossary).

Exasperated – Irritated. Frustrated.

Erratic – Not regular. Uneven.

Hesitation – The act of pausing to think.

Mesmerised – Capturing your complete attention.

Chapter 6

Plausible – Reasonable. Persuasive argument.

NVQs – National Vocational Qualifications. These could be gained in practical, work-related tasks in over a thousand subjects. In 2015, they were replaced with something similar.

Cassiopeia – Is a large constellation in the northern hemisphere, named after a queen in Greek mythology. It is known as the 'W' constellation – I wonder why.

Manoeuvre – A movement usually carried out with precision and care.

Bemused – Puzzled, confused.

Precarious – A dangerous and/or unsafe situation. Likelihood of something bad happening like an accident of some kind.

Impeccable – Faultless. To the highest standard.

Chapter 7

Wowsers – Astonished. Impressed.

Gobsmacked – Astounded. Surprised.

Catastrophe – A sudden disaster (like my book sales!).

Abyss – Deep, seemingly bottomless cave or area of water (not dissimilar to Jamie's stomach!).

Fulcrum – The point on which an object is balanced, like a seesaw with the fulcrum in the middle. If the fulcrum is moved to the left, it would take less force or effort on the right-hand side to make it move. This is very useful when levering heavy objects.

Latter – Occurring in the second part or near the end of the sentence. (Afterwards.)

Former – Occurring in the first part or near the start of the sentence. (Before.)

Effortlessly – With ease. Very little exertion.

Bowline knot – (Pronounced 'bo-lin'.) This knot makes a non-slip loop in the end of a rope. It is an essential knot used by the emergency services in rescue situations.

Jeopardy – In danger of failure.

Potassium – Is a reactive metal in the alkali metal group. Chemical symbol K. Many fruits and vegetables are high in potassium including bananas.

Diluted – Weakened/watered down (just like diluted squash).

Chapter 8

Romcom – Romantic comedy.

Clandestine – Secret.

Trepidation – Fear or anxiety of what may happen.

Composure – In control. Calm.

Olympic sport – A sport at the Olympic Games, like swimming. Five new sports are being added to the Paris 2024 Olympic Games.

Elated – Very happy.

Devouring – Eating food quickly (not a good idea unless you want to be sick!).

Oblivious – Not aware.

Gusto – Enjoyment and enthusiasm in doing something. Hopefully this is you, reading my book with gusto!

Illuminates – Lights up.

Chapter 9

Out of the frying pan into the fire – (Idiom.) A phrase to describe going from a bad situation to one that's even worse. It has been used for hundreds of years (not by me though – by someone very, very old!).

Periscope – An apparatus consisting of a tube attached to a set of mirrors or prisms, by which an observer (typically a submerged submarine or behind a high obstacle) can see things which would otherwise be out of sight.

Meticulously – Carefully and precise.

Inadvertently – Accidently. Not on purpose.

Trespassing – Being somewhere without permission.

DNA – Deoxyribonucleic acid. DNA is found in most cells of every organism. It contains the genetic code (instructions) within four bases: A, T, G and C. The body uses it for many things including replicating cells. The shape of it resembles a twisted ladder know as a double helix.

Clinical – Like a hospital. Clean, tidy. (Unlike under Lucy's bed – have you checked what's under yours?)

Vivaria – The plural of vivarium. A structure to keep pets, such as frogs or geckos, in. Like an aquarium.

Adrenaline – A hormone which prepares your body to exert itself for a fight or flight response when your body thinks you are in danger.

Chapter 10

Fortuitously – Luckily. Happened by chance and with a favourable outcome.

Regenerate – Grow back.

Unpronounceable – Too difficult to say. (So, I left it out!)

Camouflage – Hide or disguise.

Immunity – Resist infection or disease.

Venom – A poisonous substance from an animal, like a snake, scorpion, or spider. (Not the Tom Hardy films.)

Circulatory system – Where and how the blood circulates (moves) through your body using blood vessels and the heart.

Unique – One of its kind. Unlike anything else. (A bit like this book.)

Sixth sense – A supposed feeling about your surroundings, like you are being watched. Unlike your other five actual senses: sight, hearing, smell, taste and touch.

Vengeance – In this example, Lucy's urge to wee is much greater than before.

Rationalise – Thinking logically. Working something out so you can explain or justify it.

Chapter 11

Notorious – Well known. Famous.

Electrocuted – Injured or killed by an electric shock.

Conductor of electricity – A conductor will allow electrons (electricity) to flow easily through it. Good conductors are copper, aluminium, gold and silver, and these are used in electrical wires and circuits. Pure water doesn't conduct electricity but tap water isn't pure and *will* conduct electricity.

CPR – Cardiopulmonary resuscitation. Mouth-to-mouth resuscitation. First aid.

Resuscitation – The process of reviving someone using CPR.

The Rock – Dwayne Johnson, aka The Rock, is an American actor, businessman, and former professional wrestler. Referenced in this book from his song 'You're Welcome' from the Disney film *Moana*.

Besmirch – Damage someone's reputation. Talk bad about them.

Dumbfounded – Astonished. Surprised.

Apoplectic – Angry. Furious.

Topsy-turvy – Upside down.

Abracadabra – A word used by magicians when performing a trick. Doesn't normally work for me.

<u>Chapter 12</u>

Vertebrates – A type of animal that has a backbone or spinal column. (Like us.)

Amphibious – Being able to live on land and in the water. (Like frogs.)

Persevere – Continue even though it's difficult. Keep going, you are nearly halfway through the book and the best is yet to come!

Ironically – Done in a way that is opposite to what is expected. Not knowing the answer even though it is right in front of you.

Mandatory – Required by law. Compulsory.

Hypothetical – Imaginary idea. Not real.

Butterfly effect – Is the idea that a small effect over a period of time can grow exponentially to have a large impact somewhere else. The common example (which couldn't happen in this case) is when a butterfly flaps its wings at one side of the world and that tiny change in air pressure causes a tornado at the other side of the world.

Newton's three laws:

Newton's first law – If you put your phone down it doesn't move unless you push it. I'm sure Sir Isaac Newton would have used this example if there were mobile phones in existence when he was alive.

Newton's second law – F= m times a (This was covered in the first book).

Newton's third law – Every action has an equal and opposite reaction. When you're standing up (on the ground) you are pushing the earth down and the earth is pushing you up.

Chapter 13

Atoms – These are the smallest unit of matter. They are in everything. If you think of something you made from Lego, and then imagine that every piece is so small you need a very powerful microscope to see each brick.

Bluetooth – A standard for short-range wireless connection between devices like mobile phones and computers.

Theory – A set of ideas intended to explain something.

Indignantly – In annoyance at what is suggested, as Jamie wouldn't wear a dress for anybody!

Fibonacci – Was an Italian mathematician. This is his infinite number sequence. The next number is worked out by adding the two previous numbers together. The number after 2 and 3 is 5. (2+3=5).

Succession – One after another.

Willy Wonka – The fictional character from *Charlie and the Chocolate Factory*. What a great story!

OTIS – Otis is the world's leading lift and escalator manufacturing company.

DENNIS – Dennis is a specialist commercial vehicle manufacturer. Well known for making fire engines and refuse trucks.

Chapter 14

Decor – The way in which a room is decorated, in terms of colours and furniture etc.

Blind Cave Fish – Are a freshwater fish that doesn't have any eyes. They normally live in dark caves, so they don't have any use for eyes. They have the amazing ability to regenerate their heart after injury.

Inquisitively – Showing an interest. Curious.

Reconnaissance op – An observation in advance to discover information. (Op – operation.)

Exploration – Exploring an unfamiliar area.

Extraterrestrials – (ET.) Not from our planet. (Terrestrial meaning earth.)

Temperamental – Not consistent. Doesn't always work.

Handicap – Is where something has been made more difficult. In Lucy's case, her handicap is currently due to her wearing a wrist brace.

Chapter 15

Stalactites – Formed by dripping water depositing calcium salts, these structures hang down from the ceiling in caves and look like icicles. This process takes thousands of years. Don't stand and wait for this to happen, it would be a little boring!

Stalagmites – Same as stalactites but this time the icicle shape is on the floor pointing upwards. Usually under a stalactite.

Product – In mathematical terms this means to multiply. The product of 2 and 3 is 6 (2x3=6).

Mnemonics – A way to remember something, usually using letters but can be other ideas also.

Instinctively – Without thinking about it. An instant reaction.

Befuddled – Confused. Not sure why it happened.

Diabetic – Diabetes is a disease that means your blood glucose (blood sugar) is out of balance. Millions of people suffer from this, and are known as diabetics, and it can be very serious.

Obedient – Someone or thing that always does what it is told to do.

Chapter 16

Formidable – Inspiring fear or respect through being impressively large, powerful, intense, or capable.

Vlog – Personal video blog on a social media account.

Million – A thousand times a thousand or 1,000,000 or 106.

Billion – A thousand times a million or 1,000,000,000 or 109.

Proxima Centauri – Is the nearest star to us, after our sun. It is 4.2465 light years away. (A long way away.)

Trillion – A million times a million or 1,000,000,000,000 or 1012.

Galaxy – the Milky Way – Our solar system is in the Milky Way galaxy. It's a spiral galaxy and its appearance, from earth, is a milky band through the night sky, hence the name.

100 thousand million – 100 billion or 100,000,000,000 or 1011.

Concur – To agree and be of the same opinion.

Light years – An astronomical unit which is equivalent to the distance light travels in one year. This is 9.4607 x 1012 km (about 6 trillion miles). The *Millennium Falcon*, from *Star Wars*, maybe able to travel at the speed of light. Just think of all the planets we could visit if we had one of those.

Bedlam – A scene of uproar and confusion.

Ferocious – Fierce. Violent.

Chapter 17

Elements – A chemical element cannot be broken down into a simpler substance. Elements are what everything is made up of. (Water is made from two hydrogen elements and one oxygen element.)

Acronyms – An abbreviation. A series of letters comprising of the first letters of the words it refers to. An example is LOL which stands for **l**aughs **o**ut **l**oud.

Natural instinct – An automatic reaction to the current circumstances. A reflex.

Kaput – Broken or useless.

Apollo 13 – Was the seventh crewed mission in the USA's Apollo space programme and the third mission planned to land on the moon. Due to an oxygen tank malfunction, the mission was aborted and the only thing on everyone's mind was if they could get home safely. It is also a very good film starring Tom Hanks.

Bedraggled – Untidy, dirty, not looking one's best.

Chapter 18

Eerie – Quiet, deserted, a ghostlike feel to the place.

Infirmary – A hospital.

Ridiculed – To mock something. Make fun of it.

Bobby Charlton – Sir Robert Charlton CBE, known as Bobby, is a former England football player. He was a member of the England team who won the FIFA World Cup in 1966. Sadly, no relation to me (or not that I'm aware of any way!).

Alton Towers – The biggest theme park and resort in the UK. Set in over 500 acres in Staffordshire, England.

Corkscrew – This was a steel roller coaster in Alton Towers (UK) between 1980 and 2008. It was the first of its kind which turned people upside down – twice. It was replaced by Th13teen. A small section of it can still be seen in the entrance to the park. The steel track was originally painted yellow.

Rita: Queen of Speed – Rita, in Alton Towers UK, is the fifth fastest roller coaster in the UK. From 0-100km per hour in 2.5 seconds with a G-force of +4.7G.

Th13teen – The world's first vertical freefall drop roller coaster, located in Alton Towers, UK. The freefall drop is approximately 5 metres, in darkness.

Perplexed – Confused, puzzled.

Breakneck – Extremely fast.

Scalextric – Is a brand of slot car racing sets which first appeared in the late 1950s and is still sold today.

Open University – A university for everyone. Students, of any age, can study courses over a period of time to suit themselves utilising distance and open learning processes.

Incredulously – Surprised. Showing disbelief.

ChildLine – This is free, confidential support, in the UK, for anyone under 19 to help with any issues they are dealing with. They can be contacted on 0800 11 11 or via chat at their website www.childline.org.uk.

Approachable – Friendly and easy to talk to.

Momentarily – For a short period of time.

Chapter 19

Circumference – If you draw a circle on the ground and walk around the circle, you've just walked the circumference of the circle.

Perimeter – Similar to a circumference but can be of any shape (circumference is generally circular). The perimeter relates to the outermost boundary, so the perimeter of your bedroom is your four walls.

Formality – Something that happens as a matter of course.

Surreptitious – Kept secret, especially because it would not be approved of.

Chapter 20

Pterodactyl – An extinct flying dinosaur. (Technically, they aren't a dinosaur, but they are close enough – for me.)

Vain – Showing excessive pride in your appearance.

Mercury – Mercury, the element (not the planet), is commonly known as quicksilver because it's a liquid at room temperature and was once used in thermometers.

Density – How compact a substance is; a sponge is less dense than a brick.

Hydrogen – Is the lightest element and appears first on the periodic table. It is the most abundant chemical substance in the universe, so we are not going to run out of it.

Fortnite – This is a very popular online video game for children age 12+.

Scrumdiddlyumptious – Extremely tasty. Delicious.

Thermodynamics – The study of the relationships between heat, work, temperature and energy. (Thermo relates to heat/temperature.)

Envisage – Visualise and plan something in your head.

Chapter 21

Canoodling – Kissing and cuddling amorously.

Dramatically – Done with great flare and overly exaggerated.

Distinctive – Qualities of something allowing you to easily identify it.

Potent – Powerful and strong.

Lassoed – Caught (with a lasso).

Made a rod for my own back – (Idiom.) To do something that inadvertently creates more work or problems.

Egghead – A highly academic or studious person. An intellectual.

Han Solo – A character from *Star Wars*.

Filament – The wire inside old light bulbs that glowed and got incredibly hot; not very energy-efficient. Most new bulbs now use LED.

LED – A light-emitting diode. Very popular now with most lighting, as it uses less power and is long lasting.

Elaborate – Detailed, ornate, complicated design.

The Hay Wain **by John Constable** – An incredibly popular oil painting depicting a rural scene with a wooden wagon (wain) carrying hay. Completed by the artist in 1821.

Deduce – Come to a logical conclusion by reasoning.

Decade – Ten years.

Thesis – A piece of work on a subject or idea written after an extended amount of research.

Tsunamis – Giant waves generally formed by an underwater earthquake.

Chapter 22
Despondently – Fed up. Loss of hope.

Trillion microplastic particles – Trillion is a million million (1012). Microplastic particles are any type of plastic typically less than 5mm in size. There are literally millions everywhere and are getting eaten and digested by animals and ourselves without us even knowing it. Plastic has many uses, but it shouldn't be eaten. In my opinion (which doesn't mean a lot), over the next 20 years this will be just like the asbestos issues we have been facing over the last three decades.

Peripheral vision – Seeing out of the corner of your eye. As you are looking forwards, it's what you see at the very left or right of where you are.

Nerve-racking – Stressful, causing anxiety.

Chapter 23

Petrified – Terrified. So frightened you are unable to move or speak.

Medusa – In Greek mythology. She had snakes instead of hair and anyone who made eye contact with her turned to stone; handy if you want some garden ornaments but other than that a bit of a nuisance.

Comeuppance – A punishment or fate that we deserve.

Nanobots – A microscopically small robot. Currently being tested to repair damaged cells in living things. They can use your blood vessels as roads to get to where they need to go.

Host – An animal or plant in which a parasite organism lives. Could also be someone who receives or entertains guests.

Anxiously – Nervously or uneasily.

Predicament – A difficult or unfortunate situation.

Ingenious – A clever idea or invention.

Gargantuan – Very large. Enormous.

Habitats – A home or environment for us, animals, or plants.

Heebie-jeebies – Shivers. Creeps. A fear that something isn't right.

Chapter 24

Flummoxed – Bewildered. Confused.

Whatchamacallit – (What-cha-ma-call-it). Used to refer to a name of something you are unable to remember.

Juggernaut – A powerful, overwhelming force.

Megabytes – One million bytes of information. (106.)

Gigabyte – A thousand million bytes of information. (109.)

Terabyte – One million million bytes of information. (1012.)

Petabytes – A thousand million million bytes of information. (1015.)

Humongous – Very big. Huge. Enormous.

USB ports – Universal serial bus ports. These are places on a computer where you can plug in a memory stick or USB cable. These were first introduced in 1996.

Ribena – A blackcurrant-based soft drink.

Condensation – This occurs when the warm water molecules in the air hit a cold surface and cool resulting in liquid water being produced. (Gas changes back to liquid.) You can prove this by taking a cold bottle out of the fridge and placing it somewhere warm.

Blubbers – Cry uncontrollably.

Insurmountable – Too great a problem to overcome.

Chapter 25

Sympathetic – Feeling sorrow for someone else's misfortune. Understanding their pain.

Uncharacteristically – Not something they would normally do.

Caviar – Fish eggs. A delicacy not normally found in fast-food outlets!

Ghastly – To look unwell. Can also mean great horror or fear.

Insightfulness – Perceptive. Showing deep understanding.

Awesomeness – Extremely impressive.

Louboutin – A brand of expensive and fashionable women's shoes.

Entourage – A group of people following an important person.

Chapter 26

Anxious – Worried, nervous, or uneasy about something.

Gothic architecture – The style and design of buildings common between the 12th and 16th centuries and copied up to the 18th century. Famous for its pointed arches throughout, it has a kind of spooky, but beautiful, feel to it.

Genetically engineer – The process of altering DNA of an organism.

Amalgamation – The result of combining different things.

Greek mythology – Is a collection of stories involving gods, heroes, monsters, and rituals of ancient Greeks. The Greeks sometimes used these stories to explain natural phenomena.

Cryogenically frozen – This is the practice of deep-freezing someone who has died with the hope that they can be brought back to life when a cure has been found to cure them of their illness. Don't try this at home!

Tree frog – Some species of frogs can produce a natural antifreeze in their blood so even in freezing temperatures they don't fully freeze and are still alive, albeit in a hibernation state.